# Wild Turkeys Can Fly

# Wild Turkeys Can Fly

A NOVEL BY
*Henry A. Reed*

**DIAMOND BOOKS**   ◇   **Austin, Texas**

*To my love, my Dulcinea*

All things are possible —
first the dream, then the fulfillment.

*Don Quixote*

# Introduction

I was lying on an examination table in Dr. Heath's consulting room, waiting for his return. Breathing had become a struggle. I could hardly move my arms and legs. I felt panic. I overheard Dr. Heath tell his assistant that he suspected polio; he told him to order an ambulance immediately.

Shortly, the doctor returned with two men who put me on a stretcher. Leaning over me, Dr. Heath said in a half whisper, "Listen, Harvey, I think you have polio. I am sending you to an Army hospital. The Army has the best facilities for the kind of care you need, and as a veteran, you are eligible." He took my weak groan for consent.

An ambulance drove me to the emergency room at Brooke Army Hospital at Fort Sam Houston in northeast San Antonio. There a spinal tap confirmed that I had polio. I was accepted as a patient, and within three hours the doctors who were monitoring my labored breathing put me in an iron lung.

A nurse took my temperature, and I heard her tell the doctor that my fever was a hundred and four. The doctor replied, "Let's hope the fever doesn't last more than three days. After the fourth

1

day, the nerve damage becomes extensive and many patients die. I'll bet 1950 will turn out to be one of the worst years in this polio epidemic. It's only September and we have had more cases to date than all of last year. I hope this fellow makes it."

I tried to speak, but I could not. I wondered about my business, my family, and if all would be lost.

I lay in an iron lung in a small isolated room. Nurses with masks would enter occasionally to check me for fever, stay only a moment, and walk out quickly. This was the infectious stage of the disease.

On the second day I woke burning with fever. I wondered if I would die. How ironic if I should die now, at the age of twenty-eight, after all the close calls of the past twelve years.

How would it be to die? I wondered. I thought of my mother and the quest. My mind started racing, and it turned to the past. I thought of my youth and became calmer, and then I remembered.

# PART 1

# The
# Ranch

# Chapter 1

The year was 1938, and in Texas the effects of the Depression were beginning to disappear. We were in that hopeful period when the hard times seemed to be fading — and we could not yet see the war that was coming.

But nothing was farther from my mind that day than the economy or national affairs. I was sixteen and spending the summer as a cowboy on my Uncle Jonathan's ranch, and loving every minute of it.

This was the third summer Papa had allowed me to come to the Double R, and although the previous visits had been only a few weeks each, I was already considered a good hand. On this bright June day I had been sent out to meet Jeff, one of the ranch hands, to help him replace cedar fence posts.

I sat comfortably in the saddle as Ranger ambled along the fence line toward the morning sun. I was headed toward the northeastern corner of the ranch to rendezvous with Jeff, and at this leisurely pace there was time to smell the pungent scent of mountain laurel and watch the jackrabbits dash in and out of the brush.

Almost a mile from the northeast corner, I noticed white smoke rising toward the sky. I urged Ranger to a trot, and in another half mile I spotted Jeff galloping toward me waving his hat.

"Fire, Harvey!" he yelled. "A big brush fire!" He barely slowed as he reached me, shouting, "On the next ranch, but it's heading for us. Got to get help."

I turned Ranger, spurred him, and took off. Since my horse was faster, I was soon far ahead of Jeff on the way back to the ranch house. In five minutes, I had such a lead that the cowboy was out of sight. I cut across a creek bottom, and as I came up the other side, on a hill to the left stood a big deer — a spectacular twelve-pointer, the kind you dream about.

In one motion I pulled my rifle from the scabbard and brought Ranger to a halt. The buck had started running across a field in front of me. I took aim, leading him about a foot, and fired, and he tumbled and dropped a hundred yards directly in front of me. I galloped up to the body, jumped off my horse, checked to make sure the deer was dead, leaped back on my horse, and continued at a gallop, mentally marking the spot so I could come back for my trophy buck. It all happened so fast that Jeff was still not in sight.

By the time we had gathered the other ranch hands, including Uncle Jonathan and Juan Delgado, and returned to the place I had seen the smoke, the wind had shifted, blowing the fire away from the direction of our ranch. When the flames reached a rocky ravine where there was nothing to feed upon, the fire extinguished itself.

As we turned back, I told Uncle Jonathan about killing the twelve-point deer. He was excited for me — but he was also surprised. For two years, he explained, every man on the ranch had been hunting that big buck. He called to Juan Delgado, and the three of us headed for the spot where I had left the carcass.

As we rode, I was thinking of my uncle's love for his Texas ranch, a love for a place which I was coming to share. This was a wild and beautiful land, with thousands of live oaks, elms, mountain laurels, and a wild profusion of plants and flowers — a rough land of hills, rugged ravines, springs, and small lakes. The Double R covered over 9,000 acres, and the Blanco River cut almost through the center — a sparkling stream with giant cypress trees along its banks. In some areas large cliffs faced the river, exposing marvelous rock formations that glistened in the sunlight with a rainbow of colors. There were still Indian arrowheads and pieces of pottery in the caves that burrowed into the cliffs.

Now we reached the spot where I had left the buck and . . . it wasn't there!

Uncle Jonathan said, "Maybe you only wounded him."

I objected. "I saw him. I got off and checked him. I know a dead animal when I see one."

"Well, you see, Harvey," Uncle Jonathan explained, "it is possible to hit a buck on the horns and the bullet will ricochet off but knock him cold. Then after a few minutes, the deer will recover and run off."

I had not known this, but I was sure it was not the explanation for this mystery because I had seen where I hit him and it had broken his neck.

Juan and I searched the terrain, and finally we found the spot where the deer had bled. When Uncle Jonathan saw the amount of blood on the ground, he agreed it must have been killed. But the buck was gone.

Juan kept searching and soon found hoofprints going in a northerly direction. In Spanish, he said, "The deer was loaded on a horse here. The hoofprints are deeper on the way to the fence line." He turned to Uncle Jonathan and said, "Roscoe."

My uncle answered, "Roscoe has a lot of pride. I can't imagine him claiming a deer he did not kill." He turned to me, rubbing his hand across his chin as he considered the possibilities. "Did you see anyone around when you shot the deer?"

"I didn't look," I answered. "I was in a hurry to get to the ranch house to report the fire. But I know I killed it and I know the buck is gone. Who is Roscoe?"

"A neighbor. Not sure it was him. Let's go."

"If you don't mind, Uncle Jonathan, I'm going to search around and check out the area."

"Okay, Harvey. Don't stay too long." He was glancing across the north fence as he added, "And I want Juan to stay with you." I looked toward the Mexican and he nodded.

My uncle turned his horse and nudged it to a canter as he headed for the house.

Juan asked where I had first spotted the deer and I took him to the spot. We tied our horses to a limb and started walking in circles, increasing the diameter by twenty feet with each turn. Finally, about seventy-five yards from where the deer had been standing, we discovered bootprints on soft clay behind some bushes. Juan explained that the cedar bushes facing toward the north were perfectly shaped to create a good hunting blind. And following the bootprints over a small mound we found the tracks of the hunter's horse.

"Now I see the whole picture," Juan said, speaking to me in Spanish as he always did. "Harvey, you came upon a standing buck that someone was about to shoot. When the buck saw you, it took off and you dropped it on the run before the hunter could make his kill."

He took me back to where the deer had originally stood and pointed to a clump of cedars where the trampled brush showed the impression of its big body. It must have rested here often. Someone had been studying the deer's habits, its movements, and its resting places, carefully planning how to kill it. This was the work of a meticulous hunter, and I — in a split second — had wasted all his hard work, all his research, all his tracking, and all the time he had devoted to it.

Juan turned to me and with a grave expression he said, "Regardless of the hunter's fine skills, he has been poaching and trespassing on your uncle's ranch — and he had no right to that deer in the first place. As far as I am concerned, I am happy you killed it, and I consider that hunter a thief. And I am sure that the hunter is Roscoe Rafferty, the son of our neighbor to the north."

And so that day I heard for the first time the name of the man who was to be my nemesis and who would appear at strangely significant moments of my life.

The following morning, I prepared to head out for my day's work. My uncle had told me to inspect the northern boundary line for any breaks in the fence and for posts that needed replacement, do minor repairs, and make mental notes of major fence breaks that the other ranch hands would take care of later. Fence repairs and post replacements were always done in early summer. I was also to move cattle away from the fence line as I rode.

Riding the fences would take two days, allowing me to spend one night on the range. I had learned to love lying alone on the open ground, staring up at the immensity of the starry heavens over Texas.

Juan was standing at the corral gate when I started to leave, and he quietly cautioned me, "Be alert and aware. You will be on the Rafferty Ranch line. You have your rifle?"

I answered him by patting the .30-.30 Winchester in its scabbard next to my saddle, but my mind was on the job at hand and on the joy of working on the ranch, so I dismissed the warning with little thought. I leaned forward, lifted the reins slightly, and Ranger headed out the north trail.

By mid-afternoon, I had checked two miles of fence line and was lost in the fascination of the ranch. The vastness of the land, the huge sky, the sound of the wind with its own constant melody. Never lonely, I talked occasionally to Ranger as we followed the fence, but for now, neither wanted nor needed anyone else.

Suddenly I was startled back to reality by the crack of a rifle shot. I heard the whish of a bullet passing close to my ear and the thud of the bullet as it buried itself in a tree. Ranger jumped slightly, his ears came erect, and I felt myself tremble. Thick brush had forced me away from the fence, and I was a hundred and fifty yards from the line and from the direction of the shot. Instinctively I galloped toward the fence line, drawing my rifle from the scabbard as my eyes checked the brush for movement toward the north. Was this an accidental near-miss from a hunter, or a deliberate shot at me? I intended to find out.

I caught a glimpse of a grey horse galloping up a hill on the next ranch. The rider was dressed in black — black shirt and black hat — that made him seem evil. I reached the fence, turned along it until I found a place where the wires were low. Wheeling Ranger to give him some distance, I spurred and headed him straight for the fence and over. At full speed, I went after the grey horse that had now disappeared over the hill and must have been at least three hundred yards ahead of me. At the top of the hill I stopped and saw nothing. The back side of the slope was thick with cedar. I waited.

After a moment or two, I saw the grey horse coming out of the brush down below, heading toward a little creek in a small clearing. The rider stopped, turned, and looked up directly at me. Even at that distance I could sense the intensity in his bold stare. He slowly withdrew his rifle from the scabbard and placed it across his saddle, and then it seemed as if his body suddenly relaxed. He turned away and slowly trotted off, occasionally glancing back at me to check my reaction. He was almost daring me to follow, but I couldn't figure if he was hoping I would or confident that I wouldn't. I guessed it was Rafferty and he felt safe on his own ranch. I was sorely tempted to follow him, but I knew I was trespassing and not sure what I would run into. My better judgment won the day.

Still slightly shaken, I reached the place where I had jumped the fence and jumped it again. For a moment I thought of going back to the ranch house and reporting the incident to my uncle. But I decided, since it was already late in the afternoon, to continue my job on the fence line, camp for the night, finish up tomorrow, and get back to the house in the afternoon.

I felt a surge of pride in myself because, despite the feeling of danger and tension, I had actually enjoyed the excitement and I had not felt fear. And although I realized that I must be alert, I felt I was ready for any event. Despite my youth, I was very self-assured — I had proven to be a good athlete during my first year in high school and had probably developed a dangerous over-confidence.

At sunset, I turned my horse to the right, toward the center of the ranch, and pitched camp on a small cliffside where it would be difficult for anyone to sneak up on me during the night. After a supper of jerky, hardtack biscuits, and an apple, I lay propped against my saddle and wondered why anyone would want to shoot at me or kill me. It must have been Roscoe Rafferty. But what had I done that warranted such a violent reaction? Frontier days when men would fight for land or rustle cattle were long behind us. The only reason we carried rifles now was for hunting or protection from snakes — not from men.

Then my mind wandered to the curious relationship between

Uncle Jonathan and Juan Delgado. My older brother Paul and I joked about our uncle's shadow. Juan was tall and slender — a good-looking man but with something mysterious and deadly about him. When he looked hard at someone, you could see them wilt. My older married sister once told me that Uncle Jonathan had rescued Juan from a prison in Mexico. He was to be executed the next day for killing a madman who had gone berserk in the open market in Durango. The fellow had already killed a man and his wife. Juan warned him to drop his knife. He refused. Juan shot him. But unfortunately the crazed man was the brother of the local chief of police.

There was also a mysterious story about Uncle Jonathan. My sister said that a man had made an accusation against our uncle about a land claim. It seems the man had lost his small ranch because of back taxes and was evicted. His wife developed pneumonia and died. When Uncle Jonathan bought the ranch at auction, the man, sick with grief, blamed my uncle for all his misfortunes — the loss of his wife and his ranch. He vowed to kill Uncle Jonathan and made a serious attempt to keep his promise. Since that day, Juan Delgado had always been at Jonathan Reese's side.

The night was uneventful. The next day I arrived at the ranch house in mid-afternoon and was disappointed to learn that Uncle Jonathan and Juan Delgado had gone to Luling where my uncle had his home. His wife kept a comfortable house for him there, and as far as I could see they loved each other very much, but he necessarily spent more than half of his time at the ranch, and the ranch was obviously an all-male territory.

The main house was plain — a practical headquarters for the ranching operation. The bare wood floors were the mark of a bachelor house; a woman would have wanted some rugs somewhere. A large pot-bellied stove separated the living area from the kitchen, and there were two small bedrooms. At the back was a screened sleeping porch, where I usually slept, and the porch in front held two chairs and a swing. Beyond the main house was the bunkhouse, and then a small corral where cattle were loaded, usually into Uncle Jonathan's two-ton, flat-bed, Chevrolet stake truck, for shipment to market. And farther off was a larger corral where horses were trained and wild horses were broken.

All the other hands were there. Wade was the oldest — thirty-four or thirty-five, I would guess — tall, slender, tough, and the most experienced. He was always nice to me. There were two brothers, Joe and Jeff. Joe, the younger, was nineteen, short and chubby, with a constant scowl on his face and an obnoxious habit of cursing to demonstrate how tough he was. I found him hard to like. Jeff, the hand who had discovered the fire, was medium height and stocky, and usually very quiet. The other hand was Porky, who despite his name was not really fat but just big and broad, and always jovial.

Porky was skinning a calf that had broken a front leg and had to be killed. I was delighted because this would mean fresh barbecue, which was the custom when a calf or steer was slaughtered. Otherwise, the menu consisted of beans, corn bread, and a boiled vegetable.

I found Wade lying on his bunk looking miserable, and I sat down on the next cot to talk to him.

"Do you know when Uncle Jonathan is supposed to get back?" I asked.

"Any minute now, I hope." Wade had been in constant pain the last few days due to a boil on the back of his neck. It was larger than a quarter and had swelled to almost half an inch in thickness. He could hardly turn his head now.

"Wade," I said, "somebody tried to kill me yesterday. Barely missed me."

He looked up, startled. "What fence line were you working?" he asked.

When I told him it was the north fence, he immediately said, "Rafferty. The Rafferty Ranch. Did you see him? How was he dressed?"

"Grey horse, black shirt, black hat."

He sat up and hit the floor with his heels. "Roscoe Rafferty!" he blurted out. "That guy is crazy! Listen, Harvey, my advice is to keep away from that wild man. He's bad business. I saw him in a fight a while back in Lockhart. He went nuts. He beat a guy a lot bigger than him — beat him to a pulp! The other guy's face was a bloody mess, and he had bites on his arms and shoulders — and I mean big gashes. Roscoe's mouth was dripping with the feller's blood, and when he knocked the poor sucker down he started kicking him. It took four men to pull him off."

For a minute, Wade had gotten so excited he forgot about his misery. Now he eased back on the bed and stretched out again as he went on in a calmer voice. "But if you want to know more about him, talk to Joe. He knows that family pretty well. He's Roscoe's friend, God knows why." He paused for a moment and reached up to touch his neck near the boil. The pain must have been pretty bad, but he went on. "They say Old Man Rafferty has killed three or four men and gotten away with it. No witnesses. I keep clear of them. But you ought to wait for your uncle and tell him about this problem. I just don't like it. And talk to Joe."

Joe was sitting on a rocker on the small front porch of the bunkhouse. As I started over to him, I heard the rattling of the truck coming down the dirt road so I turned and headed for my uncle instead. Wade got there before I did, and the pain was evident in his voice as he asked for some relief from the boil on his neck.

Uncle Jonathan slipped from the seat of his truck and landed on the heels of his boots. He told Wade to go to the ranch house and wait, and then asked me to get some hot water. I went to the outdoor kitchen in the yard where a pot was always on the boil for coffee, grabbed the kettle, and returned to the house. As I entered, Uncle Jonathan was slicing the boil on Wade's neck with a razor blade. He made two incisions crosswise. It was revolting to me — the pus and the blood. As Wade clutched one of the bedposts, Uncle Jonathan kept sponging the ugly gaping wound. He took hot water, cleaned the cuts with antiseptic, and applied the bandage with pressure, using long strips of adhesive tape.

When the operation was over, my uncle and I stepped out on the porch and I told him about my close call the day before. He heard me out, then he said, "Maybe it was just an accident. Maybe he was shooting at something else."

"No sir!" I insisted. "The way he galloped off, the way he stopped and looked at me again — there's no doubt in my mind."

Uncle Jonathan said, "Let me look into this matter a bit more, and I'll speak to you later."

I followed as he went back to his truck where the squealing of an angry horse was getting louder and louder. Juan and the other men were trying to unload a beautiful horse that Uncle Jonathan had bought and named "The Black." Despite the four ropes that held him, the horse seemed to be able to rear up on his hind legs at will. His nostrils flared and he snorted in defiance.

Juan said in Spanish, "This is a black devil. It will take a real man *(un hombre)* to ride him."

The horse's coloring was not just black, but so shiny a black it looked dark red, almost a burgundy. What a beautiful animal, I thought to myself. His lines are almost perfect. I would love to own him.

They backed the truck up to a small slanting ramp leading into the large corral. The men had a difficult time backing the horse down the ramp, snorting and kicking, but eventually he was down. Once in the high-fenced corral, he bucked and cantered around the fence while the men watched with admiration.

Uncle Jonathan leaned on the top rail and considered his purchase with pleasure. "We'll let him settle down a couple of days, and then we're going to see if we have a man among us who can bring that horse down a notch or two," he said with a crooked smile in the corner of his mouth and with his blue eyes flashing.

As we all walked back to the campfire, I pulled Joe aside and asked, "Do you know Roscoe Rafferty well?"

"Yeah, I suppose so," he answered. "Why?"

"I think he took a shot at me."

"You're kidding!"

"No. I was going east on the north fence line yesterday afternoon when he shot but missed. I'm sure it was him. I never saw his face closely, but I'm sure it was him."

"Look, kid," he said, assuming a cocky stance. "I think you might be wrong. I know Roscoe pretty well. He's an eighteen-year-old wild kid, but I don't think he would try that kind of shit. Can I talk to you about this tomorrow? I'm supposed to be watching the fire and the meat, and I had a hell of a day today. I started at sunrise and I'm beat. Tomorrow, okay?"

That night, as I lay on a cot on the sleeping porch that was next to Uncle Jonathan's small bedroom, I could hear him snoring, sleeping very deeply. I lay awake, going over in my mind the exciting events of that day — thinking of the grey horse and the rider in black who had tried to kill me. In some ways, the horse and the rider did not seem real, yet they were very ominous.

# Chapter 2

A little later, still wide awake, my thoughts went back two years to the summer when I was fourteen. That was the year I came to the ranch for the first time. I learned to ride well and Uncle Jonathan was impressed with my aptitude as a cowboy. When I was fifteen, Papa gave me permission to come again, and by then my uncle was letting me work alongside the other men, for he had found that I could keep up with them at every job. In fact, I felt that I could handle horses and cattle better than some of the old hands, and this included Joe — which made me especially resent his accusing me of being my uncle's pet. Joe was only a couple of years older than I was, but he had grown up on ranches, and I hadn't forgotten that first summer when I overheard him making cracks about "the city boy."

But during those previous summers I never heard of the Rafferty Ranch nor the Rafferty family, and it seemed strange to me now that I had not heard of Roscoe Rafferty, who was only my senior by a year.

My thoughts then drifted back to San Antonio, my home, the grocery store that my father owned, and to my mother. I thought especially about the events of last month, the close of the school year. Many things happened during those last weeks of May. Because I had studied hard all year, my report card showed good grades. I had gone steady for six months with Joanne, one of the prettiest girls in school, and I had, as always, taken part in many sports. Every afternoon and on Saturdays I had helped in the grocery store.

By far the most exciting event that May was when Uncle Jonathan asked Papa if I could work on the Double R all summer, starting the first of June. My father hesitated because he actually needed my help in the grocery store. With his brother Jesse, he had started a soft-drink bottling company in San Luis Potosi, Mexico, and at times it was necessary for him to go down there. This left the store shorthanded since my older brother, Paul, had entered college and was taking summer courses in an effort to graduate a year early.

My work at the store was not hard, but it wasn't very exciting either. Papa and I would go to the San Antonio farmer's market every morning at sunrise where he would buy fresh vegetables and produce. He bought rice, sugar, pinto beans, and potatoes in hundred-pound sacks. It was my job then to sack those items into one- and five-pound bags. I usually would do this in the mornings, and in the afternoons I would make deliveries, at times on my bicycle, other times with Charley, our deliveryman and part-time butcher, in Papa's little red Model A truck.

I enjoyed making deliveries, mostly because it got me outdoors. Sacking pinto beans and potatoes in the small confines of the grocery store was pretty dull, but most Saturdays my father would allow me to leave by one thirty to have fun with my friends.

Mama would occasionally help in the store, especially at the checkout counter during the rush hours. Whenever she entered, I found myself staring at her. She was fascinating, almost hypnotic, to me. My mother, Delia Leon Reese, was a woman of unbelievable grace, charm, culture, and beauty. Her eyes were wonderfully magnetic and her skin tones seemed like a master's painting, the skin so fair it looked almost transparent. Her face was the reflection of love. I have never known anyone like her before nor since, and this

15

was not just the adoration of a boy for his mother for I discovered that everybody who met her held her in awe.

Her voice was melodious, and yet showed a firmness, an underlying strength of character. Every night at bedtime she would read to me. At this time we were at the end of *Don Quixote.* The book and her explanations held me spellbound — the quest, the search for one's true self, his lady Dulcinea, honor, and chivalry . . . I did not realize then how firmly my mother and this book were molding my attitudes and setting the pattern for the rest of my life.

There was something about Mama which was so gentle, so utterly feminine and ladylike, that I found it impossible to speak to her about anything violent. She was aware that I participated in football, basketball, baseball, and that I enjoyed boxing, but we never spoke of those activities. Before she left the store she would always come by and touch my face. At home, I would never leave a room where she was without kissing her. And although Papa spoke with me many times about integrity, it was Mama's talks that influenced me the most.

Recently she had twice mentioned that before I left for the ranch she would speak with me of something special. Both times she said, "The time has come." I could not imagine what she was referring to. In the past, she had talked to me about most of the great values of life. While I worked, the thought would come to me again, wondering what she would tell me, and when.

The grocery store was a stucco building on a corner, and our house was just behind it. The store entrance was a double door which cut across the front corner and opened out on a small, triangular concrete porch. Just across Elmira Street was an embankment which sloped down to San Pedro Creek. The creek, in turn, flowed into the San Antonio River and then to the Gulf of Mexico. When I was little, I had spent many an hour catching crawfish and perch in the creek, and dreaming about how it would be to follow the streams clear to the Gulf and on out to sea.

On Tuesday, the second week of May, in the middle of the afternoon, I was on my last sack of potatoes in the back corner of the store when I noticed a slender man in dark clothing and wearing a cap come in the front door. There was no one in the store except Papa and me and a lady who had just paid for her groceries and was walking out the door. The man stood aside to let her pass, then stepped up to the counter where my father was still occupied at the register. By the time the stranger reached the counter, he had pulled up a handkerchief over the lower part of his face and had pulled the cap down so that only his deepset eyes and heavy brows were visible. He had a pistol and was aiming it at Papa.

"Put all the money in a bag. I don't want to hurt you," he blurted out. He glanced toward me, then looked back at my father. I could see that he was very nervous. The gun was shaking in his hands.

I was startled at my father's expression. His face had gone hard and his eyes had narrowed. He stood there rigid but poised as though he was ready to spring. I had a large potato in my hand and I thought about throwing the potato very hard at the man, feeling certain I would hit him. But then if I should miss, the man would probably kill my father. I dropped the idea.

Papa glanced under the counter where he kept his gun. The man noticed and waved him back. Papa backed away about five feet. The man went around the counter, grabbed the gun and a paper bag, and started putting money into the bag as fast as he could, in such a hurry that he was spilling the change. Then he sat on the counter, slung his legs over it, and started backing out the door. When he got to the entrance he turned, jumped off the porch, and ran across the street toward the creek.

Papa went to the opposite counter and to my surprise grabbed another pistol hidden under some paper bags, and he ran out after the robber. By the time Papa reached the front door, the man had crossed the street, reached the creek, and had gone down the embankment, and he was out of sight. Papa ran across the street clutching his pistol, crossed the small grassy area next to the creek, and cautiously went down the slope, looking in both directions.

I followed about ten feet behind and caught up with him at the embankment. The man was nowhere to be seen. Papa hesitated for a moment, shrugged his shoulders, turned, and went back to the store. The robber had taken $24.68 — a great deal of money in those days.

My father turned to me, his expression softened, and he said, "Harvey, it's time for you to go play. You've done a good job," as if nothing had happened. I realized with a shock how little I really knew this man.

"Thank you, Papa. See you later."

I took off at a run to join my three best friends, Bob Barton, Jimmy Watkins, and Theo Gonzalez. They were in the back yard at Jimmy's house, working on our raft. We had bolted four large metal drums to the corners of a two-by-four frame. After we nailed on a deck of old boards we had collected, we had a sturdy raft six feet wide and eight feet long.

The drums were a gift from my father. He stocked kerosene oil for lamps at the store, and he had purchased a number of drums from a company that had gone broke. When I asked for the empties, telling him that we were building a raft, he agreed without hesitating, although he could have received a deposit refund. It was typical of his generosity with his children when he could manage it.

Our plan was to go down the San Antonio River and explore the area to the south. We were hoping for a great adventure. We expected to finish the raft in the next two weeks and then ask Papa's permission for Charley, our butcher, to transport it to the river on the Model A truck. I found myself rushing the others to finish the raft because I would be leaving for the ranch in three weeks, and I sure did not want to miss out on the river adventure.


Two weeks later the raft was ready. Papa said, "Harvey, if you will work with me Sunday morning till noon — till the store closes — you don't have to work the rest of next week." That would give me time for the raft trip before I left for the ranch. I quickly accepted his kind offer.

Sunday morning I waited on customers, made change, and closed the door at twelve sharp. The only job left after closing was to sweep the floor and then spread sawdust on it. As we were about to leave, a man came to the front door. He stood on the triangular porch outside and tapped on the glass of the closed door, shouting that he was desperate for a dozen eggs.

My father merely waved his hand and said, "We are closed." But the man persisted, pounding on the door, saying, "I must have a dozen eggs."

"Papa," I said with a sudden tingle of excitement, "I think

that's that fellow who robbed us." There were the same deepset eyes and heavy eyebrows.

The man continued to insist.

Finally my father said, "Okay. Wait just a minute." He went behind the counter, got a dozen eggs, and slipped out the back door with his gun in his hand. I walked around the counter to the front door just as Papa came up behind the man on the porch, taking him completely by surprise. He jumped nearly a foot as Papa pointed the pistol at his face and said, "Here's your dozen eggs. They are three dollars a dozen."

"Three dollars!" exclaimed the man.

"Yes, three dollars," Papa said as he cocked the hammer of his pistol. "And next week they will be six dollars."

The man's mouth dropped open, but he slowly reached into his pocket, pulled out three dollars and handed them over, took the sack with the eggs, then inched gingerly down the steps. Papa had a tight, hard grin on his mouth, his eyes were narrowed, and he seemed cool as a cucumber. I truly believe that if the man had flinched the slightest bit, my father would have blown his head off.

When Papa reentered the store, I said excitedly, "That's the same guy! I know it was him. Tall and skinny, same cheekbones, same eyebrows, same cap. That was him!"

"I know," he replied quietly as he put the gun back under the counter and rang up the sale.

# Chapter 3

E arly next morning, Jimmy, Theo, and I loaded the raft onto the Model A. Charley drove us to Mrs. Schultz's boardinghouse to pick up the last member of our gang, Bob Barton.

The four of us had been buddies for several years. Bob Barton, blond and tall, was my closest friend. Theo Gonzalez was a plump, happy little guy who always made us laugh. Jimmy Watkins was the serious one — and he had reason to be. His father was a drunkard, a mean man who became abusive when he drank. Jimmy told me that his father regularly beat up his mother, and on occasion would strike him with his fist. We had talked for a long time about building a raft to run away down the river as pirates, and though we said it as a joke, Jimmy, at least, wished it could happen.

We unloaded the raft into the San Antonio River just beyond the southern city limits. A six-foot pole was attached to the back brace and a large blue bandana-flag waved from it in the breeze. Our supplies consisted of a large jug of water, two loaves of bread, four apples, four oranges, and a dozen hardboiled eggs. We launched our raft with great excitement.

We floated down the river without any difficulty for three

hours, and then south of town I became aware that the current was running faster. Each of us had an eight-foot pole that we used to propel the raft by pushing against the bottom of the river which had now deepened to some five to six feet.

Bob, who was standing at the rear to steer, had noticed the swifter current too. He asked, "Is that another river that has joined the San Antonio?"

"Yes," I answered. "The Medina."

I looked back at him and saw some concern on his face. "The river sure has gotten wider and deeper," he said. "You think it's okay?"

Jimmy had been poling hard on his side of the raft. When he heard this he turned and asked, with slight panic in his voice, "What do you mean by that?" But before anyone could answer him, he exclaimed, "My God, look at the alligators!" and pointed toward the east bank. Six alligators were sleeping on the banks of a shallow cove. "Suppose they attack?" Jimmy asked.

"Don't worry," I said. "We can beat them with our poles."

Theo, who was very small but always spunky, said, "I got my .22 rifle. If they make a move, I'll shoot them in the head!"

His statement struck me as funny and I started to laugh, but Jimmy looked at me with such concern that I bit my tongue. The alligators hardly noticed as we went past.

Soon we forgot the alligators, and Theo said as he pointed to the sky, "Look at the ducks. There's hundreds! And look at those other strange birds." He grabbed his .22 and took a shot. Not a chance, I thought to myself. I had been duck hunting with Papa and knew how hard it was to bring a duck down even with a twelve-gauge shotgun.

The vegetation on the banks had become heavier, more lush, and Bob asked, "Have you guys noticed all the flowers? You'd think we were in a different country. It's like a tropical jungle."

"Harvey, how far down the river have we drifted?" Jimmy asked.

"I'm not sure," I returned. "I believe it's past noon. Let's pull into shore, have lunch, and rest awhile."

As we approached the bank, we noticed two black snakes near the shoreline. "Those are cottonmouths!" Theo screamed. "Let's kill them. Don't let them get away."

When we got within reach, we started beating them with our poles and killed one, but the other slithered away as Theo took a shot at it with his .22.

The water near the bank was very shallow and we could not pole the raft all the way to the shore. None of us enjoyed walking in the shallow water to the bank after seeing the snakes.

We tied up to a small tree and walked up a rise to a beautiful spot under two big oaks to have our lunch. Then we lay on our backs looking up toward the sky, chewing on grass blades, watching the lazy clouds glide by.

I turned to Theo and asked, "What do you want to be when you grow up?"

We weren't surprised by his first answer. He jumped up, made a funny face, and said, "I want to be a comedian like Charlie Chaplin." He strutted for a minute like the Little Tramp, then went on, "If not, then I want to be a butcher. My grandfather was a butcher for the Comanche Packing Company. He had lots of money. The company went broke in the Depression. He died of a heart attack. He croaked!"

As he said the word, he dropped his pants, fell to the ground, grabbed his throat, and kicked his feet as if he was dying of a heart attack. He was so funny that we laughed for five minutes.

Bob stood and said, "I'm going to be a reporter and work for a large city newspaper, maybe New York or Chicago, and I'm going to write stories about crime and sex. I'm going to expose all the corruption I can discover. That's why I work so hard at English. I always make A's."

Jimmy started talking without looking at us directly, as if he was talking to himself. "I want to travel the world," he said. "I'm never going to have a home. Always on the move. I want to see every country, learn how they live, stay awhile and then move on. Maybe I'll write about my adventures."

The others turned toward me. I had not realized what I was going to say until it came my turn. I started, "Don Quixote set out to find honor, glory, and his lady. He was like a knight of old in shining armor, always trying to help those in need. My mother has convinced me that I should also go about helping and saving people everywhere along my way, and that I should never turn my back on anybody who needs help."

They laughed. Bob said, "You're joking, aren't you?"

"I guess," I said, smiling. And yet, as I thought of Mama I wasn't sure. It did not seem practical, but I wasn't sure.

Finally we lay there quietly . . . and then asleep. About an hour later, I was startled awake by raindrops. It worried me a bit. I woke the others and said, "Let's get going. It's beginning to rain."

By the time we waded out to the raft, the rain came pouring down. We looked at each other with panic, and then I calmed down and said to myself there was really nothing to worry about. The temperature was warm, and while the rain would soak us, I didn't see how it could affect the river in any way. What I did not realize was how difficult it was going to be to push the raft with our poles against the current.

For three hours we struggled, and we must have only gone one mile. I tried to calculate how far down the river we might have drifted and estimated thirty miles or more. We could not possibly make it back to town before dark. By now the river was out of its banks, in floodstage. I concluded that water from the sporadic heavy thunderstorms north of the city in the past two days were reaching this section of the river, adding to the new rainfall. The current became swifter and I began to feel we might be in real danger.

I suggested we go to shore. Jimmy Watkins turned and objected, almost hysterically. "My dad will beat me if we don't get home by sunset. He told me so!"

"But Jimmy," I returned, "it has to be late afternoon. There is no way we can make it. We're miles away."

The water was now at least three feet above the banks. We tried to maneuver to shore, but we weren't very successful. A new shoreline had been created by the rising water, and the drums of our raft drew too much water for us to get closer than thirty feet. When we stopped pushing with our poles, we drifted downstream. Everybody was giving commands at once and there was panic in every voice. Jimmy looked scared to death, and I remembered that he could hardly swim. We kept pushing, we kept trying, but we weren't getting any closer to land, just drifting downstream faster and faster.

Bob Barton said, "The hell with this!" and dived in and swam to shore. Theo followed but he was washed downstream fifty feet before he found his footing.

Jimmy turned to me and said frantically, "Harvey, I'm gonna drown. What am I gonna do? I've got to get off this thing."

"Hold on, hold on. We'll get to shore . . ." I answered, but before I could finish he jumped off the raft. I jumped after him. We drifted down the river. All the while he was splashing wildly.

I came up behind and grabbed him from the back and said, "Jimmy, don't fight me or we'll both drown." But he was gasping and struggling. We came to a slight curve of the bank and I shoved him toward the shore. There the water was shallow enough for him to get a foothold and walk to the bank.

I was washed another forty feet downstream. A big tree came floating by and I grabbed one of the branches, then the tree rolled and the branch on which I hung carried me underwater. I struggled to come up, but the branch pinned me down. The tree swung up again and I came above water, gasping for air. Suddenly I was back down underneath and being dragged across the bottom. Just as I thought my lungs would burst, I hit a large rock and it broke me loose from the branch. I surfaced, drifted another fifty feet, and finally managed to get to shore.

I lay on the bank gasping. Despite swallowing a lot of water, I was okay. I stood and looked downstream hoping to learn the fate of our raft. It was gone forever . . . except for the pole with the blue bandana that stood at an angle, stuck in brush, trapped against some large rocks in the middle of the river. The little flag was still waving bravely in the wind.

I remembered about Jimmy, so I ran back up the bank and found him sitting there huddled, wet and shaking. I put my arm around him and said, "It's okay. We all made it."

Bob and Theo came up and sat next to me. Nobody had much to say. We were all soaked, shaken by the close call, and concerned about getting back to San Antonio. Our wonderful adventure had turned into disaster.

Half an hour later we started walking north along the bank of the river, with the rain still pouring and the terrain so rough we decided to cut across country, hoping we would find a road. Just at dark we found a narrow caliche road and followed it until we came to a small wooden house set back under a tree. In the dark and rainy night it looked sort of spooky, but there was a dim light from one window.

We stood hesitating, but things couldn't get much worse, so finally Theo stepped up and knocked on the door. Nothing happened and he had to knock again before the door opened, and there stood a tall, skinny old man, holding a lamp high and peering at us with fear. His stooped and wrinkled old wife stood just behind him. When they saw we were boys they relaxed and invited us in. Bob asked about the possibility of transportation back to San Antonio, but they said they had none. They explained it would likely be possible to catch a ride early the next morning with one of the farmers that lived below them who would be going north to San Antonio's market.

# Chapter 4

We spent the night in their barn, hanging our clothes up to dry, and huddling together wrapped in horse blankets and burrowed deep in the hay. Hardly a word was spoken. Our thoughts were on our worried parents at home, and the punishment we would probably get.

At dawn we were awakened by the old man, who had waved down a truck headed to San Antonio and obtained a ride for us. We dressed in a hurry, grabbed the biscuits which the kind old lady handed us, and piled into the truck. The dirt farmer was hauling a load of corn to the market less than two miles from where we lived. We must have looked like a sorry crew of bedraggled waifs, but our spirits were improving as we reached the outskirts of town. The rain had stopped and the sun was beginning to come through the thin clouds. Only . . . we still had to face our parents.

As we walked home from the farmer's market, Jimmy asked, "Harvey, will you come home with me first and help me explain?"

I hesitated because I was so concerned about my own predicament, but the expression on his face convinced me that I should help my friend. "Sure, but let's hurry," I told him.

Jimmy lived across the street from me, about two houses down. We walked around to his back yard and were startled to find his father sitting there on a stump. It was obvious that he had been drinking, and a jug was on the ground between his feet. He had a scowl on his face that made him look even meaner than usual.

Knowing Jimmy was afraid of him, I stepped forward and spoke. "Mr. Watkins, we had a close call. We're sorry we're late."

He stood up, and sort of shoved me aside to get at his son, and struck him on the side of his face. Jimmy fell to the ground with a thud, and as he gasped with pain and put his arms over his head to protect it, his father kicked him twice, striking his leg and his back.

I started toward Jimmy to see if I could help him, then turned toward Mr. Watkins as he leaned over his son. I was yelling, "No! Don't!" but he didn't even hear me as he screamed at Jimmy.

"You little pissant! You son of a bitch! Always playing. Never considering how hard life is for your poor Pa."

He landed another kick with his heavy workshoe on his son's hip, and then suddenly Jimmy jumped to his feet and lunged at his father with clenched fists. He had to reach up to do it, but he hit the drunken man with a well-placed shot to the jaw, and Mr. Watkins stumbled back. Jimmy turned and ran down the street, with me close behind.

"Where are you going?" I called to him as we ran.

"I'm getting the hell out of here," he gasped. "And I'm never coming back. But some day I'll see you again, Harvey." He turned to look back at me and slowed for a minute. "I'll see you again," he said.

I watched him run until he turned the corner at the end of the block, and I stood there remembering his desire to leave home and travel the world. This was his chance, and I guess he had a sort of quest of his own, but the trouble was that he was running away from something instead of *toward* a dream.

Anyway, I never found out if he got what he thought he wanted, for that was the last time I ever saw Jimmy Watkins.

I walked on down the street, watching the big red and white sign REESE GROCERY getting closer and closer, not sure what I was in for. My father was a fair and patient man, but perhaps this time he would not be so forgiving. Squaring my shoulders, I walked on, up the steps, and into the store.

Both my parents were there, and the relief on their faces when I walked in made me feel worse than any punishment they could offer. They listened to my story of the raft and the rain and the flood and our night in the barn, then Papa told me to go to the house and change clothes and wash the hay out of my hair.

But he added sternly, "You should not have worried your mother. I think you have just lost your trip to the ranch."

As I walked past my mother she reached out a hand and pulled me to her. Embracing me, she kissed my face tenderly and whispered, "We'll talk later."

That night and the next day I kept waiting for the promised talk, but nothing happened. Three more days went by, and I began to wonder what was to be my punishment — not going to the ranch, or not knowing whether I was going, or it just never being mentioned again.

Then it was Friday evening and Uncle Jonathan was supposed to come the following morning to pick me up — if he was coming, and if I was going. I went to bed quite early that night, hoping against hope.

Twenty minutes after I turned out my light, as I lay there wondering, my door opened and Papa came in and stood by my bed. He was silhouetted by the light from the hall as he looked down at me.

"Harvey," he said, "your mother has always been afraid for you to work at the ranch. Always afraid you might get hurt. But this time, she has convinced me to let you go." He sat down on the edge of my bed, and his voice was soft but firm as he went on. "It angers me when you are not considerate of her, especially when you cause her to worry. You must know that there is no other person in the world like your mother. Someday you will realize how incredible she is."

"I know, Papa, and I truly am sorry."

His words surprised me. I was aware that Mama was wonderful, but I had never thought about how he regarded her. As he got up and turned to leave, he asked, "By the way, was the river a great experience?" and I could hear the smile in his voice.

"Yes," I answered. "It was. It was a great adventure."

He smiled and said, "Good. Be tough, my boy."

As he walked out and closed the door to my small bedroom, I felt a surge of love for him and realized for the first time how much he adored my mother. His visit to my room had lifted my spirits incredibly. I was going to the ranch, and for now, that was all that mattered. And so, with the excitement, I had difficulty going to sleep.

Just as I was about to drift under, the door opened again, and my mother stood there — but she looked so different that at first I thought she was an apparition. She was wearing a white gown, sheer and very lacy, and instead of her black hair clinging to her head with a bun in the back as she wore it in the daytime, now it floated lustrous, full, and free below her shoulders. One long lock fell across her left shoulder and hung above her heart. The backlight of the hallway filtered through the gown and through her hair and outlined her graceful figure. I could not speak, and I would not have known what to call her if I had, for she seemed more angel than human, and "Mama" did not seem the proper word to use.

This was a magical moment. It was as though now a spell was cast over me and my life, a dedication and a purpose established, an inspiration instilled into my soul forever. I have referred to this event in my mind as The Day of the Riddle or The Day of the White Scarf — and I have never related the following experience to anyone, for fear of being misunderstood or ridiculed.

Mama stood there for a few seconds and then called me by her pet name, *"Mi Havito."* She walked toward me with slow and floating steps that scarcely seemed to touch the floor. She sat on the bed and leaned toward me, kissed me, and then with her left hand caressed my face.

She spoke to me in melodious Spanish, softly . . . and yet to this day the words thunder in my ear. To this day, the spirit of her message reverberates in my brain and then repeats and repeats.

She said, "Listen, my son, listen. Do you hear the music?"

We sat for a long moment silently. Aware of the question on my face, she smiled and said, "You will. In time, you will. The wind, the trees, the earth have music for those who listen." Her hand moved to push the stray lock of hair behind her shoulder as I watched with fascination. "Honor is a word difficult to understand. Honor is illusive for most men, and a mystery to others. Honor is to live truthfully and with nobility in all aspects of life. Always with justice. You, my son, cannot live without honor. You must not live without honor. Your adventure is about to begin."

We were quiet again, her soft eyes holding me. Then, in formal Spanish, she continued. "This is the riddle of the five illusions. Someday you will answer the riddle. The first of the five illusions asks, 'Who art thou?' Men think they know their own character. That is the illusion. The second, 'Where dost thou go?' You cannot answer the second if the first is in error. The third, 'Whom dost thou challenge?' The fourth, 'Whom dost thou fear?' The fifth, 'What dost thou seek?' Again, Who are you? Where do you go? Whom do you challenge? Whom do you fear? What do you seek? Don't try to solve the riddle today — you cannot. Someday, perhaps. You must have anguish and the scars therefrom to sharpen your senses, to make you keen and aware. Perhaps then.

"Live with honor. Let truth, integrity, uprighteousness always be at your side. Consider all men and all women your brothers and your sisters. Reject no one. Help those who ask, but especially those who do not ask. Reject no one."

"No one?" I asked.

"Yes, no one in need," she said. "Search for good among so much bad, and be triumphant."

She took my hand in hers and caressed it as she continued. "No one will tell you what is right. You will know. The world is your vessel, your ship, and you are the voyager." She paused, and an angelic smile appeared as she added, "Life to you will be a dashing and bold adventure. You must unfurl your wings and fly. After sorrow and despair, you will find a very special lady who will walk with you and will share with you. She will be a wonderful loving adventure. This quest will be elusive. Pursue it relentlessly. Do not lose heart when seeds of doubt appear."

She fell silent and I heard only her breathing. Though I felt overwhelmed by the emotion of that moment, it was to be years before I realized its true value.

She reached behind her and brought forth a white silk scarf, spreading one end so I could see the "H" embroidered on it. Then she put the scarf behind my head and around my neck.

"It is white, like your essence, my son," she said. "It is as your heart is today — pure, courageous, and stainless. Let your heart always be thus — pure and stainless — that you may have the right to wear this scarf, forever white. Wear it and be invincible."

Her beautiful brown eyes flooded me with love. She leaned down and kissed me. Her beauty was supernatural. . . ethereal. She stood, and without another word seemed to float from the room.

My mother never spoke about that night again, but there were times when she would look at me and merely say, *"Mi Havito,"* and her words would come back to me, and I would hear again every musical sound, the quest, the riddle, and "Honor — man cannot live without honor."

# Chapter 5

I lay on the porch next to Uncle Jonathan's bedroom in the small ranch house with the moonlight streaming through the screen, almost touching my bed, and as I drifted off to sleep my mother's face was transfixed upon my mind's eye.

I was startled when Joe called my name at sunrise. "You and me," he growled, "have to go to the south pasture and bring back about twenty steers that Porky saw trapped in a ravine near the river. Let's hurry. I want to get back because late this afternoon my brother's going to try and break that devil horse. They say that black devil has already hurt five men bad, but Jeff says he can ride it, and I think he will. So haul ass, kid, haul ass. We're leaving in half an hour."

As Joe walked away, I realized that he was the only one of the men that I disliked. He always acted cocky with me and had the reputation of carrying tales from one man to another. He spoke disrespectfully about women, always describing explicit details of his latest conquest. However, today I was happy he had a big mouth because I was hoping to learn more about his pal, Roscoe Rafferty.

Pulling on my jeans and shirt and boots fast, I walked into the kitchen and found Uncle Jonathan sipping his coffee from the saucer — his method of cooling it because he did not like his coffee too hot.

He gave me a big smile and said good morning, but then grew serious. "I think that Rafferty kid is capable of harming people," he warned. "I want you to avoid him, if at all possible. Roscoe could be dangerous.

"I heard Joe tell you about your job for today," he went on, "and I want you to hurry back in time to see the bronco ride. Jeff claims he can ride the black. I don't think so. Jeff is not the man. I wish I could let Juan break him. I think he could. But it would cause hard feelings among the men if he did." He shook his head sadly. "Juan is a Mexican, but he is more of a man than all of them put together. I don't give a damn what they think, and neither does Juan, but they could make it hard for him later."

As Uncle Jonathan talked, I wolfed down the pancakes that he had served me. I drank a glass of milk, grabbed three pieces of jerky and three biscuits for later and put them in my pocket.

"Take it easy out there, boy," he said as I headed for the door. With a backward wave, I was off and running to the small corral. Throwing the saddle on Ranger as fast as I could, I swung into the saddle, and met Joe just as he trotted his horse through the gate of the corral.

"I'll race you to the split oak," he challenged me, and took off, but within a few seconds I was alongside and flew by him. Ranger was a wonderful quarterhorse. Uncle Jonathan had trained him with great care and he could stop dead on a penny, take off like a bullet, and respond to commands almost instantly. You could even guide him and ride him just with knee pressure.

When I reached the split oak, I jumped off the saddle and lay down under the oak as if I was taking a nap, tactlessly rubbing in my victory. When Joe arrived I could see the dark cloud on his face and realized I had gone too far if I wanted to keep on his good side, so I made light of the whole thing, explaining that he was the better horseman but Ranger was such a great mount that it wasn't my riding skills but my horse that made the difference. I hated the idea of buttering up to a guy who was so obnoxious, but I still needed some information from him.

He seemed to relax a bit as we rode on, and at the right moment I said, "Joe, I sure do admire the way you control a horse and the way you handle cattle. I know the other fellows feel the same, and Uncle Jonathan thinks you are an excellent hand."

A big smile appeared on his face and he sat a little straighter as he remarked, "I know I'm pretty good, but most people are jealous as shit."

I went on, "Joe, I think those are the finest pair of boots that I have ever seen, and that hat of yours — if I can ever save enough money I am going to buy one just like it."

He had bought the boots in San Antonio, and they were handmade and good looking, but the hat was a bit grotesque and too big for him — black, with a snake band. The rest of the men actually laughed at it behind his back but he thought he looked terrific and obviously considered himself quite a dandy.

We rode on in silence for another mile. Then Joe suddenly started talking.

"Listen, kid. I'm going to tell you some things about the Rafferty family and Roscoe. I know them pretty well, but you've got to promise that you will never repeat anything I tell you. Okay?"

"Okay."

"Roscoe can be bad tempered. I'm even a little afraid of him sometimes myself. When he gets that murder look on his face — then I just get away from him. But a lot of things have happened to the poor guy. Old Man Rafferty, he's a mean son of a bitch. Up till a couple of years ago, he used to beat the shit out of the kid on a regular basis but it doesn't happen any more. Roscoe'll fight back. One time, the old bastard broke four or five ribs and Roscoe had to go to the hospital. Another time, he cut the guy's face bad around one eye and for awhile the doctors thought he was gonna lose it. If you ever see him up close, you'll see the bad scars at the corner of his right eye."

The sun was beating down hard now, and the sweat was beginning to trickle down my chest under my shirt, but I listened intently to Joe's story and made no gesture that would interrupt him. He tilted his hat lower over his face to shade his eyes and continued.

"Miz Rafferty was a good lady, but Old Man Rafferty used to beat her. They say two years ago she finally died from one of his beatings. They said she bled inside and died slow, and the old man wouldn't let nobody call a doctor. They told me Roscoe's kid sister,

Amy, kept holding on to her mother's hand while they was trying to close the casket. She didn't want them to bury her. I think Miz Rafferty tried to protect Amy from the old man but he still beat the girl anyway, specially when he was drunk, which was at least once a week.

"Well, kid, about a year ago I went over to visit Roscoe. They were having a pool match in town, partners only, and I wanted Roscoe for a partner because he's a damned good pool player. When I rode up to that dirty old shack they call their home, everything was real quiet. I walked round back and found Roscoe braced against the wall of the house. He had his fists clenched and his jaw locked, and his eyes squeezed down tight. I heard sounds coming from inside the house. Old Man Rafferty was screwing Amy. You could hear the poor girl moaning. I don't know what else he was doing to her, but it was terrible. Then Roscoe saw me and he lunged at me. He put a hand over my mouth and dragged me away from the house, took me to the barn, and told me with those god awful eyes staring at me that if I ever told what I'd heard he'd cut my heart out. I knew he sure as hell meant it, kid. That's why you better never tell nobody. Roscoe will kill me."

"I don't know what gave me the guts to ask him how long this had been going on, but he answered, almost before he had time to think. He said, 'Even before Ma was dead.' Then he pushed me against the wall hard, looking surprised that he said it, and made me swear I'd never tell anybody."

I asked curiously, "Joe, did you swear?"

"Sure I did," he answered. "But that don't mean a shit. I guess all that shit is why Roscoe is so goddamned mean."

We had reached the ravine, with the trapped cattle below, so it was time to move out. And besides, I had listened to about all of that story I could stand. As I trotted off I yelled at Joe, "You really like the word *caca*, don't you?"

"What does that mean?" he asked.

"Shit. By any other name it's still shit," I said, recalling my high school Shakespeare. That uncomfortable feeling came over me — the feeling that always followed the use of vulgarity. I hated it.

As we drove the cattle back, my thoughts were on Roscoe. I felt a little bit sorry for him but I still couldn't understand his action against me. I made up my mind that regardless of the situation, that fellow could never force me to back down. He was a year older than I, but not any bigger. I was five eleven and weighed about a hundred and seventy pounds, and I had plenty of confidence in my ability to defend myself.

After we drove the twenty-three head of cattle two miles north, gathering three or four other strays on the way, we left them and returned to camp at a gallop, eager to see Jeff's attempt to ride the big black stallion. When we arrived at the corral, Porky and Wade had managed to get lassos on the stallion and were holding him by the ears as Jeff tried to buckle the saddle. Uncle Jonathan and Juan Delgado were leaning on the top rail of the corral, watching intently.

As I walked up and leaned on the rail next to Uncle Jonathan, he remarked to me, "Jeff will never ride that horse. He doesn't have the skills nor the spark. I didn't want him to try, but he said he had to. Dumb, Harvey. That's dumb."

Jeff put his foot in the stirrup and was up. Wade and Porky let go. The beautiful stallion bucked violently. I had been to many rodeos but had never seen a horse that bucked with such raw violence. Jeff was whipped about like a rag doll. Suddenly the big black reared high and fell over, landing on his back and crushing Jeff under him.

Every man was over the fence in an instant and into the corral. Juan opened the gate to let the black go into the next corral and shut it after him. The rest of the men rushed to Jeff where he lay groaning in the dust.

Uncle Jonathan examined him gently and shook his head as he said, "His left leg. The bone has broken through. Pick him up and bring him into the house."

They put Jeff on the bed, and as three of us held him, Uncle Jonathan tugged on his leg three times unsuccessfully, trying to pull the shattered bone back inside the skin. Every time he failed, the jagged bone would tear more of Jeff's flesh. I felt shock and horror at the nightmarish scene — Uncle Jonathan straining, Jeff screaming, and the looks on the faces of the other men showing intense concern and empathy.

On the fourth try, the bone was pulled back inside. Joe helped my uncle strap two boards to the leg, then he and Wade carried Jeff out and laid him on a mattress in the back of the stake truck. I jumped in front with Uncle Jonathan, and Joe, Wade, and Juan rode in the back with Jeff. We drove him to the hospital in Gonzales. Uncle Jonathan and Joe went with Jeff and the doctor into the examination room. The rest of us waited.

In a few minutes, Joe came out and sat next to me. He was pale, and obviously upset. He twisted his hat round and round in his hands, and I became conscious of his rumbling voice as he stared down at his hands and talked to himself. Then suddenly he looked up at me and spoke with an urgent vehemence.

"That son of a bitch black devil horse . . . we ought to kill him! I told Mr. Reese we ought to kill him but he said no." Now he sat up straight and put his hand on my shoulder, squeezing it as he said, "Harvey, talk to your uncle. We ought to kill that devil horse. No one can ride him. He's going to hurt other men bad. We ought to kill him. You can persuade Jonathan. Make him see that."

I hardly knew what to say, and as I tried to think how to handle this I was relieved to see Uncle Jonathan come through the door gesturing to us.

"Come on," he told us. "There's nothing more we can do for him right now. He's in good hands, and we'll check on him again tomorrow. It's a bad break, but they'll fix him up."

As we drove back to the ranch, I was again riding in the front with Uncle Jonathan and he began to sing the song he always sang. I thought singing was a bit inappropriate right then, but he was nodding his head thoughtfully to a slow beat and making it low and solemn so it sounded like a hymn.

"She'll be comin' round the mountain when she comes/She'll be comin' round the mountain when she comes/She'll be ridin' six white horses, she'll be ridin' six white horses/She'll be ridin' six white horses when she comes." Maybe it was the only song he knew, because he made it fit every occasion.

I had stayed silent since we left the hospital, and finally he turned to me and asked, "Are you okay?"

"Yes sir," I replied. Then I added, "Joe and the others seem to think the big black ought to be destroyed because he's a killer, a devil horse."

Uncle Jonathan, who had always seemed to me a mild-mannered man, swung his head around with violence in his face. He hit the steering wheel with his hand as he almost shouted, "Never! I'll never kill that horse. No one will. Never!"

That night I heard Joe arguing with Uncle Jonathan about the big stallion again. He said he would pay for the horse just to have the right to kill him but my uncle was adamant.

"The horse is not for sale to you or anyone else. No one is going to kill him, and you — you just keep away from him."


A couple of days later, Wade announced that his neck was okay and he was ready to ride the big black. He stuck about five seconds before the stallion threw him against the fence. Wade cut his hip and took a hard blow to his head. He was okay, but he limped for a week. The black was truly wild, but he was the most beautiful horse I had ever seen. Joe kept on saying to anyone who would listen that the animal ought to be killed, that he was a wild horse, a devil horse.

The day after Wade's short ride, the doctor who had worked on Jeff drove up to the ranch house in a black Model T with a canvas top and asked for my uncle and they went inside. The rest of us waited in front of the bunk house. Ten minutes later, Uncle Jonathan and the doctor appeared, walked to the Model T, shook hands, and the doctor drove off.

Uncle Jonathan stood for a moment, looking after the car as it raised a cloud of dust up the road. Then he turned toward us, walked up to Joe, and said, "Jeff died last night." He put his hand gently on Joe's shoulder. "The doctor wasn't sure . . . it may have been an infection, blood poisoning, or even shock. They are not sure why. He died in his sleep, peacefully. I'm sure sorry, Joe. It's rough."

Joe seemed to find it hard to believe. He opened his mouth to speak but no words came out. Finally he just managed a deep, long-drawn "Aw, no . . ." and then, "Oh hell!"

Uncle Jonathan was quiet while the realization sank into Joe that his brother was gone. Then he explained, "Joe, unless he's got family that need to come, the doctor thinks you should have the funeral right away. If you want to go get ready, I'll drive you into town to make the arrangements, and we'll all go to the funeral with you."

It was still early in the day, and when we got to town everything moved so fast I couldn't believe it. Before evening the grave was dug, the funeral was held, and Jeff was in the ground. It seemed awfully quick, but Joe said there was no other family and the ranch hands were the only friends they had, so there really was no reason to put it off. I had been to funerals before but never one which left me as unsettled as this one.

The next morning, Wade and Joe asked me to go with them to the corral. When we were well out of earshot of the house, Wade started in on me, adding his urging to Joe's that I persuade my uncle to kill the horse. I was beginning to resent the position they were putting me in, and when I saw Uncle Jonathan walk out of the house and mount his big tan gelding, I gestured to the cowhands that I would follow him.

Quickly saddling Ranger, I cantered after my uncle, gathering my thoughts as I rode. I was fully aware of his strong sentiment concerning the black and I wasn't sure I should even make this suggestion one more time.

I finally caught up with him at the big oak. He stopped and looked at me with his warm smile. "Something you want, Harvey?"

"Yes sir," I answered. "All the men think the big black should be destroyed."

"And what do you think, Harvey?" he asked. "That's what should matter to you. What do you think?"

"I don't know," I said. "He's so beautiful."

"Get off your horse, Harvey. Let's sit here under this big old live oak tree."

We sat on the ground with our backs against the big oak, looking out over the rolling green hills to the east beyond the Blanco River. The horses stood still with dropped reins, hip-shot and patient. Uncle Jonathan crossed his long legs at the ankles and chewed thoughtfully on a piece of grass he had pulled up.

"I'm going to tell you something I hope you never forget," he began, speaking in the slow, soft Texas drawl he used to soothe both men and beasts. "The big black horse is a wild animal, and that wildness is partly what makes him exceptional and beautiful. To destroy him is the same as destroying the spark that is within us all. Harvey, have you ever seen a wild turkey?" He did not wait for an answer, but his voice took on more force and he emphasized his words with his hands. "A wild turkey's intelligence is ten times that of his domestic cousin. In fact, there's hardly a similarity between the two. The wild turkey has unbelievable senses and eyesight which makes him most difficult to hunt. He is the wariest of all gamebirds. Some wild turkeys weigh as much as twenty-five pounds, and yet, Harvey, wild turkeys can fly. They can fly a half-mile. Do you understand? *Wild turkeys can fly.* They fly beautifully."

He spoke with such intensity that it made me shiver. It was years before I really understood the total meaning of his words, years before Juan Delgado drove home the lesson that Uncle Jonathan began for me that day.

# Chapter 6

Soon after sunup the next morning, a man rode up on a pinto horse that carried Indian markings and dismounted by the corral. Uncle Jonathan had spotted him out of the window and came out to greet him. He was evidently expected.

I couldn't help staring at this visitor. Though obviously a cowhand, he was a most unusual looking fellow. One word described him: leather. In fact, that is how I always thought of him — he looked like a piece of rough leather. He was tall and thin, yet there was no doubt about his strength. His face, his hands, they all looked like leather. Something in the way he walked said you couldn't break or hurt this man. He wore chaps, a red handkerchief around his neck, and his hat showed years of rough wear and indicated a rugged life. This was a Man.

He had come from the ranch where he worked near Floresville, at Uncle Jonathan's invitation, to ride the horse, the big black. All the hands quickly gathered around to watch the show.

When the stallion was turned out into the big corral, Leather stood still with his feet planted solidly and hands on hips, watching him pace around the fence. Finally he gave an affirmative shake of his head and turned to Uncle Jonathan.

"Ay, yes. He's everything you said, Mister Reese. He's a beaut!"

Three of the men threw lassos around the black's neck. The *bosal* was slipped on and Wade and Porky helped Leather get the blanket and saddle on the skittish and pitching animal. The two men held the horse's ears as the Man of Leather jumped on.

Wade and Porky let go, and the ride began. The man and the horse seemed all of one piece, going through wild gyrations with turf and dust flying high into the air. It was incredible to watch. Once, the horse rolled on his side. Leather merely stepped off and stepped right back into the saddle as the stallion scrambled to his feet again. The ride might have been forty-five seconds, yet seemed almost endless. Dust flying, mud flying, and the terrible heavy breathing of the big black added to the thunder and excitement of that ride. Leather's sleeves were rolled up and his hands and arms resembled sinewy leather that had been bonded together as part of the reins. It was no longer a man and a horse, but one entity in a terrible struggle against itself, a merging that had come from tenacious determination as if fire had welded them into one. The horse's nostrils dilated as he snorted, he was foaming at the mouth, and it seemed the fight would go on and on as he tried every twist and trick to rid his back of its burden.

Finally and suddenly, the horse ended the challenge, and at a slow gallop, horse and rider circled round the corral. After two turns, Leather slipped off the black, patted him on the neck, and walked away. The rest of us sat in silence, still stunned by what we had seen. Then the men began talking about it in wondering tones, and the spell was broken.

At the fence, Leather put his hands on the top rail and leaped over, easily and gracefully. Uncle Jonathan asked him, "Did you break him?"

Leather answered, "You can't break that horse, but the right man can ride him. You've got to have the right man."

Uncle Jonathan smiled and said, "That's your horse."

Leather looked at him, "I'll pay for it."

"You already have," responded Uncle Jonathan.

Startled, the strange man hesitated a moment, then held out his hand to shake on the deal and said, "I'll come back tomorrow and get my horse."

As he mounted the pinto to leave, he saw Juan Delgado next to Uncle Jonathan. Their eyes locked for a long moment. Every man felt the tension in the air. Then both faces relaxed and a slight smile showed at the corner of each man's mouth. There was a kinship here, a mutual recognition of Man to Man, which needed no words to express. The tension dissolved. Leather stopped his horse in front of Juan and said, "Goodbye, *hombre*."

Juan responded, *"Adios, amigo."*

Leather turned to Uncle Jonathan and said, "This man could have ridden the black." He turned the pinto and rode off.


In the late afternoons I liked to take a walk, generally following a path from the back side of the big corral through a grove of lush woods to a fresh flowing spring. The waters there cascaded down big varicolored stones more than a hundred feet into three small lakes which made watering holes for all kinds of wildlife. The little lakes were surrounded by large oaks and elms. It was a wonderful place for a young man to sit and think — or just dream — and I considered this spot my personal magical place.

That afternoon when I started my walk and circled the large corral toward the path, I saw a horse and rider on the far side of the fence. As I moved on I saw clearly the rider in a black hat and black shirt and knew it was Roscoe. He had pulled his rifle from the scabbard and was drawing a bead on the big black, which had become aware of the rider and was moving nervously in the corral.

I yelled, "Hey, what are you doing?"

He turned his horse and looked at me, and I saw the face of my mortal enemy for the first time. I was surprised to find him most handsome, except for the scars at the corner of his right eye, which did not detract from his good looks. Yet there was the hardness of the mouth, with severe intensity in his eyes that made him seem deadly serious and ominous.

He looked at me, apparently unconcerned by my appearance. I stopped. Our eyes locked. I asked again, "What are you doing?"

Without answering, he turned his horse and loped away, not hurrying and never glancing back, slipping his rifle back into its scabbard as he went.

I went back to the house and found Uncle Jonathan sitting in his favorite chair. "Uncle Jonathan," I told him, "I just found Roscoe Rafferty behind the big corral preparing to shoot the big black. I'm sure he would have killed the horse if I had not come up on him."

He leaped to his feet as he asked, "Is he still there?"

"No. He galloped off."

Uncle Jonathan headed for the door, his boot heels whacking the board floors. He was off the porch in one stride, across the yard and straight through the bunkhouse door, and I followed just two steps behind. Walking over to the bunk where Joe was lying, he slapped the cigarette from his fingers, grabbed the man by the belt with one hand, and pulled him out of the bunk. He held Joe six inches from the floor and with his other hand grabbed him by the chin and squeezed so hard you could hear the poor kid wince with pain.

For a moment I thought he was going to break Joe's jaw. Uncle Jonathan spoke very deliberately, with venom in his voice, holding Joe's face just four inches from his own. "If anything happens to that horse, I'm going to kill you."

This was that other side of Uncle Jonathan I had seen first in the truck — this wonderful, jovial man with wisdom and kindness, suddenly becoming deadly in front of my eyes and with a physical strength I had not suspected.

Then he literally threw Joe back into his bunk, breaking the mattress supports, which caused both man and mattress to hit the floor. Joe's eyes reflected abject fear and I suddenly became aware that the rest of the hands were there and no one had moved nor spoken a word.

Walking back to the ranch house, Uncle Jonathan's mood

changed almost miraculously. He slapped me on the back and said, "Let me get my hat and I'll take that walk with you."

"Great!" I answered.

As we walked, I asked Uncle Jonathan, "Why would Roscoe want to kill the big black?"

"Roscoe was just doing what Joe asked him — or paid him — to do." He shook his head sadly. "I really feel a little bit sorry for that boy. Some bad things have happened to him. He lost his mother, you know. But Harvey, be careful. I warned you before that I think he can be dangerous."

We had reached the spring now, and he stopped and let his eyes rest on the tumbling water. The thought crossed my mind that this special place did not belong just to me. He was looking at it with such a fond familiarity that I felt sure he responded to it as I did, and ever after when I thought of my magic place, my mental picture included him as he was that day.

"The Rafferty Ranch is only 630 acres," he went on. "I've been trying to buy it from Old Man Rafferty for a number of years. I'd like to improve it. It could be a good place. Right now something evil hangs over it. You see, a year ago Old Man Rafferty's sister died in Oklahoma and left him some money. She had a small piece of land where they drilled for oil, and they hit it. The well petered out, but not before she had $25,000 in the bank. Then she got bit by a rattlesnake and she died. Old Man Rafferty was the only surviving relative, so he got the cash. Right before all that happened, I really thought Rafferty was going to sell me the ranch, but now he doesn't need the money so he's being bullheaded. He's spending it fast on women and liquor. What a shame, considering all the repairs and improvements needed on the place. In a couple of months, all the money will probably be gone. Anyway, Harvey, you keep away from young Roscoe."

"Uncle Jonathan, I'm not afraid of him. I'm not afraid of anybody."

"Good, Harvey. I know that about you. But nevertheless, you have to be smart," he replied.

On Saturdays we all usually went into Luling, ate lunch at the local Chinese restaurant, and played pool at the billiard hall the rest of the afternoon. This Saturday morning we were all waiting patiently for Uncle Jonathan to take us into town when we saw a beat-up old Chevrolet pickup coming down the road. The driver headed directly to the big corral and as he slowed down, the man I called Leather stepped out, pulled his saddle from the back of the pickup, and slung it over the top rail of the corral. He leaped the corral fence, grabbed the saddle, and walked up to the big black as it stood motionless and watched his approach. He slapped the saddle on the horse's back, put the bit into its mouth quickly but gently, tightened the girth once more, and slipped smoothly into the saddle.

We watched in amazement. We were sure that today the big black would be ready to buck off anybody who tried to ride him. Instead, it seemed as if he welcomed Leather onto his back. Wade went over to the corral gate and opened it. Leather gave us a slight wave of his hand as he moved off; then the horse and his rider walked out the gate and turned up the small road. That rider on that horse was a thing of beauty to behold.


After lunch at the Chinese restaurant, Uncle Jonathan announced, "Juan and I are going shopping at the hardware store and the feed store. Need to pick up a few supplies. Where will you fellows be?"

"At the pool hall," replied Wade. Wade was the best pool player, but I was a close second. Porky was fair. Joe was terrible, and every time he missed a shot, a stream of profanity would slip from his mouth. For some reason, I had imagined that after Jeff's death, Joe would no longer curse. Instead, he seemed to be using even more profanity and delighted in giving us gross details about his intentions toward a woman that night.

We finished the first game, and each paid Wade ten cents for losing. He gleefully said, "Rack 'em up again, Harvey. I want to take you guys one more time."

There were four tables in the pool hall, and all were occupied with at least four players. I was carefully racking the balls on our table when silence fell upon the room. I looked up to see Roscoe walking toward us. He stopped at the other end of the table and stared at me with a hard grin on his face. I stood straight and stared right back into his eyes, and even as I reacted, some part of me was standing aside and judging my own performance. I knew I was ready. I wasn't about to flinch from him or anybody else.

We stood frozen for an endless moment, and I'm not sure how the stand-off would have been broken if Uncle Jonathan and Juan Delgado had not walked in the door just then. They came to the side of our table, looked from one of us to another, and then without warning Uncle Jonathan yelled, "Okay fellows, draw!"

Everybody in the pool hall burst out laughing. Roscoe looked around angrily and stalked out the door, and as he disappeared Wade gave a piercing rebel yell.

Laughing loudly, Wade said, "Harvey, you made Roscoe madder'n a stepped-on rattlesnake!"

Uncle Jonathan walked over to me, and with a broad grin said, "Good man. Follow me outside. I want to speak to you."

I thought it was going to be something about Roscoe and our peculiar situation, but I was wrong. As we sat on a bench on the sidewalk next to the pool hall door, Uncle Jonathan told me he had been to the post office and found a letter from my father.

He saw my anxious look and added quickly, "Harvey, it's not about you. Your father wants me to go to Mexico in three weeks and take a piece of equipment that your Uncle Jesse needs in San Luis Potosi for the bottling plant. I don't want to leave you here at the ranch, so I have decided to take you with me, and your father left it up to me. Juan has agreed to stay here and keep an eye on things. You know I am an investor in the bottling plant too, and Jesse has been asking me to come there for almost a year to sign some legal papers. I'm looking forward to going and spending two or three weeks down there. I love Mexico and its people. I know you like working on the ranch, but I'm afraid you'll have to go with me. Okay?"

"Sure," I replied, actually quite excited about the prospect of traveling to Mexico.

"Your mother also sends her love."

His bright blue eyes suddenly sparkled as he said earnestly, "Harvey, I wonder if you truly appreciate your mother. She is the loveliest creature in the world. There is no other woman like her. She makes life seem beautiful. When I am near her . . ."

He stopped and flushed. I was most surprised. He looked away and said casually, "I wonder if it is going to rain? Thunderheads are building up to the south."

The day before we were to leave for Mexico, I spent the day on the range, struggling to bring in Uncle Jonathan's prize bull, "Mr. Thomas," from the farthest point of the ranch. All the hands had been looking for the bull, and it was by accident that I found him. He was an ornery critter, with a mind of his own, and it took me six hours, alternately kicking and prodding him, to cover the seven miles to the big corral. Uncle Jonathan wouldn't let us use a bullwhip on Mr. Thomas. He spoke of him as if he were part of the family. As we finally approached the ranch house, the other cowhands spotted us and cheered me on, the last hundred yards to the corral.

As I wearily trudged up to the porch after unsaddling Ranger and turning him out, Uncle Jonathan opened the screen door and patted me on the back. "Good work, Harvey. Come on in. Your Uncle Andrew just got here and we're having a cup of coffee. Want one?"

"Yes sir, I sure do," I answered.

Uncle Andrew was another Reese brother, and he was the county sheriff. I had only met him a few times before. Now he looked at me and then back at Uncle Jonathan. "You sure you want Harvey to hear? Some pretty serious stuff about the Rafferty family."

"Sure do. Harvey has had some problems with Roscoe. He needs to know."

Uncle Andrew stirred his coffee a few times, then shook off the spoon and laid it carefully on the table. Uncle Jonathan handed me a cup and sat down to listen to his brother.

"Well," said the sheriff, "three days ago Roscoe came to see me. He asked me to come out to the ranch with him. I told him I was pretty busy, was there a problem. He said there was a bad problem. I said, 'Okay, wait for me an hour, let me clean up a few things, then I'll go with you.' When we got to the ranch house — and by the way, Jon, it's a pigsty — I knew something was wrong. Roscoe didn't talk the whole way out, and he led me to the barn still clammed up. I walked inside and there was Old Man Rafferty, dead as a doornail. His head was covered with blood and he was lying in a big pool of it that must have been every drop the old bastard had in him. I looked over at Roscoe and he was standing stiff, just staring down at the old man with pure hate in his eyes. I took him by the arm and led him outside. The smell was pretty bad so I moved him over to the house and we sat on the back steps. I said, 'Roscoe, tell me everything. Don't leave nothing out. I want to know everything, if you're asking me to help you.'

"Then he told me the godawful story. He claimed that he had taken his sister Amy to Gonzales because she was pregnant and was about to have a baby by her father. The poor girl died during the delivery. The baby is okay. I went to Gonzales myself to make sure this part was true. The doctors told me that Amy had been beaten severely before Roscoe brought her in. They were not sure exactly what killed her. Might have been the birth of the baby or might have been the beating. Anyway, when they told Roscoe that Amy was dead, he broke down and cried like a kid.

"Roscoe told me he come back to the ranch to confront his father and the old man accused Roscoe of getting Amy pregnant. By the way, he swore to me that he never touched Amy. It was always his father, and always a little bit brutal. Roscoe said his father went out to the barn to get a bullwhip 'to teach Roscoe a lesson he was never going to forget.' Roscoe followed him, and on the way he grabbed a pick handle. When the old man turned with the whip, Roscoe hit him on the side of the head. I'm not sure if the old man died then, but he did die and he was hit more than once. But Jon, what I think is terrible is that Roscoe had gouged out the old man's eyes. I have a feeling that he did that before he died . . . and he died slowly, bleeding to death, with Roscoe just watching.

"Anyway, I believe the poor bastard. He's a bad penny, but he had to put up with a lot of crap from his old man. So I told him, 'I have to get a warrant for your arrest. I won't be back for a couple of days, so if I was you, son, I'd head for Mexico and I wouldn't look back. I wouldn't look back, not for a moment.' I'm on my way over there right now with a warrant, but I don't expect to find him — leastwise, I hope I don't."

As the sheriff stopped talking and took a last gulp of coffee, Uncle Jonathan sat staring at him and then slowly shook his head from side to side. "Godamighty," he sighed.

Uncle Andrew pushed back his chair and got up. "Better mosey along now and make sure he's gone. I don't know what's going to happen to that baby. I thought you ought to know about your neighbors." He took his hat off the post of his chair and jammed it on his head, mumbling, "Hate this damn job sometimes."

As Uncle Andrew drove off in his Model A, I thought about my own father and mother, and thanked God for them.

# PART 2

# Mexico

# Chapter 7

T hree days later, Uncle Jonathan and I arrived at the bottling plant in San Luis Potosi, where production had begun six months earlier. Uncle Jonathan owned ten percent of the plant, and the balance was owned equally by my father and their brother Jesse.

Uncle Jesse was so different from his brothers that this trip — my first real chance to get to know him — was an education for me. His last trip to San Antonio had been more than two years ago, and I was seeing him now from a more mature viewpoint. Physically, he was tall and handsome, a man of considerable strength and agility and probably the most striking of the four Reese brothers. There was much to admire about him, but he also lent himself to profanity, vulgar jokes, and loose women. Although married, with four children all younger than me, he went wherever he wanted and whenever he wanted without regard to his family. He usually had a big smile on his face but it did not disguise the fact that he was rough and tough and most men feared him. He was considered a bit of a rascal, yet he was respected and his company sought after. He had a reputation both as a great hunter and as a womanizer.

When we drove up to his home, which was next door to the bottling plant, he rushed out to meet us. He embraced Uncle Jonathan and then turned to me and hugged me so hard I could not breathe for a few seconds.

"Harvey," he exclaimed, "you look pretty husky now. Are you tough?"

"I think so, Uncle Jesse."

"Can you fight? Are you good at it? And do you win?"

"Yeah, usually I win," I replied.

"Okay. Don't you ever lose a fight. Don't forget your name is Reese, a good noble Irish name."

"Well, sometimes you can't help losing," I said.

"Yes you can. Go back with a baseball bat and beat the hell out of them, but don't lose a fight," he returned sharply.

I was beginning to feel awkward as we stood there in the broiling sun on the busy street, so to end the discussion, I said, "Well, okay." It was inconceivable to me that one could not lose a fight like a gentleman and shake your opponent's hand. And the idea of going back with a baseball bat made me want to laugh. Yet I saw that Uncle Jesse was dead serious.

Now he waved at the big building next door and said, "Come see the plant," and led the way.

I fell in behind my two uncles as they walked slowly past the machines and the people who were hard at work. The noise was tremendous and it was necessary to shout to be heard. I had had no idea the operation was so big — at that time it produced more than 24,000 bottles per day.

Uncle Jesse suddenly turned around to me and asked, "Harvey, what do you think of it? Did you know that your father created this whole idea, laid out the plant, and bought all the equipment in the U.S. from companies that were going broke? He's quite a man. But I'm the one who put it together, and I know how to run it and market the product. Someday I would like to see you in your own business."

He turned back to Uncle Jonathan and said, "Let's go to my office now and get the paperwork out of the way, because tomorrow I have a surprise for you."

At that moment one of the workers dropped a case of bottles to the floor with a loud crash. Uncle Jesse turned and yelled in Spanish in a voice that roared and vibrated across the plant. "What the hell is the matter with you, José? One more dumb-ass mistake and you're out!" His sudden scream made us all jump. Then he turned and calmly led Uncle Jonathan into the office.

I spent the rest of the day watching and talking to the Mexican workers in the bottling plant and learned to respect them.


The next morning at early breakfast, Uncle Jonathan told me that we were leaving in two hours to hunt in southern Mexico. It seemed that Uncle Jesse had made these plans two months earlier with his good friend Dr. Rafael Montemayor. Last night, Uncle Jesse had told his brother he was counting on him to join the hunt. I had not been expected, but I was included in the invitation after Uncle Jonathan explained that I was a proven good shot and an excellent horseman.

After breakfast, we went into the living room where a bootmaker was waiting to fit us for hunting boots. Uncle Jonathan was wearing his cowboy boots and refused the offer, but I was delighted to accept. The boots on display were beautiful. The bootmaker had brought twenty pairs, all sizes of different designs for us to choose from. The pair I selected were handcrafted hunting boots that served me for many years thereafter.

By the time the fitting was over, Dr. Montemayor had arrived. He was a short, smiling, balding man with a rounded belly and spindly legs, who wore horn-rimmed glasses at all times — even when asleep, as I later learned. We left San Luis Potosi in a 1929 Dodge sedan, followed by a canvas-covered Ford Model A pickup truck with two men from the plant. The Model A was loaded with our equipment and baggage.

Very late that night we arrived in Queretaro, 125 miles north of Mexico City, checked into a hotel and after a light supper went straight to bed. The next morning, Sunday, we had a late breakfast and then headed for the bullring. The great bullfighter Ernesto Martinez was on the bill to fight two bulls.

El Matador Martinez was a hero throughout Mexico. On this Sunday afternoon, he was to fight and kill animals from the Reforma Hacienda which were considered the bravest, most vicious and dangerous bulls in Mexico. Ernesto Martinez was also a second cousin of Dr. Montemayor, so our party took a personal interest in the event.

No spectator event can equal the excitement of a bullfight in Mexico. No one speaks of death, but the word is ominously present. Yet the mood is not somber. On the contrary, fiesta is in the air. The women are dressed in a variety of striking outfits, and as always I would find one or two beautiful exquisite ladies who demanded homage. Most men wear hats; the majority were light-colored straws, but I also saw traditional charro, western, and even top hats — these worn by the judges. There are banners flying, vendors selling beer, candied apples, cotton candy, fresh fruits, and flowers. The band plays stirring music, trying to compete with the spontaneous roars from the crowd triggered by events on the sands below in the arena. The poignant smells of perfumes, mixed with beer, fruit, and those odors peculiar to the elegant parade horses that ushered in the bullfighters and their entourage, then the mule teams that would drag out the slain bulls.

I had seen bullfights before so the pure spectacle of it was not new to me, but it wasn't until this Sunday that I understood and appreciated the valor, the integrity, and the dignity of the bullfight.

The first bull hooked his horn around the leg of the matador and threw him to the ground but was unable to effect a fatal thrust. The matador regained his feet, continued working the bull, and finally killed him. The second bull, a black massive animal that charged at the matador like a railroad train with lightning speed, brought the crowd to its feet.

It was halfway through this performance that I finally understood the beauty of the *corrida*: a mere man on foot, standing with princely splendor in his "suit of light" with his small red cape, defying the huge black death that stood in front of him. Only when a man can stand facing death without fear and with dignity does he have the right to wear the "suit of light" and stand in the full sight of God. It is a fascinating dance of death . . . Man, fearless, maneuvering the black beast around him as if it were a puppet.

The matador performed a perfect *veronica*, a graceful pass with the cape, followed by a *rebolera,* a sweeping semicircular pass that allows the man to "fix" the bull. And with the *muleta,* the small cape, he performed beautiful right-handed and left-handed *naturales* followed by a *pase por alto.* The *pase de rodellas,* on his knees, brought the crowd to its feet, and the *pase de la muerte,* the pass of death, brought a gasping silence from the stands.

Finally the bull came to a stop, exhausted and profoundly perplexed at his inability to inflict injury on his conqueror. At that moment, the matador knelt in front of his adversary with his back toward him and faced the people. Then gracefully and elegantly he walked away and accepted the tribute of his admiring public while the bull stood motionless. The band started playing and the crowd joined in loud adoration.

Now comes the Moment of Truth, when the matador must make the kill. He must plant the bull with his front hoofs together; only then are the shoulder blades separated, allowing the thrust of the sword to reach the heart of the beast. To make a perfect kill, to place a perfect thrust, the matador himself for the first time must be the moving object, instead of the cape.

Martinez aimed the sword, the bull charged. With the cape in his left hand, El Matador covered the bull's face, blinding him momentarily, then lunged forward over the deadly horns and made the thrust . . . and the beast fell.

With emotion in my breast and a lump in my throat, I watched as the matador paraded around the arena, the band playing, with the women throwing flowers and men slinging their hats into the arena. Magnificent!

That night we went to a special cafe where the four of us were to dine with Ernesto Martinez and his wife. Our party arrived first and we were already seated when El Matador walked in. Everyone in the restaurant stood and applauded, and the band played an exciting Mexican bolero. Uncle Jesse exclaimed in a loud voice, "It's wonderful to be Mexican!"

Mrs. Martinez was beautiful — an exquisite Mexican woman so stunningly attractive that all evening I could hardly keep from staring at her. Once Uncle Jonathan kicked me under the table and I realized my fascination was showing.

I heard a waiter speaking to another customer, wondering why El Matador was with *gringos*. They were not referring to Uncle Jesse, because he spoke Spanish boldly, with the confidence of the affluent Mexican. They meant Uncle Jonathan and me. Although I thought I spoke good Spanish, most Mexicans still considered me a *gringo*. And yet it seemed to me that after I had spoken only a few words there was a tacit brotherhood, an allegiance, between most Mexicans I met and myself.

Two days later, we were in the town of Oaxaca some 300 miles south of the capital. We arrived at midday, and Uncle Jesse immediately took us to the open market, a riotous place of narrow aisles flooded with people, many of them Indians selling fruits, vegetables, and their handcrafted items of silver, wood, leather, and onyx.

Trailing along after Uncle Jesse, we came to a stall that featured animal skins and was manned by two Indians who seemed to be different from the other tribal types I had observed. They were serious, stocky, and short, with handsome faces showing an unmistakable self-confidence.

Uncle Jesse asked us to examine the beautiful animal skins that were on display. The Indians called them "tigre," which means tiger, but the markings were clearly those of a South American jaguar, yellow with black markings. The skins were perfect, without even a bullethole.

"Tomorrow morning," he told us with a broad grin, "we will travel to the town of Matias Romero. You will learn how to kill *el tigre* and have a perfect skin." Then he turned and addressed one of the Indians in Spanish. "Chulpe, will you and your brother be ready? We want to leave tomorrow morning right after breakfast."

"*Sí, señor,*" was the response.

After supper that night, Uncle Jonathan and Dr. Montemayor excused themselves early and retired. As I settled myself across the table from this rugged eccentric uncle of mine, I thought of the curious contrast between the two close friends — Jesse Reese and Rafael Montemayor. I had been impressed by the doctor's good manners. He was always formal, and his education and his intelligence were evident. It was surprising that a man of such obvious culture could be Uncle Jesse's best friend.

For the next half hour I sat there, captivated by Uncle Jesse's tales of hunting experiences and adventures as he drank his beer leisurely. Suddenly he stood and said, "Come on, Harvey, you have to go with me. I might need your help."

I followed closely as he walked out of the small hotel. His pace was brisk. He knew where he was going and I had to walk fast to keep up.

We came to a small street, almost an alley, and he turned right, went up to a door, and knocked. The door opened and a handsome woman stood there. She had large hips, a small waist, and a very large bosom. The light from the single kerosene lamp on the table behind her filtered through her transparent dress and made her look naked. I was shocked and I think I actually gasped at the sensuality that she exuded. A woman of thirty-five or thirty-seven, I would guess.

Soberly she said, *"Pase, Don Jesse."*

Without a word to me, he walked in, closed the door, and left me standing there feeling awkward and self-conscious. I leaned against the wall trying to look casual, and then noticed a young girl standing across the alley. She had been watching the scene too. Now she walked ten feet to another doorway and sat huddled and still. As she curled her feet under her and wrapped her arms around her thin body I heard her crying, though she was trying hard to muffle her sobs.

She looked so pathetic that I could not bear to just watch her cry. I walked slowly toward her, moving gently so she wouldn't panic. She couldn't have been more than ten years old. She looked up at me with some fear, but somehow knew that I meant her no harm and returned to her sobbing. I sat next to her for a few minutes and then I put my arms around her. She looked up at my face for a long moment, then, evidently reassured, she put her head on my shoulder and continued to sob for another ten minutes before she ran out of tears. There we both sat, silently waiting, I for my uncle, she for . . . I was afraid it was for her mother in that same house.

An hour later I heard my uncle talking and laughing inside the house. The door opened, he stepped out, turned back to the handsome woman, grabbed her and kissed her on the mouth for a long minute.

*"Adios, mujer.* I will be back in a year," he said in Spanish.

*"Vamonos, Havito,"* he said to me, and as I stood up to join him,

the girl squeezed my hand and slipped past him and into her house. My guess had been right.

Uncle Jesse and I started back down the alley, when suddenly from the shadows a man leaped out at us. He wore a large hat, and a serape crossed one shoulder, and I caught the glint of a knife in his hand.

I could not believe how swiftly my uncle reacted. He reached into his back pocket, pulled out a pistol that I wasn't even aware he had, stepped toward the man, and struck him across the head. The man dropped like a sack of potatoes.

"Harvey," he exclaimed, "I just coldcocked a Mexican."

I was as startled by his statement as by his action. "I thought you considered yourself a Mexican," I said.

"Not today. Today I am an Irishman." He bent down and picked up the knife which had fallen into the dust and handed it to me. "Here," he said. "A reminder of tonight." Then he turned on his heel. I closed my mouth with a conscious effort and followed.

We walked in silence for two blocks in the opposite direction from the hotel. I finally asked, "Uncle Jesse, where are we going?"

"I have some business with El Brujo Orozco."

"El Brujo?" I repeated, knowing that the word meant witch or someone involved in witchcraft.

We reached an intersection that bustled with activity, despite the late hour. The contrast from the quiet streets we had just walked was like emerging from a sound sleep in the middle of a Mardi Gras. Two saloons with wide doors and large windows were at opposite corners, and both were filled with men and women talking, laughing, and drinking. A big fruitstand occupied another corner, and in front of it on the wide sidewalk, half a dozen street vendors offered foods to the colorful crowd which eddied back and forth and in and out of the bars. There were tacos of a dozen varieties, fruit juices, *raspa* (flavored snowcones), *cabrito* (young goat), sweet breads and rolls, cracklings, candies — the whole array of fiesta foods. On the fourth corner a mariachi band played, and many of the people were dancing to its native rhythms.

To add further variety to the carnival-like scene, in the four streets which came together at this intersection there were groups of dancers, each representing a different region of Mexico. Each of the four groups consisted of twenty couples dressed in traditional costumes of their area. The costumes of one group were the type worn by peasants, but very neat and festive. Their dance depicted rural life and customs. Another group was from Vera Cruz. These women were beautiful — tall, with delicate features and large eyes, and their dresses were long, feminine, and colorful. Their dance was elegant and graceful. The third group's dance was more provocative. The women's costumes were off the shoulder and their movements were sexual and suggestive. A particular movement or step by a female would bring an aggressive response from the male. The fourth group depicted the dance of the cock or flight of the hawk and other birds.

The music for each group was different, but all were exciting and beautiful. At one point, all 160 dancers were performing at the same time, and the large crowd of spectators went wild with enthusiasm and applause.

We watched for thirty minutes, then Uncle Jesse tapped me on the shoulder. He led me into one of the bars and asked if I drank.

"Only beer," I answered, "and not very often."

He ordered two beers at the bar, and when they were handed to him he shoved through the crowd to a small table in the corner where three young Mexicans sat. Uncle Jesse stood there and looked down at the young fellows, staring hard into the eyes of each one in turn. By the time he had locked eyes with the third, all three men got up and melted into the crowd, carrying their beer bottles with them.

"Have a seat, Harvey," he said, as though nothing unusual had occurred.

After a deep swig of beer, he leaned forward confidentially. "You may not realize that there are *brujos* all over Mexico," he explained. "Some are good people, others evil and diabolical. I have heard of one *brujo* that terrorized an entire village, actually holding the town hostage while he demanded tribute and promised terrible consequences for anyone that dared to not pay up. Some *brujos* call upon black evil for power; others are truly gifted in strange ways, born with clairvoyant power and the ability to foresee the future. People visit these *brujos* for various reasons. Unfortunately, most of the reasons are in relation to evil, one person asking for illness or accident to happen to another — an enemy, someone you envy, to settle a dispute, or hoping to have power over a woman or man you desire, forcing the other individual to desire you and to lust for you. Simply diabolical." I seemed to be getting a textbook course in witchcraft, and I wondered where it would lead.

"The *brujos* use an assortment of aids — dried blood of a goat, tarot cards, scented oils, and potions of God knows what. Many swear to their power. Many illnesses and even deaths have been attributed to the *brujos*. Some of them are men, others women. The illness of the son of Julio Peralta, a dear friend of mine, has been attributed to El Brujo Orozco. Don Julio's son has developed boils all over his body and is in terrible pain. The doctor can neither help nor explain the reason. They are afraid he's going to die.

"My friend lives in a beautiful *hacienda* six miles east of San Luis Potosi, but El Brujo lives here in Oaxaca. Julio has asked me to help. I plan to confront the bastard right now. He's only a short distance from here. You don't have to go. You can stay here and I'll return in an hour or so."

"No sir," I replied. "I go where you go."

"Good," he said, with a big smile. "I thought you would. Let's go."

We pushed and shoved our way through the crowds once more and finally turned down a dark and narrow street where the music and the shouting faded far away. We must have walked for twenty minutes before we reached a small house where Uncle Jesse barged right through the door without knocking — and I was right on his heels.

A handsome woman with a red bandana on her head was sitting in the small front room. "Do you have an appointment with El Maestro Orozco?" she asked haughtily.

Uncle Jesse did not answer her. He looked at two doors and decided to try the one on the left. I followed him into the big dark room where El Brujo Orozco was sitting at a long table facing us. Two ladies standing in front of him gasped at our intrusion, quickly covered their faces from our view, and rushed out of the door.

An assortment of strange objects was on the table in front of us — jars with colored liquids, vials of many sizes, one jar with a dead lizard. His tarot cards were spread in front of him, and on the wall behind him were images of evil subjects — human bodies with animal heads. To the left, a table with at least fifty candles sent forth pungent fragrances that were strange and foreign. Beneath the table were small dolls of cloth, rag dolls that represented victims, some with needles, others with small ropes around their necks. Each doll had a different appearance.

But it was El Brujo himself that dominated the room. He was a big man, slender but powerful, and even seated one could see he was tall. His deep, dark, penetrating eyes were frighteningly hypnotic. As I stared at him, almost mesmerized, I could feel the very essence of evil emanating from him.

He raised his hand and said in a loud deep voice that chilled, "Don't come closer or you die!"

We both stopped. He turned to me and asked, "Do you have a coin in your pocket?"

I answered, "Yes."

"Hold it in your hand and close your fist," he commanded. He stared directly into my eyes as my right hand reached into my pants pocket and pulled out a quarter. Suddenly I realized the coin was burning my hand. I jumped and released the red hot coin, dropping it onto the floor. El Brujo had a slight smile of victory on his face.

But Uncle Jesse reached down and picked up the coin. He stood and his eyes bored into El Brujo's. Through clenched teeth he said, "Make the coin burn me, you lowlife bastard!" He raised his fist with the coin and repeated, "Make the coin burn me!" He laughed, stepped up to the table and reached across it. He grabbed El Brujo by the front of his shirt and with a one-handed heave pulled him to his feet and slapped him across the face so hard the startled man's head spun halfway around. He slapped him again and again.

Then he pulled him across the table, dragging cards and jars that crashed against the floor. He shoved him down until El Brujo was on his knees with blood flowing from his nose and mouth. I saw genuine fear on his face.

Uncle Jesse leaned over the man and said, "I am only going to tell you this one time. Listen carefully. I have a friend, Julio Peralta, near San Luis Potosi. His son is sick. I will be in San Luis Potosi in four weeks. If his son is still sick, I will return and kill you, but first I will cut your balls off. I might kill you anyway, you evil son of a bitch." He hit El Brujo in the face with his fist and it was obvious the man lost some front teeth. He collapsed on the floor.

Uncle Jesse reached for the jar with the lizard in colored water, opened it, and poured the contents over El Brujo's head. He cringed and let out a whimpering sound of despair. Uncle Jesse reached down and pulled him back to his knees. The man's face now reflected pure terror. It was obvious that no one had ever used violence against him. Uncle Jesse left him on his knees while he proceeded to tear down all the symbols from the walls, and with his pistol in his hand he broke all the jars and turned over all the candles and incense burners. He returned once more to El Brujo and grabbed him by the throat and started to squeeze. El Brujo gasped for air, trying desperately to pull the hand from his throat, but he could not.

I started to worry that Uncle Jesse might kill him. El Brujo's eyes opened wide as if pleading for life. My uncle said, "In four weeks I will kill you if that boy is not well."

He released El Brujo and turned to me. "Let's go, my boy. Here's your coin. Never let it burn you again. Understand?"

"Yes sir," I answered.

As we stepped out of the room, the woman with the red bandana spoke to Uncle Jesse. "Tonight you will die for having touched the Chosen One. In the morning, you will not exist."

Uncle Jesse laughed and said, "Come to our hotel at seven in the morning and see for yourself. I will offer you a cup of coffee."


I was relieved when I finally got to my room at the hotel, but I was so tense and excited that I could not sleep. The face of El Brujo was still vividly in my mind. My room was only on the second floor, and the french windows were open onto the balcony. I could hear melodious guitar music coming from below. I stepped out onto the balcony and sat on a bench and listened to the sounds of the romantic night. As I listened, witchcraft, Tarot cards, lizards in colored water melted away. I reached in my pocket and drew out the coin that had burned my hand. I stared at it . . . and then, with a shrug, flipped it over the rail to the street below.

A block away a young man with his guitar was singing to a girl indoors at a window. The words spoke poetically of his unending love for her. Directly across the street from the hotel, another man, alone, leaned against a lamppost playing his guitar and singing about the loss of his loyal friend. Two blocks in another direction I could hear three men and a woman singing about the beautiful state of Jalisco.

In Mexico, no matter where you are, music will be with you. It is part of the Mexican soul.

At breakfast the next morning Uncle Jesse looked fine, joking about the service at the hotel. I saw the handsome woman with the red bandana enter the dining room through a side door. When she saw Uncle Jesse, she physically cringed and I heard her gasp with shock.

Uncle Jesse saw her and yelled, "You come for your coffee. Good. Come. Sit down."

But the woman turned awkwardly, losing all her composure and dignity as she pulled up her long skirt and ran out the front door.

# Chapter 8

At ten o'clock that same morning, we started out on horseback from a little village twelve miles southeast of the town of Matias Romero. We plunged immediately into a heavily wooded forest, with the two Indians trotting in front of us at a steady pace. This went on for five hours. I could not believe the endurance, the stamina, of our two guides, especially since it seemed to me that we were steadily going upgrade to a much higher elevation.

Finally we came out of the forest onto a big plateau that seemed to extend for miles in all directions, and about twenty miles across this ocean of grass the mountains jutted suddenly out of the earth. The grass was similar to our Texas Johnson grass, taller — about four feet — but quite sparse and easy enough to walk through. Occasionally there were patches of grass so thick that we were forced to maneuver around them.

We rested for a half hour and had a quick lunch washed down with water. While we ate, I noticed that the two Indians were wrapping their left arms with many rags, forming layer upon layer, tying each layer with thin leather strips as they added more to them until the arm was about twelve inches in diameter.

We left the horses tied under some large trees and started walking across the grassy plateau. The grass came to the center of my chest, but it reached to the chins of the two Indian guides who were walking fifty feet ahead of us. We were spread in a line ten feet apart, walking slowly and cautiously, on the watch for small animals and snakes. I flushed rabbits and rodents right and left, but saw only two snakes, which our guides told me were non-poisonous and fed mostly on the mice and rats. *El Tigre,* the jaguar, would come onto this plateau to hunt the other small animals.

The four of us were carrying high-powered rifles, but the Indians were armed only with the curved knives in their right hands. Periodically they would stop and scan the grass in all directions for movement. At one of these stops, they looked back toward us and pointed to the left. At first I could not see anything unusual. They continued to point and to look back for acknowledgement from us. Uncle Jesse was the first one to point in the direction that the Indians had indicated.

I asked in a whisper, "What are you pointing at?"

"Look way over there," he said softly. "Look at the grass. Watch the grass."

Then I noticed the grass blades two hundred yards away were moving slightly. They would part and then gather again. One of the Indians whispered, *"El Tigre. Abajo. Abajo."*

We started crawling, moving toward the right to intercept the jaguar. Occasionally we would stand with our heads just above the grass to confirm our angle. By the time we had closed the interval to a hundred yards, we were directly in front of the animal and we turned left and began crawling straight toward it.

Until that moment, I had not been aware that my heart was pounding. I caught Uncle Jonathan's eye and I could tell that he was feeling the same excitement. I looked toward the Indians as we crawled forward, expecting them at any moment to fall behind us, but instead, about fifty yards from the jaguar they stood again to confirm that the big cat was still coming toward us.

The Indians would move up a short distance, then come to a dead stop. They moved, we moved. They stopped, we would stop. Finally, through the blades, I could see the shadow that had to be the jaguar moving toward us in a crouching crawl, tense and poised to leap at any moment. By now, it was not more than a hundred feet away and headed for an area of thick grass just in front of us.

One of the Indians crawled within ten feet of the clump of thick grass, expecting the jaguar to come through and confront him. I looked toward Uncle Jesse, hoping that he would recall the Indian from his reckless advance. Inside the area of thick grass, we clearly saw the jaguar leap forward at some small game. We heard thrashing, growling, and then the death squeal of the little animal. Then there was silence.

I was stunned. I pushed the safety of my rifle forward and felt every muscle tense for the next move. The jaguar came out of the thick grass directly in front of the Indian. A red fox was hanging from his jaws, and his head looked huge. When he saw the Indian he squatted, and the fox came rolling out of his mouth. I could see the red blood on his lips and dripping from his fangs. For a moment he was sizing up the situation; then he crouched in a coiled position. The muscles of his powerful shoulders flexed beneath the fur, and his yellow eyes were hypnotic and penetrating.

The stand-off continued with almost unbearable tension and I thought it would never end. And then, without warning, the Indian leaped to his feet and uttered a scream that vibrated across the whole plateau and sent a shiver up my spine. The jaguar charged, and four feet from the Indian he rose on his back paws. His front legs were spread high, the black claws outstretched, paws silhouetted against the skyline, and his mouth opening wide as he leaped upon the man.

The Indian shoved his padded left arm directly into the bloody jaws. The cat bit down, and with his two short powerful front legs struck at the arm from both sides, tearing into the white rags. The Indian was falling backwards from the force of the beast's charge, but at the same time he plunged his knife into the exposed upper part of the jaguar's stomach and with one thrust ripped him open almost to the hip. The jaguar slammed to the ground, but although he was fatally wounded he regained his feet and dashed off toward the left. We all leaped up and raced after him. He left a trail of blood as he ran.

After a rush of a hundred yards, the jaguar stopped running and the struggle to give up life began. Thrashing and tumbling, completely disemboweled, the beast fought tenaciously against death. But it was over. He stopped and lay on his side, and as the blood left his body, so did life.

A great sadness fell upon me and I thought I might weep, but then Uncle Jonathan walked up to the dead jaguar, knelt beside him, stroked his neck, and patted him two or three times — a salute to the courage, vitality, and beauty of the beast. It was a gesture I needed to see.

Uncle Jesse turned to me and said, "A perfect skin, Harvey. More sporting than rifles, don't you agree?"

"Yes sir," I said slowly, thinking back over the excitement of the last few minutes, and then added with enthusiasm, "Yes sir, a perfect skin."

Later we learned that the jaguar weighed 165 pounds dressed — thirty pounds more than the Indian who killed him.

It was late when we got back to the village, and Uncle Jesse told us, "Let's get to bed quickly. Tomorrow we are going to penetrate that jungle," pointing to the east. "It will take us three days before we get to the high country, and we want to be as fresh as possible." He instructed the two men from the plant to drive the Dodge sedan and Ford pickup to a village called Pataloutan, sixty miles southeast, where we would rendezvous in two weeks.

The next morning we entered the jungle, the four of us on horseback and the two Indians following on foot, each leading a mule loaded with supplies. This wasn't my idea of a true jungle — more of a semi-tropical rain forest. I had expected a thick wood that we would have to hack our way through, but although this vegetation was wild and in some places quite thick, we had no difficulty riding through it.

We crossed many brooks and springs, and it rained every afternoon for about an hour. This forest was at a high elevation, and the temperature rarely varied, normally staying between eighty-five and ninety degrees which I found quite pleasant. The trees were tall, rising high into the sky, but they did not block out the sun completely. Filtering magically through the leaves, the sun sparkled on flowers of all kinds as if purposely spotlighting the flame-vined bougainvilleas, gardenias, orchids, and a hundred other species that were not familiar to me. There were huge pines, cypress, black walnut trees, and many others that I had never seen before. Most of the trees bore a myriad of beautiful air plants, gorgeous orchids in red, purple, white, and some with several colors within one flower.

There was food on every hand — papaya, mangoes, bananas which we could reach out and pick as we rode. Butterflies were everywhere and sometimes there would be one of such stunning and vivid colors that we would come to a full stop and stare in awe. Hundreds of monkeys chattered at us, and parrots of every color imaginable — brilliant reds, greens, yellows, and incredible blues — flew among the trees.

At sunset, our two Indian guides found a place for us to camp — a large clearing that allowed us to see the sky and the stars between the big trees. The plan was to spend one night here and by noon the next day reach an Indian village, where we would go through the formalities that were expected by the village elders.

Our two guides started a campfire in the center of the clearing. There was still enough light for us to spot a large deer with beautiful antlers at the edge of the clearing. We stood very still, observing the handsome buck . . . except for Dr. Montemayor, who whipped out his rifle, fell to the ground, took aim, and shot. The deer was hit in the neck and fell where he stood.

The doctor leaped up excitedly and ran to the buck. The Indians and Uncle Jesse yelled for him to stop, but by that time he had reached the buck, grabbed it by the horns, and started to drag it toward the campfire. Again Uncle Jesse yelled at him to leave the buck where it lay, and I began to understand what was wrong. He was trying to explain that the bucks in this forest were full of parasites and other insects. By this time, the guides were laughing, anticipating what was to come.

That night, Dr. Montemayor, stripped naked, had to jump back and forth over an open fire for hours. The deer in that jungle were covered with millions of tiny ticks half the size of a pinhead, and the doctor was covered with them. The only way to get them off was to jump repeatedly over an open fire naked. All night long we could hear the good doctor exclaiming, "Ouch! Oh! Ouch!" Sympathizing with him kept me awake for an hour or so and then I drifted off. By the next morning he had rid himself of most of the parasites, but before he dressed, the Indians examined him carefully and plucked off one or two strays that had escaped the flames.

At noon we arrived on schedule at the beautiful Indian village. The houses had grass roofs, and most sat on four huge posts. They had no walls and the floors were made of wood planks that had been split from trees by hand and rubbed smooth with stones. There were straw mats for beds. Some of the houses had tables and stools. The floors were four steps off the ground, probably to guard against snakes and other varmints.

The women wore skirts that were tied at one side, revealing their shapely thighs when they walked, and their bodies were bare above the waist. The girls were very pretty, with features more delicate than I had expected. They did not speak Spanish, but apparently they had no difficulty understanding us, and I felt sure they recognized my embarrassment at their exposed bosoms.

We were escorted to the main hut, which was some thirty feet in length with eight posts holding up the roof. We sat on benches at a long handsome table made from walnut that had been rubbed down by hand with abrasive clay. Three of the elders sat with us for lunch. Beautiful young women served us bean soup with the herb cilantro that was incredibly good. There were also corn tortillas and pieces of iguana meat on a wooden skewer cooked over an open fire — surprisingly delicious, though it was only later that I found out what I had eaten.

Halfway through the meal, a big tarantula fell from the ceiling, landing at the other end of the table. One of the women pushed the big spider off the table and immediately picked up all the food, took it away, and brought us fresh dishes. Uncle Jesse told us that the fuzz on the legs of tarantulas was the only thing dangerous about them. When they fall in that manner, the fuzz from their legs flies about, and some might have landed in the food. If any of this tiny needle-like fuzz is ingested with the food, it will attack the intestines, causing illness and perhaps death.

After our meal, and an hour's visit with the chiefs, we prepared to move on. However, our party had grown. Besides our two guides, we were accompanied now by ten Indian men and three women. One of the females was a girl of eighteen that I had noticed when we first rode into the village. She was taller than the other girls, with a lovely face and an exquisite body. When she saw me looking at her, she smiled and lowered her head, but she quickly moved next to my horse and walked alongside me for the next three hours.

I was riding in some sort of dream world I think — the heat, the beauty of the forest, the whole fantastic situation lulling me into a sense of unreality — when suddenly we were out of the jungle and facing rugged mountains directly in front of us. It was as if someone had drawn a line and said, "The tropical rain forest ends here!"

Uncle Jesse asked us to join him in a conference. We dismounted, walked over to some rocks, and sat down. The pretty Indian girl, whose name I learned was Concha, left my side and went to join the rest of the Indians sitting on the ground. As she walked away I saw her bare bust and felt myself flush. I looked about, self-conscious, to see if I was being observed. No one seemed to care.

"It will take us about six hours to get to the top of those mountains," Uncle Jesse told us. "There is not enough daylight left today, so we will spend the night here and start early in the morning. It will take us about an hour to get beyond the timberline. We should be able to find a passage up the mountains that will let us to go on horseback all the way instead of using the longer route through the canyons. But this is where the danger lies. Many Indians live up in these mountains peacefully and happily, but there are also bandit gangs. Be on your guard and ready to act in case we meet any of these cutthroats."

Guards were posted in shifts that night, but I was not aware of anything happening until dawn, when Uncle Jesse shook me and said, "Get your gun, Harvey, get behind that big rock, and keep your eyes open looking up that hill."

I crouched behind the rock and waited. The light of day came quickly and soon I could see three men on horseback a hundred yards up the hill. They wore large straw hats, gunbelts on each shoulder crisscrossing in front, and carried rifles. On my left, Uncle Jesse and Uncle Jonathan waited for two more horsemen who were riding up the ravine toward them.

The first man rode a high-stepping pinto which danced restlessly as he pulled it to a halt. "We would like to buy a mule and some supplies, *amigo*," he said. His Spanish words sounded innocent enough, but the guttural tone and his villainous appearance seemed menacing. The second man, astride a white stallion, stopped behind him.

Uncle Jesse answered him in a growl. "We have nothing for sale." Both of my uncles had rifles in their hands.

In a flash, the first man drew a pistol from its holster and fired. Uncle Jonathan's rifle went off from the hip, striking the man on the painted horse dead center, dropping him grotesquely to the ground. The rifle shot echoed through the mountains.

The second rider hesitated, and then slowly raised his hands and said, "No, *amigo,* we only want to buy supplies." And his white horse, without a command, apparently from knee pressure, backed up quickly. Then he swung his horse around and galloped off. The three horsemen on the side of the hill above turned their horses in the same direction and galloped after him.

The dead rider on the ground had gotten off a shot and hit someone behind me. The women were crying hysterically, looking down at a young Indian who had been hit on the thigh, shattering the bone. I rushed back to where the young man was lying, knelt beside him, and tried to stop the bleeding with my hands. I was soon covered with blood.

Uncle Jesse arrived just a few seconds later, moved me aside, took his belt and formed a tourniquet. For the next half hour, he worked frantically with the boy. But at last he rose and announced that the young man was dead.

I said, "How can that be? It was just his leg."

"That was a hollow-point bullet that shattered his leg and tore the arteries all the way to the hip. There was no way to stop the bleeding," he answered.

In the next thirty minutes, we buried two men with hardly a spoken word except for a short prayer that Uncle Jonathan insisted on reciting at each grave.

# Chapter 9

Four riders, plus eleven men and three women on foot, started up the side of the mountains. The climb was not difficult but there were some places where we had to dismount and lead our horses when the narrow trail had a rock wall on one side and a steep precipice on the other. I admired the horses' ability to handle the rough incline. They were sure-footed and I never once saw one of them slip. At times as the trail wound around we would be only a hundred or so yards from the next mountain across a small valley.

Dr. Montemayor seemed terrified whenever we got to one of these narrow places in the trail. The man's fear was obvious but everyone pretended to ignore it. I tried to make light of the danger and kept assuring him that every area could be maneuvered.

At one point when I was working my way up a steep incline leading my horse, I was bending over so far that my hands were almost touching the toes of my boots. Suddenly I nearly collided head-on with another body directly in my path. Straightening up, I gasped in astonishment when I saw it was an Indian woman who had a child in her arms and a large load of supplies on her back.

Her burden caused her to bend over too, as she made her way down the trail.

An hour later, we reached the top of the timberline. Uncle Jesse, who was in the lead, pulled up his horse at a wide spot on the trail and dismounted with his rifle in his hands. There was an air of urgency and tension in his manner, so I jumped off my horse and quickly walked to his side. Motioning for everyone to stand still and be as quiet as possible, he pointed across to the next mountain that was just a hundred yards away. There, right above the timberline, was a big brown bear staring directly at us.

The bear was a large, beautiful specimen. It continued to stare at us, not moving a muscle. Uncle Jesse was on one knee, taking aim, when the animal suddenly moved forward, and at that instant the thunder of my uncle's shot split the quiet of the valley, ending with the thud of a bullet hitting heavy flesh.

The bear lunged into the air, turned, and started down the side of the mountain into the brush and timberland. Uncle Jesse ejected the spent shell, threw a new one into the barrel, and rushed down the side of his own mountain. He would slide and slip feet first where the earth was loose, occasionally sliding on his seat, then coming to his feet and taking a few jumps. He was making surprising speed by this erratic method. The rest of us watched this drama from above like spectators in a theater — the bear going down the side of his mountain and Uncle Jesse going down over here.

Because of the brush, it wasn't likely that the two main characters in this play could see each other. But from above we could see that they were going directly toward each other on collision courses that would converge at the small valley three hundred feet below where a stream of rushing water filled the cleft between the mountains.

The bear would run a short distance, then trip, tumble, and roll a couple of times, regain his feet and continue his run to the bottom, mowing down bushes and small trees on his way. He was obviously wounded and surely a very dangerous creature at this point. As Uncle Jesse continued his descent toward the bear, the rest of us, quite helpless, resorted to screaming warnings which he ignored.

Uncle Jesse's route to the clearing below was shorter than that of the bear. They arrived at the same time, no more than a hundred feet apart. Uncle Jesse immediately went to one knee and brought his rifle to his shoulder. When the bear reached the water's edge it changed direction, turned to the right, and started running along the bank. Uncle Jesse's rifle followed the bear as it turned. Then he squeezed the trigger and the bear tumbled, landed on its side, and was still.

Ejecting the spent shell from his gun, Uncle Jesse slipped a new shell into the chamber. He walked cautiously to the bank of the stream, sat down, and waited. One did not take chances with a downed bear until it was guaranteed dead. By this time, most of the Indian men were sliding down the side of the mountain. There was no hesitation on their part. They jumped into the stream, came out on the other side, and headed for the bear, confident that he was dead, and immediately started the skinning process.

Dr. Montemayor asked them to stop long enough for him to take a picture of Uncle Jesse with his rifle and the bear, using a black box camera that he was carrying. Then the men got on with the process. The skin and the head were rolled up, tied together, and placed on one of the pack mules. The animal's fat was removed carefully — a valuable commodity for the Indians. One of them would return to the village weighted down with more than a hundred pounds of lard.


We wound our way up the side of the mountain, and a short time later I saw a spectacular waterfall across the valley, the water cascading down the rocks more than three hundred feet. I borrowed Uncle Jonathan's binoculars and waited for the entire party to pass. Then I slid off my horse, sat on the edge of the trail, and with the binoculars made a very careful examination of the beautiful torrent. The falls were a quarter of a mile from where I was sitting, but I could clearly hear its roar.

Halfway down the falls, the water hit large boulders, most of it cascading to the right but some splashing like a shower to the left. And there beneath this spray which created all the colors of the spectrum in the rays of the sun, were two nude figures, bathing on the cliff. A young girl of seventeen or eighteen, bronzed and glittering in the sunlight, and a dark, handsome man were playing and splashing, laughing, giggling, and chattering.

I was fascinated. It was an intimate moment to which I was an unseen observer, but there was a feeling of unreality. Were these lovers real or were they part of some fantasy or dream that only existed in my head?

The corner of my eye caught two eagles circling high above the waterfall. I found them in my binoculars. I had heard that when eagles flew in circles in that way it was part of the mating ritual. I turned back to the two nude figures that were still splashing in the shallow pond which the water created on the ledge. Suddenly the playing and the splashing stopped. They turned to each other and embraced and melted onto the ground. Violently they made love. I imagined that I could hear the heavy breathing. And just as suddenly they parted and lay silently on their backs next to each other, facing the sky. I watched for a few more minutes, but the bodies never moved except for their hands that were now grasping each other. The eagles had disappeared.

Slowly, quietly, as though I were in church, I stood, then mounted my horse and caught up with our party. Concha had lagged behind, waiting for me. When I saw her naked bust and exposed thigh, the same excitement I had felt while watching the lovers under the waterfall returned. There were desires in me that caused an unfamiliar hunger.


We continued to the top of the mountain and reached our destination two hours later. We were cautioned to be very quiet the moment we reached the plateau at the top. Instead of the rugged mountain peaks I had expected, the ground was flat as far as the eye could see. The terrain was the color of cream or perhaps more like chalk — slightly yellow. There were strange trees and bushes scattered widely apart.

Uncle Jesse drew his rifle and asked us to get ours quietly. I could not understand. There was nothing up here — just the bare land as far as the eye could see.

One of the Indians came up to me and pointed and said, *"Venados,"* which means deer.

"Where?" I asked.

*"Alla. Alla,"* whispered the Indian.

Then I saw them. Hundreds of them, I thought, at a hundred yards or more, standing still, looking at us but well-camouflaged because of their coloring which exactly matched the color of the terrain. Only after you played tricks with the focus of your eyes did you start noticing the little black outline of their tails or their ears. And then you would begin to see an ear flick or a tail wag, and finally, as your eyes adjusted to the trick of color, the deer came to life. Later I was told that one of the Indians had actually counted seventy deer in this herd.

The Indians were squatting behind us. The four of us spread out and dropped to a kneeling position. We took aim and at a given signal we all fired. I managed to shoot twice before the deer scattered, and I knew I brought down two deer. Dr. Montemayor must have missed because only four deer were killed with that first volley. As if by magic, the rest of them disappeared.

We started running toward the fallen animals. Uncle Jonathan and Dr. Montemayor, who had the largest tummies, were the last to arrive. I had killed a seven-point and a ten-point buck with my two shots.

This land which had at first appeared to be so flat was actually scarred with ravines over the entire plateau. It looked as though a million years ago the area had been a delta with hundreds of rivers and creeks, and that through volcanic eruption it had become a mountainous plateau. The ravines were eight to ten feet with steep sides, and some twelve feet wide. While most of them were dry, a few carried small spring-fed streams. However, it rained every afternoon and the water would rush through the gullies for a brief time. There was a plant or shrub that grew here that seemed to be the favorite food of the deer.

In pairs, we climbed down to the bottom of a ravine and started to walk along it, moving quietly and ready to confront a deer. The ravines turned and meandered, and often as we were making a sharp turn we would come upon a deer. Other times we would wait near a turn in the ravine for the deer to come to us. I could usually hear them approaching as their hoofs clacked against the hard clay. It was exciting. There would be the clack clack clack of a deer coming right toward you. I would wait till it appeared from around a turn and caught sight of me. Startled, the deer would jump for the top of the ravine wall. Its leap would take its front hoofs to the top of the wall; a hesitation followed as it struggled to get its hind hoofs over the top. At the moment of hesitation, I would take my shot and drop the deer. We killed thirty-nine deer that day, all of them trophy bucks.

The Indians would come to the sound of the shot and field dress the carcass at the spot. Then two of them would carry it to the camp clearing where it was skinned and the meat processed. Some of it was cut into long strips and hung to dry on a long pole supported by two forked sticks. Other meat was put into big sacks and covered with salt, one layer after another. By the time the hunt was over, the Indians had covered a large area of ground with hundreds of poles supporting strips of deer meat. A man was to remain and guard it from predators. The plateau was the only area where the Indians hunted deer, usually trapping them. Here the meat was pure and had a sweet and delicate taste, untainted by the parasites which spoiled the game in the jungle below. That evening the Indian women prepared deer meat in three different ways, all delicious. When night fell on the high plateau the stars were so bright you could actually see another person's features clearly. After supper we lay on our backs and silently stared at the Mexican sky.

The next morning, the hunt started before sunrise and lasted till two o'clock. We killed nine more deer and three large javelinas. Then we started packing and preparing for the trip to the north side of the plateau and the descent to the river below. There we were to meet a forty-foot steamboat that would take us downstream to a village at the very end of an isolated backwoods road where Uncle Jesse's men would meet us.

As we prepared to leave the campsite, I started feeling very ill. Dr. Montemayor brought out his black medical bag, took my temperature, and announced that I had fever of a hundred and two. He gave me aspirin and some medicine to take every four hours, but he advised against my traveling until the following morning and then only if my temperature was back to normal.

Uncle Jesse came to where I was lying down. He knelt beside me and explained, "Harvey, we don't want to leave you, but if we are not down to the river in two days, I'm afraid old Captain Galindo is going to think we are not coming and leave. We will go on ahead and hold the boat, and wait there for you. I'm going to leave Paco behind to help you, and one of the girls to cook for you and Paco. You'll be all right, and you can come along as soon as you're able."

Then with a sly wink, he added, "Don't worry. It's Concha I'm going to leave for you."

I was embarrassed to realize that he was aware of my attraction to Conchita, but nevertheless I was able to smile as I looked upon his devilish face, knowing that although I could never respect him as I did my father, I did love the old rascal.

Only two Indians followed Uncle Jesse, Uncle Jonathan, and Dr. Montemayor as they left. One Indian was to be left behind to guard the meat that was drying. The rest of them, loaded with packs on their backs, started the descent that led to their village. They had not been paid any money but they had not expected any. Their reward was the huge supply of deer meat.

# Chapter 10

As my uncles went out of sight, I was feeling quite sorry for myself. Concha brought a bowl of soup, knelt at my side, and began to serve me. She was smiling as she held the bowl to my lips, and as I rested between gulps, I was conscious of her beauty, her face, her golden-tan skin, her nude bust as it rose with each breath. I forgot about my uncles . . . but the fever, or perhaps the medicine, was having its effect, and soon sleep overcame me. My eyes closed with her image before me as I fell asleep.

I awoke in the middle of the night, shaking violently. Paco and Concha were already aware of my condition and they stripped all my clothes from my body, then covered me with three blankets and put a large fur over the whole bundle. I continued to shake. They built a big campfire. I saw Conchita standing by the fire. The voluptuous movement of her naked breasts as she came toward me captured my interest in spite of my chill. As she stood above me, the moonlight silhouetted one side of her body and the light from the campfire made her golden-brown skin glisten.

She looked down and smiled, untied her sarong, threw it aside, and stood for a moment, nude and beautiful — perhaps to allow me to gaze at her. She knelt beside me, pulled the covers back, and slid next to me. Her arms and her legs enfolded me. The warmth of her body engulfed me. I remember that night as a fantasy — it was a dream, and yet I know it really happened.

I was awakened the next morning by the movement of Concha as she left my side. I rolled over and found Paco squatting next to me with a big smile on his face, uncharacteristic of this type of Indian.

He spoke in broken Spanish. *"Vamos, sí? Vamos, esta bien?"*

I replied, *"Sí. Vamos. Estoy bien."* And indeed, my fever had broken and I felt able to ride again.

The trip back was slow, but most pleasant. The descent on the north side was not nearly as difficult as the ascent we had made on the east side to the plateau. Halfway down the mountain, I asked Paco if he thought it would be all right for Conchita to ride on the saddle with me. An hour earlier she had stubbed her toe, it had bled a bit, and she continued to limp.

He gave me a big smile and helped her up onto the saddle in front of me. I felt her nude body leaning against me, and occasionally she would turn and meekly smile at me, looking intensely into my eyes. She created an excitement within me that I had not known before, and I believe she was very aware of my new consciousness.

Paco was now displaying a new talent that surprised me. He would make jokes about a crooked tree, about a rabbit, or a bird in the sky, and was able to make it funny in a clownlike way. Conchita and I would laugh, responding as naively as children. My imagination at times would take over. I thought myself to be a knight on his charger, with his squire and his lady at his side, setting off in search of adventure, truth, and honor, in a foreign land full of unknowns and mysteries.

In the late afternoon we stopped and made camp. Paco built a large fire and Conchita made a supper of beans, tortillas, bananas, and mangoes. Using my saddle as a seat on the ground, I watched as she served me. I could hardly keep my eyes off her lovely body as she moved around the camp. She served Paco and herself and took a seat on the ground next to me, occasionally looking up at me and shyly smiling.

Paco, who had hardly spoken before this day, said, "Señor,

you would love El Valle y El Rio de los Santos." (The Valley and the River of the Saints.)

"*Sí,*" exclaimed Conchita. "You would love El Rio de los Santos."

I wondered what prompted these remarks. "Where is the river?" I asked. "Is it far from here?"

"Three days, four days," continued Paco. He had put aside his dish and now he leaned forward toward me and his eyes caught the glow from the sinking sun. "Señor, it is so beautiful that the soul becomes renewed. It is enchanted. I cannot describe how beautiful and wonderful and peaceful is El Rio Santo."

"People live much longer," added Conchita.

"It is to the south," continued Paco. "But you have to go over rough mountains. There is a path that goes through the mountains to the other side. Only a few know how to reach this pass. My grandfather took me there twenty years ago when I was a boy. My grandmother had died and he asked me to journey with him because he was old and needed help. He had decided to go to El Rio Santo to live the rest of his days. It was so beautiful that when I returned to my village I could not describe the river to my friends. I saw flowers that no man had seen and fruits of another world. I found gold, but my grandfather forbade me to take any because men of greed would come there and destroy the peace of the Valley. But I will take you there, Señor, if you want to go, and you can take Conchita with you."

I believed Paco was sincere, but the thought crossed my mind that he had gone with his grandfather as a boy, and perhaps through the years that followed his imagination had greatly expanded on his recollection of the visit.

"Why are you asking me to go? Why me?"

"Because," he said, "you are good. Your face shows good. You are good and I know you like us, and I know you love Conchita. If you cannot go now, when you are ready, Señor, you come and we will take you to the Valley de los Santos. I will take my woman with me, and my son, who is still small, and you and Conchita will have many sons and we will be very happy, Señor. What I have said is the truth. I would not lie to you, Señor."

I looked into Paco's face and I saw a sincerity and a truth that humbled me and a dignity that I had failed to recognize earlier. I wondered why I had not looked into the faces of these people before now. Only in the face of my mother had I seen such innocence and complete sincerity without any question or doubt. And yet, there was mystery about them that was difficult to fathom.

Paco finished, "When you are ready to go to El Rio Santo, Señor, we will take you," and fell silent.

Concha, who had been following the conversation intently, now rose and walked away, disappearing among the trees. After she had been gone for twenty minutes I became concerned and asked Paco, "Where do you think Conchita went?"

"There is a waterfall a short distance from here," he answered. "I will take you if you wish. You can bathe there. But you can find the way. Just stay on this path."

Then I remembered that Conchita had carried a towel as she left. I picked up another towel and started down the path, my imagination racing ahead. After a quarter mile, I caught a glimpse of her in a wooded area where she was bathing under a small waterfall, the water splashing against her sensuous bronze body. When she saw me she grinned with delight and came to meet me. She unbuttoned my shirt and slipped it off, then the rest of my clothes, and when I was nude she took me by the hand and led me under the flowing waters. She splashed my face, and I in turn splashed hers. We both laughed.

She rubbed my back with soap and motioned that we must hurry because the night was approaching fast. She took my hand and pulled me from the falls and started to help me dry. I then, still nude, impulsively reached for her naked body, drew her to me, and kissed her . . . a long, gentle kiss. She drew back, and looked at me, hesitant. Then she smiled, grabbed her sarong, and ran back up the path, laughing as she went. I dressed and followed slowly, completely captivated by still another precious moment.

Later I lay on the ground, using my saddle as a headrest, gazing at an orange moon rising in the eastern sky. Paco was on one side of me and Conchita on the other, and I felt an overwhelming sense of gratefulness. Conchita fell asleep facing me, with her body brushing mine. The mystery of Mexico, I thought to myself, cannot truly be related to another. You must live it.

The next morning when I woke, I felt well. The sickness was completely gone. I urged my friends to hurry with the breakfast so we could be on our way. As we set out, Conchita was on the saddle in front of me as before, but now there was a change. Now we three were fellow travelers and comrades, friends, with Conchita as my girl and Paco as my compadre, joking and laughing with whole-hearted enthusiasm.

We continued down the north side of the plateau through the timber area of the mountains. Two hours later we entered the jungle, and within an hour we were at the river called Jesus Domingo. The river was wide and deep, and flowed lazily through the jungle. We followed it downstream for six miles and as we went over a small rise we saw the clearing below and the small dock where a forty-foot steamboat was tied up.

Uncle Jonathan, Uncle Jesse, Dr. Montemayor, and three crew members were on the dock waiting for us. We came to a stop at the top of the rise and Conchita, who was still in the saddle with me, swung her leg around and sat sideways facing me. For a long moment she looked deeply into my eyes, then brushed her lips across mine and started to drop to the ground.

I held her for a moment and softly said, *"Adios, Conchita, adios."*

Almost in a whisper, she responded, *"Adios, Señor,"* and slipped to the ground, resuming her role as a guide and a servant. Paco's farewell was hardly audible. They did not follow but remained at the top of the rise as I went on toward the dock.

Uncle Jonathan came running up the rise and almost pulled me off the saddle. He hugged me and said, "Harvey, I am sure glad to see you. I was very worried about you, son, but it's a good thing we came ahead because we barely got here in time. Captain Galindo had given up on us and the boat was about to pull out."

Uncle Jesse and Dr. Montemayor also greeted me affectionately, both of them embracing me and inquiring about my health. As we walked toward the boat, I glanced back to the rise where I had left Conchita and Paco. They were gone, and I felt a great sense of loss.

I thought to myself, I'll come back and we will go to El Rio Santo. Some day I must go to El Rio de los Santos.

For the next three days, we hunted from the deck of the beatup old steamboat as we drifted downstream with its small engine chugging, chugging under minimum power. The hunting was incredible. Using twelve-gauge shotguns, we brought down all kinds of game birds, ducks, and some birds that were entirely new to me. There were also wild hogs, javelinas, a small variety of deer, and lots of other small game along the shore. But hunting alligators in the River Jesus Domingo was the most exciting. When we would shoot one, the Indian guides would jump into the water, grab the alligator by the tail, and drag the huge beast to the shore, where the skin was removed with astonishing speed. Occasionally, one of the alligators was only wounded, and it would dive to the bottom of the river. One of the Indian guides would jump in with his knife in his teeth and the struggle that followed was dramatic, the Indian riding the back of the alligator, trying to plunge his knife into its soft underbelly.

We drank, we ate, we loafed and napped on the deck, and for further diversion we fished, catching a variety, some as large as thirty pounds. We were always ready to drop our fishing rods, grab a rifle or shotgun, and squeeze off a shot at a target. The river banks were lush with thousands of gorgeous flowers, a wonderland complete with the music of colorful birds singing their many songs. Butterflies, monkeys, and incredible sunsets added to the magic.

During the entire trip down the Jesus Domingo River, we enjoyed the music of Carlos, one of the ship's hands, as he played his guitar and sang songs of Mexico. He was skillful and had an excellent voice and seemed able to sing for hours without tiring.

By the third afternoon I was the only one hunting and fishing. My two uncles and Dr. Montemayor just sat on the deck, exhausted but filled with contentment — three sportsmen who had realized the ultimate.


We landed at the quaint village called Pataloutan, with a population I estimated at 2,000. It was located seventy-five miles from the Gulf of Mexico and three hundred and sixty miles southeast of Mexico City in semi-tropical jungle at a high elevation, and it seemed to me the cleanest village in Mexico. The houses were small but immaculate, made of adobe and timbers painted white, and with tile floors. There were flat stone sidewalks and cobblestone streets which were washed daily.

The women were very pretty, with fair skin, and wore colorful flowered blouses, very low off the shoulder, exposing the upper part of their well-rounded bosoms. They were flirtatious, readily smiling at any man. Their walk, hip and body movements were most provocative. The men of that town seemed benign and childlike; all of them were dressed in white, with identical little straw hats, and they all seemed to wear large smiles.

I remarked to Uncle Jesse, "There is no way for those little men to handle those good-looking girls."

He answered, "You couldn't be more wrong. You are only seeing their daylight image."

We headed for the local saloon, hoping to find Uncle Jesse's men. Parked at the curb were the '29 Dodge sedan and the Model A truck, but the men were not around. The saloon-cafe was on a corner and had big arches on each side opening onto the street. We ate lunch there late in the afternoon — a meal of quail, pinto beans cooked in beer, hot chili, and tortillas. The quail was prepared in *mole,* a red chili-and-chocolate sauce that was delightful.

"We will start back early tomorrow morning," announced Uncle Jesse, "but tonight we are going to the cockfights. Get your money out. The men in this village are notorious gamblers."

After lunch, my uncle inquired about his two men, Roberto and Fidel. The saloon owner said to look for them at the small infirmary on the edge of town, because the tall one had been injured. When we reached the infirmary, we found Roberto sitting on a bench outside, next to the front door. Uncle Jesse asked him for an explanation.

Roberto spoke very apologetically. He said, "Two days ago, Fidel invited one of the pretty ladies for a ride in the Dodge. They rode out of the village and were gone for two hours. When they returned, no one seemed to mind. At night, after supper, we were walking to the inn when we were confronted by four men. One pulled a knife and faced Fidel. The other three moved me aside, assuring me they intended me no harm. Fidel announced that he was unarmed. One of the men handed him a knife.

"Fidel was a bit larger than his opponent, but the little man moved like a serpent. He seemed impossible to touch. He toyed

86

with Fidel until Fidel lunged forward, missing his adversary and landing flat on his face. The little man plunged his knife into Fidel's back between his shoulderblades, then backed away, announcing he would leave his knife in Fidel's back as a souvenir. I'm sure he thought Fidel would die. Two men helped me carry Fidel to this infirmary and luckily found the doctor because they tell me he only comes to this village every two weeks for two days. He pulled out the knife and found that the thrust had missed the lungs and arteries. He treated the wound and thought Fidel could travel in three days — that's tomorrow."

Roberto looked at Uncle Jesse and waited nervously to learn his reaction. Uncle Jesse merely shrugged and said, "Roberto, we are going to the cockfights and then to the inn. You stay here with Fidel and we will return in the morning."

It was my first cockfight and I would not have imagined that the excitement would be even more intense than a boxing match. Those little smiling men in their white outfits and straw hats changed dramatically. Their smiles were gone. Their faces were intense and deadly serious as they placed their bets on the cocks. Everyone was drinking large quantities of beer. I made small bets on each fight and won almost every time.

I studied the methods of the handlers. They would bring out the viciousness of the cocks by stroking their heads and necks. The fighting cock is a species quite unlike its domestic cousin. Although the fighting cock is fierce and ruthless, he is also brave and courageous. He fights to conquer and to kill. Most of the damage is inflicted by the horny spurs on his feet. Blinding is a common injury, but even blind they will go on fighting. Great skill and centuries of breeding have created these noble birds. The two handlers would bring the cocks face to face, then turn them loose, and the cocks fought relentlessly and viciously until one was dead. Truly a fight to the death.

Twice, fistfights erupted between supporters of the different cocks. On one occasion, knives were drawn. Only a small wound was inflicted before some of the bystanders separated the two men.

During the last fight, Dr. Montemayor slipped outside — for obvious reasons after so much beer. When he returned, I could see he was distressed. He whispered that he had overhead two men discussing Fidel. One told the other that four men were going to remove Fidel from the infirmary later that night and finish the job. Apparently the offended party was tired of waiting for Fidel to die.

As soon as the cockfights were over, we went to the cars. The Model A was already loaded with our equipment. Uncle Jonathan got behind the wheel of the Dodge and Uncle Jesse followed in the pickup as we headed straight to the infirmary. We found Roberto sitting on a chair next to Fidel in a small ward.

Uncle Jesse told them, "We must leave. Fidel's life is in danger."

Roberto and I picked up Fidel in our arms and carried him out and put him on the back seat of the Dodge. Dr. Montemayor sat in the seat next to him. This time, Uncle Jesse drove the Dodge, with Uncle Jonathan at his side. Roberto and I followed in the Model A. As we started to pull out, six men appeared and took positions directly in front of the Dodge, blocking our path. Uncle Jesse and Uncle Jonathan stepped out of the car and both drew large pistols.

Uncle Jesse asked, "Which one of you sonsabitches will die first? Step aside now or die!"

The six men looked at each other and parted. My uncles jumped back into the Dodge and took off, with the Model A directly behind them. And that was the last I ever saw of Pataloutan, the village of the provocative women and the little men of strength.

# Chapter 11

When we reached Queretaro we headed straight for our hotel, eager to check in and relax in its luxury after our trip. But we began to be aware that there were not many people on the downtown streets, and just as we pulled up in front of the hotel we heard the cathedral bells tolling and it was a mournful, dirge-like sound.

We entered the lobby and as we approached the front desk, the little clerk came around the counter and extended his hand to Dr. Montemayor and said, "Let me express my sympathy regarding your great loss, and, I might add, a loss for everyone in Mexico."

Dr. Montemayor did not take the clerk's hand. "What are you talking about?" he asked, with slight panic in his voice.

"Why, señor, the death of Ernesto Martinez, Mexico's greatest matador!"

Our good doctor exclaimed, "No! *Dios*, no!" And then to our astonishment his legs seemed to simply go limp under him and he melted to the floor, and there he wept, sobbing loudly and without control.

Uncle Jesse took charge. "Harvey, help me pick him up. Jonathan, get his room key."

We carried the doctor to his room, and the hotel physician gave him a sedative. Uncle Jesse went back downstairs to learn more about the tragedy, and when Uncle Jonathan and I met him for a late lunch he gave us the story.

"Ernesto Martinez was killed Sunday afternoon," he told us, "and for the last two days his body has been lying in state. Tonight there will be the rosary." He paused for a moment in an effort to control his own emotion. "Ernesto Martinez was killed as he tried to save the life of an aspiring eighteen-year-old youth who jumped into the bull ring, unauthorized, with his own cape and started to work the bull that belonged to Ernesto. The young man was knocked to the ground, and El Matador Ernesto, trying to draw the bull away from the foolish young fellow, carelessly exposed himself and the bull managed to hook him, goring him in the chest and killing him instantly."

Uncle Jesse paused again. He was seeing the action as he described it, and he was filled with the horror of what had happened on that bloody Sunday. He swallowed hard and went on.

"The bull then turned and hooked the young man in his side, lifting him with his horn and tossing him high into the air. The young man also died. When Ernesto Martinez was carried from the bull ring, thousands of spectators were weeping loudly without shame, and for the last two days all the stores have been closed, and all the restaurants, and every hour the church bells toll his passing. The city is in total mourning. Twenty thousand have passed by his casket and the line is still moving and circles a city block."

After lunch we went to Dr. Montemayor's room to check on him and were surprised to find him dressed and about to leave. "I must go to the family," he told us, "to pay my respects and offer my services." He paused, removed his glasses and examined them self-consciously. "I apologize for my behavior. I hope I did not embarrass you. You three are dear friends and I would do nothing to threaten our comradeship."

He embraced each of us in turn, then added, "Tonight at eight o'clock I would be pleased if you could attend the rosary for Ernesto, my fallen matador."

So we knelt in the packed church where the body lay in state, along with the many thousands kneeling outside in the street as the rosary was prayed for the soul of this brave man.

90

The funeral the next day was so moving that I struggled with my emotions, all the while trying hard to suppress tears. The silence was profound and complete, although twenty thousand people attended. The prayers at the graveside were spoken almost in a whisper. For the immediate family, the moment for crying and hysteria had passed and now it was their dignity and their elegance that was evident and had to be admired, particularly the matador's wife. When the prayers were over, she stood by the graveside for a moment, turned, and faced the huge crowd of people who stood so still and motionless you could hear the soft breeze in the trees. Then she said, *"Con permiso"* ("With your permission") and her voice was clearly heard. The mass of people parted to allow her to pass and she walked through the corridor of human walls with a dignity and a presence, with such pride and elegance, that it caused a lump in my throat, and made it difficult to catch my breath.

At that moment, the band started playing "La Virgen de la Macarena," probably the most stirring of all the bullfight music. It played for her. It was for this elegant lady, the Lady of the Matador Ernesto Martinez. Not a tear in her eye, but not a dry eye among the thousands of other souls at this majestic moment.

That night, when I finally lay down on my bed I was exhausted. In retrospect, the bullfight had been a thrilling experience, but it was dwarfed by the magnificence of the people — both the bereaved family and the grieving public — standing with a pride and a character which exceeded my expectations.

At eight the following evening, we arrived at the bottling plant in San Luis Potosi. As soon as we had unpacked, Uncle Jesse asked me to drive out with him to visit his friend Julio Peralta at his *hacienda* eight miles from the plant.

The Peralta estate was a large stately home furnished in the Spanish Colonial style. Servants begged us to enter through the big ornately carved front door. Mr. and Mrs. Peralta bid us a gracious welcome, assuring us with formal but warm Mexican hospitality that their home was our home. We sat in a large living room with high ceilings, marble floors, and handsome furnishings that seemed palatial to me.

Mr. Peralta spoke to Uncle Jesse with great excitement and

joy. "Our son is cured. Two weeks ago we noticed that three or four of his boils were beginning to drain and dry. The next day ten or fifteen, and the next twenty-five, and so on. He had 143 boils and within one week they were gone. Now he is out of bed and has returned to his school. There is very little scarring. It is like a miracle."

He paused for a moment and closed his eyes as if in prayer. Then he went on. "Jesse, my friend, we know how this happened. El Brujo Orozco died. Friends tell us he went into a deep depression. He would not eat or drink anything, nor would he speak. He died a week ago. God has answered our prayer. Jesse, my friend, I know I asked you to help. I was desperate. Now you don't have to do anything. We are free of that Devil."

Uncle Jesse stood, walked towards his friend and embraced him and said, "Thank God your son is healed. I am so glad it was not necessary for me to intervene. It might have made matters worse." I marveled at his delicacy and tact as I realized that he would never let Don Julio know what he had done to save the boy's life.

He turned to Mrs. Peralta and gallantly kissed her hand. This was the first time I had seen the cavalier side of Uncle Jesse. I loved it . . . I loved him.

He nodded to me and said, "Come, my boy, it's time we say good night to these gentle people."

Once outdoors, as we walked toward the car, Uncle Jesse said, "Dolores Peralta is one of the most refined ladies in the world." He stopped and turned, facing me directly, and added, "Only your mother is superior to her. My boy, your mother is a miracle. Around her I am awed. She makes me believe that the world could truly be immaculate." His words brought tears to my eyes.


Uncle Jonathan and I said goodbye to Uncle Jesse and Dr. Montemayor in front of the bottling plant at noon two days later. The four of us had become comrades for life — *compañeros, amigos, compadres*. It was a heart-warming occasion, with hugs, back-slapping, a few jokes — and almost a few tears.

By late afternoon we reached Monterrey on the way back to Texas. We checked into the Hotel Ancira, and I was impressed by the black and white marble floors and the beautiful winding marble staircase that dominated the elegant lobby. There was exquisite hand-carved furniture of fine Mexican craftsmanship, upholstered in colorful, hand-embroidered materials. The large lounge featured a hundred-foot-long hand-carved bar with inlaid marble and a back bar of mirrors framed in onyx. At one end of the lobby was a restaurant offering Continental cuisine as well as delicious Mexican dishes.

As I stepped out of the shower in our room, Uncle Jonathan was walking out the hall door and announced that he would wait for me in the cocktail lounge downstairs. It was only five o'clock, and in Mexico that was three hours too early for supper.

When I left the elevator half an hour later and walked into the lobby, Uncle Jonathan was hurrying toward me. "Harvey," he half whispered, "Roscoe is in the bar. Let's you and me go somewhere else."

I flushed with an unfamiliar sense of anger. "No sir!" I snapped, and walked past him with long fast strides that brought me to the bar quickly. I looked to the right and saw Roscoe sitting at the far end alone, drinking a beer. There was no one else in the room except the two bartenders.

When he saw me he stood up. I walked toward him. I felt good, as I had when the assignment was to carry the ball in a football game. When I reached him, I threw a punch with everything I had to the side of his jaw, and he crashed to the floor.

"That's for the shot that you took at me," I said.

Roscoe lay there for a moment, showing shock on his face. Then his face hardened. At that moment, one of the bartenders yelled, *"Que pasa? Que pasa?"*

I turned toward the bartender and said, *"Todo esta bien. Todo esta bien."*

Roscoe was getting to his feet when he heard me speak in Spanish. His look turned to surprise, and curiously he just stood there as if in shock. My conclusion was that he thought I had allies. I don't think he realized until that moment that I could speak Spanish, and that indeed I might be on my home turf.

His face hardened again and he said, almost through clenched teeth, "You better always look behind you. You'll never know when I'm there."

But my spirits were soaring. "I'll be waiting. I love to see you crash to the floor," I said, and smiled at him tauntingly.

He wiped the corner of his lip where a trickle of blood had appeared and walked past me, circling me by at least four feet. Only then was I aware that Uncle Jonathan had walked up behind me. Roscoe almost backed out all the way to the door. Now his expression was murderous, and as he walked through the lounge I watched him until he disappeared down the hall.

I turned and looked at Uncle Jonathan and was delighted to find him grinning broadly. "Damn, Harvey," he said. "You've done grown up good. Real good."


After supper, Uncle Jonathan told me that he had sold his truck to the general manager of the hotel, and we would be returning to Texas by train. The next morning we took a taxi to the railroad station. As we entered the depot, the corner of my eye caught Roscoe stepping out of another taxi.

Uncle Jonathan glanced at him and said, "Roscoe seems to be going back to the States. He won't be able to stay in Texas. Wonder where he'll head for next?"

We went directly to the train. Roscoe was following about fifty feet behind us. When we reached the platform of the train, Uncle Jonathan stepped up. I turned, put my hands on my hips, and looked directly at Roscoe. He came to a stop about twenty feet away, and we stared at each other. The confrontation lasted for thirty seconds. Roscoe did not move. I finally laughed and went up the steps and directly to my seat. Roscoe would have to wait for the next train.

As the train began to get underway, I looked out the window and saw Roscoe still standing there, never moving, until finally he was out of sight. Very satisfied, I spoke softly to myself, "Roscoe, I'll be waiting for you," happy at the courage that I felt.

# PART 3

# World War II

# Chapter 12

The next two years of my life were dominated by high school activities. I had many girlfriends and went steady with half a dozen pretty girls — but never for long. I played football, basketball, and baseball, and did well at all of them. I boxed in the Golden Gloves, losing only one fight in twelve and that by a split decision. As we emerged from the Depression, the mood of the country changed. We were dancing to jukeboxes, to the music of Benny Goodman, Artie Shaw, and Glenn Miller. We had frequent parties in our homes. At school, students joined fraternities and sororities, and we gave our dates corsages and rented tuxedos for the proms and balls.

But after memories of the sporting events and the girls and the proms fade into the background, a man and a job stand out from this period of my life. Walter Maurer was a friend of my family, and he became like a second father to me. He owned a drugstore two blocks from my home, as well as a small manufacturing plant with eight employees where he made medicated teas and other home remedies which were distributed statewide.

Maurer was about fifty at that time. He reminded me of Lincoln. Standing a slim six feet four, he had a pleasant face with deep wrinkles and dark, deep-set, melancholy eyes. He was gentle and caring, with great sensitivity, and I thought him brilliant, not just in business but in most all areas of life. He was a druggist, a chemist, and had been an investment banker. In the twenties he had made a fortune and lost it in the crash of '29 through the fraud and dishonesty of his brother. Now he was beginning to recoup his finances.

All through my high school years I made frequent visits to Mr. Maurer's drugstore and soda fountain. I could not have explained why at first, but he was a man I admired and someone from whom I felt I could learn much. Our relationship developed almost unconsciously into that of mentor and apprentice. He would often walk home with me after my visit to his drugstore and chat with my parents.

After graduation, I decided to work with him for a year before going on to college, and it was a decision I have never regretted. My official job included inventory control, ordering supplies, and acting as Mr. Maurer's personal assistant. But I got so much more than the small salary he paid me and more than the specifics of my duties implied. He introduced me to economics, banking, the stock market, and the general field of interstate commerce. He helped me to love Shakespeare, Joyce, and Byron. He taught me business methods which I am still applying today.

During that winter came the bombing of Pearl Harbor, and the ensuing war suddenly altered the dreams and plans of all Americans forever. The times were exciting. The country was united — it was vital and alive. Everyone was busy; everyone had a purpose. There was a sense of dedication and determination. And most important, this was a war in which we knew that honor and truth were on our side. As a country we had no fear, and we were certain that we would be victorious.

I spent many hours at Mr. Maurer's home, as we read together or studied some aspect of business or discussed the effect the war would have on the nation's economy. Conscription for the armed forces had begun even before Pearl Harbor, and I discussed with him the decision that was imminent for me about joining the service.

Mrs. Maurer was a nurse, some fifteen years younger than her husband, and she was working at the county hospital to help with their finances. But she was one of the most ill-tempered women I have ever known, and if she came home while I was there, I would quickly gather my books and leave. Her abusive remarks to her husband embarrassed me, as they obviously did him, so I never lingered.

On one occasion, he helped me pick up my books and stepped out the door with me to say goodbye. As she heard the door close she screamed, "Where in the hell do you think you are going?"

He turned to me and said, "Harvey, I humbly beg your pardon." He paused for a moment, looking sadly at his feet, and surprisingly added, "Your mother is magnificent. If only all women were like her. There is a great deal of her in you. I love you both."

I remember that I embraced him before I walked away. At the corner I looked back and he was still standing there with his head bent down, looking so sad that it made my eyes fill with tears.

Educationally, this was the most rewarding year of my life. Throughout the years, I remained a son to this wonderful man who contributed so much to my growth. He continued to be my advisor until he died seven years later. When I think of him today, sadness overcomes me.


In November, I enlisted in the Army Air Corps, and after basic training was sent to Arizona State University in Tempe under the Air Force educational cadet program.

I believe that my mother's influence and instruction, and perhaps my experiences on the ranch and in Mexico — including the strange confrontations with Roscoe — had given me a chance to mature faster than my friends. Athletics too had allowed me to test myself in many ways. As a result I had developed a direct but philosophical approach to most problems, and a self-confidence and poise which I did not find in others my age. Looking back, I see myself as a self-assured youngster who still had a lot to learn but further along in the process than my fellow cadets.

During the year and a half I spent at Arizona State, the college had only forty civilian male students and a hundred and thirty cadets — a total of 170 men to enjoy the company of more than 900 coeds. And although we were taking accelerated courses that required many hours of classes, the fun never seemed to end. We had dates any night we could sacrifice the time.

I developed close friendships with many of the cadets, but particularly with two. One was Mark Evans, an intellectual, intense, good-looking fellow from Terre Haute, Indiana. The other was Michael Pruske, a tall, tough, street-smart "survivor" with a humorous, foolish streak and a quick smile that forced you to like him.

Pruske was of Polish descent, from a small coal-mining town in Pennsylvania. He and I would put on eight-ounce boxing gloves in the gym to spar. Invariably we drew a crowd because we would become quite serious, land some heavy blows, and put on a good show. I always pulled my punches because I suspected I could knock him out easily and did not want him to be aware of that fact. We always stopped before we got to the point of a knockdown and we would embrace and leave the gym together laughing, to the astonishment of the spectators who had gathered hoping to see a decisive finish.

Finally we began to hear rumors that the Army Air Force academic programs were going to be shut down and we would be shipping out. And one day we found a notice on the dorm's bulletin board signed by the area commanding general which confirmed it. All the academic programs were terminated and all personnel involved were to be reassigned for training in critical technical positions. Next to that announcement were the orders showing our individual assignments and times for departure and for reporting to the new stations.

Mark, Michael, and I were all assigned to an armament and gunnery school for B-25 bombers at a base in northern Georgia. In addition to our orders, we were given money for travel expenses and instructions to find our own transportation to Georgia and report at the base before 2200 hours in seven days.

That night Mark and I had dinner at the mess hall and then we talked for two more hours discussing our orders and the possible consequences. Most of the cadets were — at least on the surface — jubilant that they were making a move and getting closer to the time when they would be sent overseas and get into action. But the philosophical Mark was depressed. He was taking the long view and being realistic about what was to come.

"Harvey, it's very possible that within eight or nine months we will be in combat," he said, "so we must seriously consider the possibility that we won't come back. It is important that we evaluate our lives, our contribution to others, and question whether our existence has had a real meaning."

I could not share his gloom, and I felt a need to buoy up his spirits. "Oh come on, Mark, we are not going to be killed. You and I are too lucky. We're going to beat the hell out of the Germans and the Japs and then we're going to have a great life."

"I want to be optimistic," Mark went on, "but it is difficult. Every day you hear of the thousands that are killed, of the terrible slaughter that is going on. We need to do a summing up, a self-judgement. Can I justify my existence? Has my living made a difference so far and will my dying matter? And what about the effect that our death might have on our families?"

Mark's sensitivity impressed me, but I felt that he too often dwelled on the worst possible consequences. Finally I changed the subject abruptly and asked him, "How are you going to get to Georgia?"

Mark stared at me, then made a visible effort to bring his mind back to the practical. "I'm going to take a bus to Terre Haute," he said, "visit a couple of days, and then go to Georgia. I think I have enough time."


Michael Pruske was very proud of his Harley-Davidson motorcycle and was planning to ride it to Georgia. He suggested that I buy one of the surplus cycles that were being sold at an Army base a hundred and fifty miles away. He would be happy to take me to pick it up. The Army had discontinued the extensive use of motorcycles due to the many accidents that had occurred. It sounded like a great idea to me, and I was excited by the prospect of a cross-country motorcycle trip. I had saved a little money and learned to my surprise that surplus Army motorcycles, practically new, were available for less than two hundred dollars. The only models that were offered were the Indian brand motorcycles, and we found one with very little mileage, made the purchase, and I rode it back to the base.

With Mike's help, it took just a day to sand down the olive drab color and repaint the Indian cycle bright blue with red stripes. I loved the feel of its speed and power on the open highway. There was a sense of freedom and adventure you could not get by any other method of travel. In that sense, the three-day trip to Georgia was great — but traveling with Pruske made it somewhat bizarre.

In a small town in Arkansas, Michael got drunk, and wanted to fight three guys, all at one time. It was only by my appeal to their generosity that we were able to walk away — or, I should say, they allowed me to drag Michael away.

At the next small town, we stopped at a cafe on the town square and ordered steaks, which turned out to be tough. Pruske started flirting and joking with our pretty waitress. Halfway through the meal, he went over to the counter where she was serving other customers. I went on eating, looking up occasionally to check on Pruske's progress. He and the girl moved to the end of the counter and stood talking for five minutes. Then Michael came over to my table and said he was going to leave for a while and take Nancy with him.

"When will I see you?" I asked.

"Hell, I don't know. Here I've got some action going and you want to know when you're going to see me again. Two or three hours, I guess. I'll meet you here in the town square."

"It'll be pretty close to dark by then," I said.

"Don't worry. The boogey man won't get you. Hell, man. I've got something going here. If you want, I'll ask her if she's got a friend."

"No, thanks. Not my kind of action," I answered.

A couple of hours later I was sitting on a bench in the quiet town square, the Indian parked on the curb next to me. Occasionally someone would walk across the square; otherwise, nothing stirred. I had bought a beer at the cafe and sat sipping it slowly, wondering when Pruske would show up.

Finally the door of the cafe opened and three fellows came out and walked over to me. They looked burly and tough, and the biggest one put a foot up on the bench beside me as he asked, "Where is your friend?"

Their attitude was menacing, so I replied cautiously, "He went on ahead. We're on our way to Georgia."

"And you stayed behind? That's your story?" remarked the tall one.

"Yeah. I really felt tired . . . and I don't like cycling in the dark. I'll catch up with him tomorrow."

The big one then leaned forward with his face just six inches from mine, "My wife Nancy has not been at the cafe for two hours. If she's with that Yankee sonofabitch, I'm going to de-nut him after I've broken his legs. Do you understand?"

"Don't look at me," I answered. "He said he was leaving and I said okay."

He turned and walked away, followed by the other two, and I watched them head for the small bar and pool hall a block from the square. I waited for a few minutes, mounted my motorcycle, and headed east as if leaving town, but instead I turned left on the last street, moving slowly so that my cycle would not sound too loud, and started searching for Pruske's Harley-Davidson.

I went up and down the streets, stopping at intersections and looking in both directions. I kept on circling until I was on the west side of the town. Then I looked back toward the town square and saw eight men standing together there. I turned onto the main highway and headed west out of town slowly, hoping that Pruske had also gone in that direction.

As I reached the top of a small hill two miles from town, Michael was heading toward me, Nancy sitting on the back of the big seat with her arms around him. As we approached each other, I could hear Pruske singing a Polish song.

"Michael!" I yelled to him. "They're waiting to hang you! There are eight men waiting for you, and one of them is her husband."

I heard Nancy gasp. She bounced off the cycle, went to the side of the road, jumped the fence, and started trotting across the field. "Where you going?" Michael called after her.

"I gotta aunt that lives nearby, but you better git. Elmer's as mean as they come. You better git." Nancy didn't wait to see if we took her advice.

Mike turned to me and said, "We have two choices. We can take a chance and go through the town and then head east on the main highway. Or we can backtrack about thirty miles to a little farm road I saw that'll probably lead us around the whole area, but it'll also probably add a hundred miles to our trip. What do you think?"

"Mike, did you know that woman was married?" I asked.

He replied, "Sure, man. They're the best."

"Dammit, Mike," I said, "I don't approve of the kind of crap you pull, but that's your business, so I'm not going to stand in judgement of you. But dammit, when you involve me, that's something else!"

"Yeah, I know. Which way you want to go?" he said with a grin. I knew he was itching for a fight, to make up for the one I had pulled him out of earlier. "Well," I told him, "I don't mind riding an extra hundred miles, but I do mind being *forced* to ride an extra hundred miles. Going through town is the shortest way, so that's the way I'm going to go."

"Yahoo!" he yelled, slapped me on the back, skidded the back wheel of his cycle, and took off. It took me only a split second to come up alongside him.

As we entered the town, everything seemed to be quiet. We were cautious, trying to circle around the center of town, taking some of the back streets and alleyways. We reached the highway on the east side and thought we were in the clear, but then as we rounded a bend, two hundred yards ahead of us stood twelve men, each of them holding a weapon. I could not see any firearms, but I did see clubs, chains, and one guy with a machete.

We moved slowly toward them, and then suddenly I turned my accelerator to full speed. Mike followed. When we got to the men they scattered as fast as they could and I shot through, but Mike hit one of them, throwing him into the air and onto the side of the road. As we went over a rise, we saw the road a hundred yards ahead was barricaded with two trucks and three cars. Behind the barricade four cars that had been traveling west were being held up, awaiting the results of this gruesome business.

We stopped in the middle of the road. We looked back and saw a half dozen of the men we had scattered running toward us, swinging their chains and clubs. At the barricade, at least eight other men were waiting.

We looked at each other and Mike said, "Harvey, have you

103

ever gone cross-country? It's fun. Pretend we're horse thieves and the posse is after us. Follow me."

He turned to the left, went twenty feet, and then crashed through a wooden fence that splintered in front of him. I was directly behind him, sprinkled by loose dirt from the rear tire of his cycle. We bounced and swerved across country, dodging holes, bushes, and small trees for a hundred yards or so. We found a narrow trail, probably a cattle trail, turned right and followed it for a quarter mile, then found another trail that headed back to a road. Finally there was a dirt road leading to an open gate that brought us back on the highway beyond the barricade. Behind us, we saw two trucks that were following, but it was too late for them. We were flying, and there was no catching the Harley-Davidson and my good trusty Indian.

We sped on for three hours before we turned onto a side road and found a spot that was well concealed from the highway. Using our barracks bags for pillows, we settled down for a few hours of rest.

"How much territory do you think we'll cover tomorrow?" I asked.

"If we start early we might get there late in the evening," he answered.

Just before I fell asleep, I looked up at the sky. My thoughts were of my mother and of her words, "You must live with honor. Man cannot live without honor." I pondered the word *honor* and wondered its true meaning. I wondered about Michael's values and his interpretation of honor. Maybe he never thought about it. Nevertheless, he sure was fun to be with, and regardless of his values, I loved him and would defend him to the end. But it was probably better if he didn't know it.

# Chapter 13

After four months of armament and gunnery training, we were awarded sergeant's stripes and wings and assigned to a specific crew, flying B-25s. I would have four more months of training as a turret gunner and stay together with the same crew and bomber. Our plane was named "Little Stud."

For me, it was a wonderful time in the Air Force. We would fly every day, make bomb runs over targets in the Gulf of Mexico, take gunnery practice on targets both on land and water. Our training days consisted of four to six hours of flying, and the rest of the time we were relatively free to do as we wished.

Although Mark and Mike had been assigned to my squadron, we went to town together only occasionally, mostly because I had made a new friend, Roy Graham. Roy was from Kansas City, and he was our plane's radio operator and on the same schedule that I was. During those many hours of flying we were only busy while actually on target, and Roy and I would have long discussions on politics, philosophy, psychology, and the latest bestsellers. We both enjoyed reading books, usually novels, and we would swap them and have long discussions about them.

Roy was married and was trying to make arrangements to bring his wife to Georgia. I was surprised to learn the difference in their ages. He was twenty-four and Lily was only seventeen.

One Saturday I agreed to go to town with Roy to rent a room for Lily. Although we had a considerable amount of liberty, flight personnel were not allowed to sleep off base except on weekends. Roy wanted to find a room for Lily with a nice family where he could join her on the weekends.

Armed with three ads from the local newspaper, Michael, Mark, Roy, and I set off to check out the rooms. We rode double on the two cycles, Roy behind me, and Mark behind Michael. If we found a good deal, Roy would put down a deposit and then we would have some fun in Gainesville, a typical small Southern town.

Roy was satisfied with the room and the family at the first home we tried. It was a large two-story house that seemed to have been crowded onto a small lot. The house must have been at least thirty years old and it was in sad disrepair. The front porch that circled three sides had a double-seat swing and an assortment of mismatched furniture. On either side of the entry hall, large openings led to the dining room on the left and the living room on the right. The furniture showed years of wear, with nicks on the woodwork, and upholstery that was slick with exposed seams. However, the house was spotless, without a speck of dust or a dirty window anywhere, and although the varnish had worn thin on the floor, the boards were mopped and waxed.

The four of us sat in the living room on the heavily upholstered furniture, drinking ice tea and eating cookies on this hot summer afternoon, with all the windows open to allow as much breeze as possible. We listened courteously to Mrs. Ruth Lee Martin who asked each one of us about our homes, our family, and our activities in the Air Force. We were all impressed with her graciousness, her good manners, her charm, and her intelligence. She was a big woman, probably close to forty years old.

Mrs. Martin's manner demanded respect and there could be no doubt that she was a lady, but I wasn't sure what to expect from my fellow airmen, especially Pruske. I wasn't at all sure he knew how to act in such a situation. I needn't have worried. Pruske listened attentively, a little saucer with two cookies on his lap, a little napkin in his left hand and a glass of ice tea in his right, nodding at the appropriate times.

Mrs. Martin had three children, two boys — one twelve and the other fifteen — and a daughter. When the boys walked into the room, they were required to shake hands with each one of us. The daughter, Sandra, eighteen, was a real Southern beauty who met us on the porch as we were leaving after the arrangements for the room had been concluded. She said "Hi," smiled shyly, kissed her mother at the doorway, and walked past us. She was a tall girl of five foot seven at least, with a most provocative shape.


On our way to the local pool hall, both Mark and Mike told Roy they would like to visit the Martins with him again after his wife had arrived. Mark showed special interest in Mrs. Martin's beautiful daughter, and I was glad to see it because for the last two weeks he had seemed strained as if something was worrying him deeply, and at times he was despondent.

Roy, however, gleefully announced, "Mrs. Martin wouldn't allow you two reprobates to get within ten feet of that gal. But I can tell you that if Lily was not around, I might take a crack at Sandra myself."

Mark and Mike both laughed, but I considered the statement disgusting.

At the pool hall, between games, Mark and I sat on a bench and discussed the politics of small Southern towns like Gainesville. Then, almost between sentences, Mark fell into deep thought and seemed unaware of what I was saying.

Taking him by the arm, I said, "Mark, we've been friends for a long time, and I have been aware that something's bothering you. Won't you tell me?"

He turned to me with a start and searched my face as if trying to make up his mind whether to trust me. Then, with a sigh, he leaned forward with his arms on his knees and looked down at the floor between his feet. He began talking so softly I could barely hear him.

"Harvey, it's about my family. I just don't know how to handle it. You see, Mother left my dad and me when I was six years old. She moved to California with a newspaper reporter, and it was only four months ago that I finally heard from her. After all these years, suddenly she wrote begging forgiveness for having left me and promised a reunion that she hoped would last forever. Her letter was wonderful. She spoke of the great love that she had for me, and assured me that she had never loved anyone as much as she did me. She explained how her mother forced her to marry my father, who was a well-to-do man but fifteen years her senior and she didn't love him. Then she met Kenneth Stern, the man she ran away with and eventually married after getting a Reno divorce. Her plans were to send for me, and Stern had agreed; but then she got pregnant, had a daughter, and after that he wouldn't allow it. And eventually he wouldn't even let her mention my name.

"Six months ago, Stern ran off with a younger woman. My mother said she didn't care, for now she could plan our reunion. But Harvey . . ." He turned and looked at me. "Harvey," he repeated, as his eyes filled with tears, and he choked so that his voice was hardly audible. "She's dead. It's all crazy. She's dead."

Mark sat with his head in his hands, trying to control his emotions. He swallowed hard, leaned back against the wall, and went on talking in a lifeless monotone.

"She was in her back yard watering the flowers and stepped on a fallen live electrical wire and it killed her. My sister wrote and told me that somehow I was to blame for her death. She said that her father left them because of me, and that since the day her mother started writing to me she had all kinds of bad luck. I wrote and told her that Mother had not written until after her father had left them. I tried to explain what Mother had said about her father and another woman. She answered, called me a liar, and asked me never to write again, and said that as far as she was concerned I did not exist."

We sat quiet for a few minutes as I wondered how I could comfort him in the face of this awful tragedy. "Mark," I said finally, "let's go across the street to that small restaurant and eat dinner. I need to talk to you about this."

As we walked out of the pool hall, Roy came over and asked if he could borrow my cycle for a couple of hours. I nodded and said, "Okay, but not more than two hours. I want to get back to camp."

Mark and I ate dinner in silence, and it wasn't till we had gotten our final cup of coffee that I started talking. "Damn, Mark, you think you've had a lot of bad luck, but your dad and your step-mother were very good to you. You've told me this many times, and that your life growing up in Terre Haute was great. Now you find your real mother again and learn about her bad luck, and I can see how that would be depressing, but at least feel grateful that she did correspond with you and you did learn that she loved you.

"Mark, you're a smart guy. Think carefully about this and look at it clearly. You still have your home, and you have two parents who love you. And to top it all, you met a good-looking girl today and I had the impression she sort of went for you. Next week when Roy goes to help his wife move in, you should go with him and help him, and maybe . . . who knows, you might find the love of your life."

Mark forced a slight grin, then became serious again and said, "I'm having trouble with the meaning of it all."

"All what?" I asked, not sure how much he included in that remark.

"Everything," he replied. "Life, the purpose of the war, the killing, the hate — it's crazy. And then, after a while it's over. We all die."

"Yes, someday we'll die, but for now, thank God for life, and don't forget the trees and the flowers, the mountains, pretty girls, love, freedom, our great country, and honor."

Mark looked directly at me, gave me a half-hearted smile, and started to say something, but at that moment Mike and Roy came in, arm-in-arm with two girls who were obviously prostitutes. They were quite voluptuous and rather pretty, but somehow they looked a bit unkempt, a bit dirty.

It didn't bother me that Mike had a date of that type, but for Roy, with his wife on the way to join him, I thought it was callous. In later conversations, Roy told me flatly that sex with his wife was simply not enough. Sometimes he would talk about honor, truth, and morality, but always as abstractions. "Invented by kings to control the peasants," he once said. He would not equate his actions and his relationship to his wife with the question of morality.

I considered the difference between Roy's attitude and Mike's. Mike Pruske thought of girls only as a source of pleasure for him, and he hoped it was for them. He might violate them, but he remained somehow unaware of his offense. But Roy Graham knew and enjoyed the violation and the knowledge of his actions. It was clear that he had a contempt for women, and Lily was there for his pleasure. I believe that with time I might help Mike to understand honor and the dignity of women, but I did not believe that I could ever change Roy's convictions.

The following week, I caught Roy in the barracks when he was getting ready to go meet Lily's train, and I asked him if he would please take Mark with him.

"Why?" Roy asked me.

"Because he might get acquainted with Mrs. Martin's daughter Sandra. Mark needs something or somebody right now." Roy didn't seem particularly understanding or concerned, but he agreed to take him along.

Half an hour after they had left, Michael came over to my bunk, grinning broadly, and said, "It's you and me, baby. Let's go to town and raise some hell."

I smiled back. "All right, Mike. But if there's a fight, let me start it this time."


Curfew on Sunday night was eleven o'clock. When I walked into the barracks that night, Roy waved at me and beckoned me over to his bunk.

"I thought you should know," he said, "Mark didn't hit it off with Sandra. He made no impression at all. She just plain rejected him. He spent most of the weekend sitting on a bench in the park. He slept at the Y, even though Mrs. Martin invited him to stay at her house. Lily and I saw him there in the park Saturday and again on Sunday afternoon.

"And listen, man," he continued, "Mrs. Martin was very upset that you didn't show up. I think she has picked *you* for her daughter. She sure is a fine lady, and Lily loved her right away. But sit down. I'm about to give you a big shocker."

I sat on the bunk opposite him. "Yeah?"

"Get this. Her old man, Will Martin, drove up on his eighteen-wheeler and parked the huge tractor and trailer right in front of the house. Mrs. Martin, her two boys, Sandra, Lily, and I were having lunch — Swiss steak, mashed potatoes, blackeyed peas, boy, was it good — when the old man came in the dining room smelling like a brewery. He was really drunk! Had on a torn T-shirt, grease on his hands and face, looking awful. He stood there weaving, with a glare on his face that could have killed an ox. Mrs. Martin walked right up to him and said, 'Will, dear, this is Roy and Lily Graham. They will be renting the spare room. Why don't you go upstairs and wash up, then come join us?'

"He said, 'Ain't hungry,' and he shoved her real hard, obviously hurting her arm. He ignored me and Lily and stomped upstairs, and we never saw him again that afternoon. He sure doesn't look like somebody Mrs. Martin should have married."

Corporal Parker, the barracks orderly, walked in and yelled Mark's name. Somebody answered, "He's not back yet."

Parker spotted us and came over to say, "Bad news for your buddy. Evans' father just died of a heart attack. The Captain's giving him a five-day leave, effective immediately."

Just then the door at the end of the barracks opened and Mark came in and walked straight over to us. Before I could say anything, Corporal Parker repeated his news. Mark stood rigid. The color left his face. Stunned, he spun and went back out the door.

I followed him to the steps outside. He started trotting, and I ran after him, "Where are you going? What are you going to do?"

"I'm going home right now," he replied.

"Hold on, Mark. Let me try for a pass and go with you."

"No, please," he said. "I must go. I can't wait."

I stopped. I called after him, "You need a suitcase, a change of clothes, or something."

"I don't need nothing. I don't need a damned thing," he screamed as he continued to run until I lost him in the dark.

As I walked back to the barracks, I wondered if I had made the wrong decision. Maybe Mark should not be alone at this time.

# Chapter 14

The following weekend I went with Roy to meet Lily and to visit the Martin family. Actually, I was looking forward more to seeing Mrs. Martin, whom I had found captivating, than Sandra, who struck me as immature, although she was very pretty.

The big eighteen-wheel rig was parked in front of the house when Roy and I rode up on my Indian. As we walked across the yard, we realized that Mr. Martin was on the porch sitting in a rocking chair. When we went up the steps he stood and greeted us with a big smile and introduced himself. I suppose he didn't remember meeting Roy a week earlier.

"Boys," he said, "I'm Will Martin. I sure am proud of you military boys. You fellas are going to keep this country free, and the rest of us working folks are thankful to the good Lord for having you guys. Just go on in. Mrs. Martin is in there somewhere. Make yourselves to home." He spoke pleasantly, but his heavy Southern accent had a hint of the backwoods about it, and his lack of education was obvious.

Roy and I went in, and when we were out of earshot I asked

softly, "Roy, where is that mean sonofabitch you mentioned? That little guy sure doesn't seem mean to me."

Roy shook his head in amazement. "I can't believe the change. I can't believe he's the same man I met the other night!"

Mrs. Martin came down the hall. "Hello, Roy. Well, Harvey!" She took my hand. "I'm so glad to see you again. We missed you last weekend." She turned and called up the stairs, "Lily, your husband is here." Then to us, "Sandra will be home in about twenty minutes. Come in and sit down."

We went into the living room and sank into the deep, soft chairs. They were such a pleasant change from the barracks that I didn't mind their enveloping heat, and the worn spots were easy to overlook.

Mrs. Martin said, "Harvey, I see that you have met my husband. Mr. Martin is operating that truck just temporarily. His father was the famous Edwin Martin who designed and built the highway between Gainesville and Raleigh. My husband has been researching different businesses, and he's getting ready to become involved in a new enterprise very soon now." We later learned that Mr. Martin had been driving trailer trucks for the last six years. I found her attempt to believe in his ambition and respectability both brave and pitiful.

Lily came downstairs and said hello, then she and Roy went up to their room and closed the door. I was rather embarrassed because their intentions were so obvious. Sandra came home, and she and I spent the afternoon in the back yard. We talked about cars and the latest neighborhood gossip, and I pushed her in the swing which hung from a big tree, and we laughed and giggled like kids. I gave her a little kiss when she was not expecting it, and then we both laughed.

In the middle of the afternoon, Lily and Roy came out and we lounged around on the rickety lawn furniture and made smalltalk. Mrs. Martin brought out a tray of lemonade and cookies, and joined us.

A little later, Mr. Martin came around the corner of the house and called to Roy and me. We followed him to his big truck parked at the front curb. Reaching under the front seat, he pulled out a bottle of liquor that was clear as water and offered it to us. He said,

"This is the purest stuff that y'all will ever taste. It's called 'white lightnin.' Take a swig."

I took one and thought I was going to choke to death. It had to be 150 proof. Roy took two drinks and seemed to enjoy it. Will placed the bottle to his lips, threw his head back, and allowed five huge gulps to pour into his mouth. I could hardly believe it.

"Listen, boys," Martin said, "I'm about to go pick up ten quarts of this bootleg stuff. The place is just forty-five miles across the state line. It's easy. No danger, I promise. It's for some friends of mine, but I'm going to make forty bucks on the deal. My neighbor said I can use his car, and I hate to drive alone. Have to do it all the time. Come on, go with me and we'll split the bucks."

"Harvey, let's go," Roy said.

"No thanks. I think I'll just stay here," I answered. I could see that Martin was beginning to show that other side of his character — the bully Roy had described. I had no desire to see more of him. But Roy was eager to go along for the ride and the money.

"Aren't you going to say goodbye to the girls?" I asked him.

"No need," Will answered for him. "Tell them we'll be back in three hours, in time for dinner."

I went back around the house and sat down next to Mrs. Martin, and we got involved in a long discussion about the psychological effects of the war on the younger generation. She also talked about the beauty of the spring flowers in Georgia, sometimes very articulate and other times full of emotion, describing everything in loving terms. As on my last visit, I was most impressed by this gentle lady.

Occasionally during our conversation, I would glance at Sandra and Lily, and was amused at the way they entertained each other. They acted more like ten-year-olds than marriageable teenagers. They played hopscotch by drawing the squares on the ground with a stick. They sat on the sidewalk and played jacks. Then they took turns pushing each other in the swing, paying little attention to us except an occasional smile or remark.

It was late in the afternoon before Roy and Mr. Martin returned.

Early Tuesday morning, I went to headquarters and asked the

top sergeant if he had heard from Mark. "Not a word," he answered. "And if he's not back by tomorrow he'll be AWOL, and he'll get his can racked good!" I went outside to a public telephone directly in front of the headquarters building and placed a long distance call to Mark. We had exchanged home phone numbers, planning to stay in touch after the war. I let it ring ten times without response, and finally hung up and turned away, full of concern for my unhappy friend.

"Hey, Reese!"

It was the top sergeant, standing in the door of the headquarters and beckoning to me. He seemed more serious than usual. Normally he enjoyed joking and kidding the men.

He took me into his small office and gestured toward the chair across the desk from him. As soon as I sat down, he started shooting a string of questions. "What do you know about Mark Evans? Have you known him long? Is he a good guy? Is he a good soldier?"

"Of course he is," I said. "He's also one of my best friends. I would trust him with anything."

"Did he have any problems?"

I heard the change of tense, but I guess it didn't really register. "I know him very well, and sure, he has problems. Don't we all? Why the line of questions?"

The sergeant studied me for a moment. "Reese, I hate to tell you this, but Mark Evans hung himself two days ago in Terre Haute, Indiana. We just got the message a few minutes ago."

Without another word I stood and walked out.

I must have walked for hours, to the back side of the base, to the abandoned airstrip, completely around the base. I did not go to inspection. I missed my flight. And I simply did not care.

My mother's words were pounding in my head. "You must help anyone who is in distress. Anyone who needs help. You must allow others to depend on you." I wondered, could I have been more help to Mark? Maybe I should have asked for leave and gone with him to his father's funeral. God! I should have helped him somehow. He was a noble man, with all the right instincts. The world might have lost a champion.

The following week I decided not to go with Roy to the Martins' house. I had been keeping pretty much to myself and to my own thoughts, trying to understand where life leads us all, trying hard to understand the reason and purpose of Mark's life.

I wanted a fresh scene, a chance to look at things from a different direction. On Saturday morning I packed a small bag and boarded the Greyhound bus to Atlanta. I checked into a good hotel and that evening went to the Atlanta Symphony. And although I love classical music, the passionate performance of Tchaikovsky's Sixth Symphony, the "Pathetique," did not help my over-all mood.

After the program, I stood on the sidewalk watching the crowd disperse — the valet parking attendants bringing cars as fast as possible to their owners, men flagging taxis for their parties, groups maneuvering for position, men in tuxedos and women in evening dresses, most of the ladies bedecked with handsome jewelry. These were apparently the wealth and society of Atlanta.

I was a little self-conscious in my uniform, and surprised not to have seen at least one other serviceman in the audience. I hung back to wait until the rush was over before trying to catch a cab. My hotel was only ten minutes away and I could have walked, but I was not completely sure of my directions.

Finally the crowd dwindled to the last few people. The next taxi would be mine. My attention was drawn to two ladies who were arguing while evidently waiting for their car to arrive. One of them was a good-looking, middle-aged woman in a long red evening dress and wearing large diamonds in every appropriate place — including a necklace that was absolutely breathtaking. I saw three huge rings sparkling on her hands over her red silk gloves. Her poise and her carriage spoke of a wealth become habitual. The younger woman was very pretty, with a petite, cute figure. Twenty-two years, five foot three, I estimated. She wore a bright blue silk dress, cocktail length, with matching blue silk highheeled shoes.

Now that the crowd was gone, their argument became louder. Their chauffeured limousine approached the curb, and two men, one middle-aged and the other in his twenties, stepped from the car and held open the doors for the ladies . . . but the girl in blue refused to get in.

Just then my taxi pulled up and stopped directly behind the Cadillac limousine. Still watching the drama, I stepped off the curb and entered my cab, but before I could close the door, the pretty young lady turned and dashed over to me.

Holding my door open, she asked, "Could you please drop me at the Piedmont Hotel?"

Before I could answer, she was on the seat next to me and had closed the door.

I turned to the driver and commanded, "Take off." He quickly backed up, and as we sped forward the younger of the two men was trying to reach for our door, but he was too late.

I could feel her tension and agitation as she sat with her hands tightly clasped on her lap, but she said nothing, looking out her window so that I saw only the curve of her cheek and small rounded chin. After several blocks of what I felt was an increasingly awkward silence, I asked gently, "Which hotel?"

But before she might have answered, the driver answered, "I know. It's in the next block."

When we arrived at the hotel, she said, "Thank you," and stepped out.

"I'll see you in," I said.

"No, please, it's not necessary."

"I insist." I paid the driver and followed her into the lobby.

She stopped abruptly and turning toward me said, "Dear me, I have no money."

"Don't worry, I'll lend you some," I assured her.

"Thank you," she said. She looked about and added, "Let's sit for a minute here in the lobby."

She led me to a far corner of the large lobby and sat on a Victorian loveseat. I looked around for a chair to pull over, but there were none close by.

She saw my hesitation and said, "Please, sit here next to me."

When I did, she took a deep breath and then, as though she had just made a hard decision, she began to talk. Her words at first came in a rush, and I wondered if she had been preparing them in the taxi in case I did come in.

"I know this is most presumptuous," she said, "but I do need to speak to some one. I know I have no right to ask you to respect my confidence but I must and I do. My name is Vanessa. I'd rather not give you my last name. May I ask your name and where you are from?"

"Harvey. Texas," I replied.

"Do you know anyone in Atlanta?" she asked.

"No one," I answered. Then curiously I asked, "Are you not somewhat afraid of me, a stranger?"

She turned more towards me and looked into my face for a moment. Her hazel eyes were candid and honest. She answered, "There is nothing more to fear. What else can happen to me? I have been raped twice in the last two weeks." She must have seen the shock on my face, and quickly added, "I am so sorry. Please forgive me. I have no right, but . . ."

She stopped talking, lowered her head, and was silent for a moment. Then she added, "I'm so ashamed."

For several minutes we sat in silence. I remembered Mark, my dear friend. And now, looking at this sad lady I was overwhelmed with emotion. My eyes filled with tears that I could not control. Tchaikovsky's "Pathetique" with its somber melodies returned to me. When she looked at me to speak she was shocked at my emotional reaction and was visibly touched. From that moment there was a trust between us that was to remain always.

She reached for my hand and held it in both of hers. "Thank you," she whispered. "I think your sympathy has renewed my faith. But if I may burden you, I will tell you my story. I must tell someone, for I don't know what to do."

I squeezed her hand and nodded, and she sighed and relaxed a little as she began to talk.

"My mother and father divorced when I was ten. I never see my father anymore. He remarried and lives in Miami and has two daughters. When I was eleven my mother married a man who has a son three years older than me. Somehow I never did get along with my stepfather. Oh, not that we quarrelled. We were always very polite to each other. But there was no closeness. He seemed to take little interest in me, and I certainly never understood him. It's a big house. The only thing we had in common was my mother.

"Two weeks ago, in the middle of the night, this man, my 'stepfather' . . ." she spoke the word with heavy sarcasm, "came to my bedroom and raped me. I fought and screamed, but my bedroom is far from the others and no one could hear me. He overpowered me, tied my hands with my sheets, and raped and abused me in other manners. He left me tied up but I worked myself loose and went to my stepbrother's room. I told him what had happened and asked for his advice. He told me to do nothing until he could figure the best course of action. I agreed because of Mother. I wasn't sure whether to tell her and what she would do if I did.

"The next night my stepbrother came to my room. I let him in to learn his advice." She hesitated for a moment, then continued. "My stepbrother then proceeded to rape me, doing exactly what I had told him his father had done to me. I think I went into minor shock. The next day I did not leave my room the entire day, not even to eat. Late that night my mother came to my room to ask why I had not come downstairs. I let her in after she assured me she was alone. I told her what had happened to me. And Harvey, can you believe this? She sat there thinking about the situation, and I was waiting for her to comfort me and somehow make me feel less dirty, less used . . . at least, I expected her to understand what I was going through and to help me . . . Oh I don't know what I expected, but not what I got. She told me, 'I am so sorry, but we must not have a scandal in our family. I think it would be best to find someone to marry soon. Perhaps a trip to Europe would also be appropriate. In the meantime we must act as if nothing has happened.' Just like that. As cold and emotionless as if we were discussing what dress to wear to a party. I could hardly believe my ears.

"The symphony performance tonight was in honor of the sponsors, and Mother insisted that I attend. Until tonight, I had not left my room. All my meals were brought up to me. After the performance tonight I suddenly realized that I had to run away. I have no money with me, and only the clothes I am wearing. Just six weeks from now I am going to receive a trust fund from my grandfather's estate that will make me independent, but until then I must depend on others."

"Don't you have friends?" I asked.

She shook her head. "Most of them are Mother's friends, and I obviously can't expect any help from them." She thought a minute and said more hopefully, "Yes, I have a dear friend from school who lives in Savannah. Virginia Stein. I am sure I could stay with her. But what about tonight?"

I stood and said, "I am staying at the Wynecoff Hotel."

"That's on the next block," she said.

---

119

"Good. Let's go to my room." She hesitated. I looked directly into her face and softly added, "I am not like them."

She jumped up smiling and said, "Let's go."

I had the impression that telling me her misfortune partially relieved her hurt.

As soon as we got to my room I sat on the bed and phoned the Greyhound bus station. I learned that a bus left for Savannah the next morning at ten and the fare was seventeen dollars. When I put the receiver down, Vanessa, who had been standing by the door, walked to the bed and sat next to me. I reached into my pocket and pulled out all the money I was carrying, sixty-four dollars. I put fifty on the nightstand next to the bed and returned the other fourteen to my pocket.

Then I took her hand and said, "This room is paid for. Stay here tonight. Tomorrow, take a taxi to the bus station. It's only four blocks. The bus for Savannah leaves at ten. I'm lending you fifty dollars. I know it's late, but I think you should call your girlfriend Virginia now, and if she agrees for you to come, get her promise to keep your visit a secret."

Vanessa picked up the phone and got Virginia's number from the operator. She reached her friend and it was obvious she was warmly welcomed. As she replaced the receiver, Vanessa smiled broadly for the first time, and I saw how beautiful she could be when her life returned to normal.

"Vanessa, may I have Virginia's number in Savannah, and may I ask your full name? I would like to call next week, if I may."

"Vanessa Parker," she replied. "Yes, please call me whenever you wish," and she wrote down the number and handed it to me.

"My name is Harvey Reese," I said. I stood to leave.

She asked, "Where are you going?"

"There is a bus returning to Gainesville at two A.M., in two hours. I learned the schedules when I arrived," I said.

"Harvey, sit for a moment," she asked. "You have ample time. I want to ask you something important, and also to offer you again my deepest appreciation. It is most strange that you should help me this way. I truly do not understand, but first . . ." She paused, then asked, "Now that you have learned my misfortune, am I repulsive to you as a woman?"

"Of course not. Absolutely not," I quickly reassured her. "In fact, you are one of the loveliest women that I have ever met. You have nothing to be ashamed of. You have done nothing wrong." For a moment, I was so appalled that such men could do such a crime that I could hardly speak. "I would like to see them punished, but of course that would have to be your decision. It would put you through severe trauma to press charges and pursue the case. Think about it while you are in Savannah. But I can assure you, this bad time will pass, and I truly believe you will have great happiness in your life. I am looking at you and I see a vision of beauty."

I paused for a moment, leaned forward, and gently kissed her lips. Then I got up and went over to the small bag I had left in the room earlier. Taking out the new toothbrush and toothpaste, I gave them to Vanessa. I picked up the phone and called the operator to ring the room at eight the next morning. With my bag in my hand, I stood in front of Vanessa who was still sitting on the bed, took her hand and kissed it.

"Sleep well, my lovely princess."

Tears came to her eyes, but she did not speak a word as I left the room.

# Chapter 15

The next day I learned that Roy had invited Michael Pruske to the Martins' for the weekend, promising him a great time in return for the ride to town. I was concerned that Mike might make advances to Sandra and that she might be naive enough to respond. He was an exciting guy and fun to be with, but he definitely had no scruples.

My concern hung in the back of my mind until Sunday evening when Roy came back to the barracks. He reported, with his typical enthusiasm, "Harvey, we had a great time. I laid Lily three times and I ate like a pig." He sat down on the opposite bunk and grinned. "And I have a story to tell you about Mike. He really had a ball!"

I cringed and sat at attention; however, what Roy had to tell me did not involve Sandra but a new enterprise for Mike. Old Man Martin had asked Mike to make a run with him to pick up the bootleg whiskey. Pruske jumped at the idea, explaining that he had done some running back in Pennsylvania. The two of them were gone for five hours Sunday afternoon, delivered over forty gallons of white lightnin', and each made over a hundred dollars. Then they decided to make another run, this time to a place in northern Georgia. As they were going down the dirt road toward the still, the sheriff and twelve men jumped from the bushes ahead of them and raided the place. If Mike and Martin had arrived five minutes earlier they would have been arrested. When they got back to the house, they were laughing and bragging about their good luck, both of them slightly drunk.

"As the evening wore on," Roy said, "Old Will kept drinking and got pretty looped. He started using some pretty bad language and began to get this mean look on his face. Mrs. Martin had been in the kitchen cooking the meal. She came into the living room and said supper was ready, and then in that formal way she has that makes her sound so ladylike, she said, 'Mr. Martin, will you kindly sit at the head of the table and carve the roast?'

"He turned on her with murder on his face and screamed at her, 'Woman, you sassing me? You sass me and I'm gonna have a chunk of your hide!' You wouldn't believe the look on Mrs. Martin's face. It wasn't shock, it wasn't fear. It was more like shame or embarrassment . . . like she was a little girl who had gotten ink on her best dress. Her eyes filled up with tears, and she turned and went upstairs. I really felt bad for her.

"I was sure surprised when Sandra said to her father, 'Mr. Martin, sometimes you have a big mouth.' We sat down and ate supper. Old Will carved the roast pretty sloppy and nobody said much. Only Mike and Will seemed to be having any fun at all. I didn't see Mrs. Martin again until we were ready to leave. Then she came downstairs, completely calm and with her dignity back. She told me not to worry about Lily, that she would take care of her, and shook hands with me.

"And then, Harvey, she told me to be sure and invite you for next weekend. Said she was going to make chicken and dumplings especially for you, and please don't disappoint her. You really should go, buddy. She's a neat lady and she sure likes you."

The following Wednesday morning at 7:00 A.M. sharp, everybody on the base turned out on the parade field for a surprise review by the Inspector General. Colonel Powell, the base CO, accompanied him up and down the rows of soldiers as he gave close attention to everything from haircuts to shoeshines. He had already toured some of the barracks and done a white-gloves inspection of the kitchen. As they walked past me, I could tell Colonel Powell was nervous. Bad marks from the I.G. were a serious matter.

The review over, the officers stood in a huddle for a few minutes while we all remained at attention and waited for the outcome. Finally they mounted the steps to the podium and the Inspector General took the loudspeaker to address our CO. "Colonel Powell," he said, his voice booming over the parade ground, "you can be proud of this base and of your men. I suggest you give them the rest of the day off. In fact, I highly recommend it. The last two bases that I inspected were terrible!"

The Colonel thanked him and announced to us that within one hour there would be a general pass for every man who wished to leave the base for the day. Cheers rang out from the ranks.

As we walked back to the barracks, Michael came up behind me and said, "Harve, I want you to go somewhere with me." When Mike called me "Harve," it usually meant he needed something from me.

"Thanks," I replied, "but I don't feel like doing anything. I'm going to the library and get a book. Maybe go to the chapel and say a few prayers for Mark."

"Oh come on. Be a friend," he urged. "I need your help. I've got a chance to deliver eight gallons of white lightnin' and make a killing. The delivery is for a little place between here and the Tennessee border that's desperate for some stuff, but I can only carry four gallons on my cycle. You could carry the other four gallons and I could make a bundle."

"Michael, what you're doing is against the law," I said.

"No it's not. The only thing that's against the law is to own the still and make the stuff. We sure don't want to get caught at the still, but we're only going to be there for a moment, and we'll check around before we go in. Harve, you know the stuff is good. It's strong but it's not poison. It's good hooch. So hell, what's the harm? And I know something that will interest you. Those North Carolina backwoods and hills where the still is located are beautiful. I know how much you love the country. You'll be glad you went with me."

He was throwing in everything he could think of to persuade me to go along. "I've met a lot of runners," he told me. "Most of them are from the South and they use stock cars that they've souped up. The law plays hell trying to catch those boys. I only heard of one guy that's not from these parts. He uses a Harley-Davidson, same as me. But none of those guys ever get caught."

"If it's not against the law to run it, why does the law chase them?" I asked, a bit suspicious of the whole project.

"They just want you to tell them where you got it from," he answered. "After all, it's not against the law to have a bottle of whiskey, is it? So come on, go with me, please."

I let myself be persuaded. "Okay. This time only," I said. "And only because I want to see the country you describe while I'm still stationed here in Georgia, and I'm curious to see a still and the kind of characters that own them."

The backwoods and hills of northern Georgia and North Carolina were indeed beautiful — the foliage, the flowers, the tall pines, and lots of other kinds of trees. However, it did not compare to Mexico, I thought to myself.

We had a map but even so it was difficult to find the location of the still. I could see why the law enforcement people had such a difficult time finding them, and now I understood the meaning of "the backwoods." The spot was very isolated, deep in the hills.

After we were loaded and ready to leave the still, an old man told us that "the red motorcycle just loaded and left fifteen minutes ago." Pruske explained that the red cycle belonged to a runner from Texas.

When we reached the main highway and had gone three miles, we looked back to discover the sheriff's car following — and gaining on us. Pruske said, "Okay, pal. Let's show that bastard back there what kind of riders we are." We gave our cycles more power and roared off.

Going over a hill, we could see the road for a mile ahead of us weaving through the timberlands. Our motors settled down to a steady purr. We caught sight of the red cycle in the distance ahead of us and I was startled when Pruske called to me, "That's the red cycle that belongs to Roscoe from Texas. He's probably the best runner in the whole area."

"Roscoe?" I asked. "What's his last name?"

"Hell, I don't know. Let's worry about the sheriff behind us. If we get caught we might get a year," said Mike.

"A year!" I exclaimed. "You told me there was no penalty."

"I know, I know," he replied. "I lied. Hell, let's talk about it later."

We were catching up with the red bike that was cruising at a normal speed ahead of us. We could also see a rough dirt road that forked to the right a half mile ahead. The red bike passed it. We took it. The sheriff chose to follow the red bike, which was now going full speed. We went bumping and sliding up that dirt track for three miles until we came to a gravel road which led us back to the main highway.

We made our deliveries and went straight back to the base. As soon as we were parked, I walked over to Pruske. When he turned around, I planted a hard right punch to his midsection that folded him over and sat him on the ground. But his reaction was remarkable. He started laughing loudly, rolling on the grass, and between howls he said, "Harve, I knew you'd be pissed off at me. But you've got to admit it was exciting and fun." And while he gasped for air, he added, "Damn, you punch hard!" But he kept laughing.

I stood staring down at my crazy friend until suddenly my anger dissipated and I saw it from his angle. I started laughing too and sat down on the ground next to him where we both roared like idiots till we had tears in our eyes. There were eight GIs in front of the barracks watching us and wondering what the hell was going on. We sat there until our laughter gradually faded away in exhaustion and we lay panting. Our audience finally drifted off in disappointment, still puzzled.

When I felt like talking again, I sat up and said, "Mike, I want to know more about Roscoe. What can you tell me?"

"Nothing much," he said. "He's just a white lightnin' runner. Why? You just punched me for getting you involved. Why do you want to know about that runner?"

"Well," I began slowly, "back in Texas I knew a guy named Roscoe. We became enemies. And I know it seems too much of a coincidence that this should be the same fellow, but how many guys do you meet from Texas named Roscoe? I had heard he was somewhere in the Southeast. I would just like to get a look at him.

Incredible if it really is the same Roscoe, but I need to know. I want you to help me. I want you to set it up."

"Okay, Harve, old boy. I'll work on it this week. But I don't really understand. If he's your enemy, why the hell do you want to see him? By the way," he added, "my plane is grounded. They have to replace an engine. I've been assigned to your plane for tomorrow. I'll be your waist gunner during the gunnery practice runs. How 'bout that!"

He was quiet a moment and then suggested, thinking it out as he talked, "Harvey, I've got an idea. I know what I can do. I can call Lou Autry. I made three deliveries to him. I bet he knows a lot about Roscoe. Yeah, I'll call him tonight and let you know tomorrow what I find out."


The next morning I was running late. I wolfed a quick breakfast in the mess hall, went to the supply room, grabbed a parachute, and ran to the plane where I found the engine already warming up. Pruske got there at the same time, but without a parachute. He started to climb into the B-25, but I stopped him and asked, "Where's your chute?"

"I was late and I didn't have time to get one," he answered.

"You're crazy. Go back and get one," I insisted. "I'll hold the plane. Go on. You can be back in five minutes. Run!"

By the time he returned, the tower was fuming. We told the tower that one of the engines had been missing slightly, and they threatened to cancel our flight. Now we changed our story and advised that the engine was okay. If they canceled us, we would have to make up the flight on the weekend, and none of us wanted that.

Our destination that day was an old abandoned ship off the coast of Georgia in the Gulf of Mexico. Flying at only five thousand feet, we could enjoy the terrain below. We were over water for only a half hour before being advised over the intercom that the target was ahead. The pilot dived the plane and leveled off at two hundred feet. Three hundred yards from the target, the nose gunner opened fire, blasting the target ship. At a hundred yards, the waist gunners from both sides started shooting. I looked at Mike and I could tell he was enjoying it.

Then it was my turn. I opened fire from the tail turret with two fifty-caliber machine guns operating hydraulically, tracking the target through my superimposed gunsight that made it easy pickings. I could see the bullets tear into the deck, others hitting the hull and ricocheting and splashing into the water. I got off four bursts, two seconds each, each gun shooting sixteen bullets per second. Each two-second burst totaled sixty-four bullets, multiplied by four bursts, totalling 256 fifty-caliber bullets, all within eight seconds. The fire power of those guns was incredible.

The B-25 shot past and swung around for a second run at the target. This was great sport and I was getting as much kick out of it as Mike. Those B-25s may have been noisy and full of rattles, but they were tough, fast, and dependable and you couldn't help developing an affection for them. We made eight runs at the target before we broke off and headed home at an elevation of four thousand feet. On the way back, I climbed out of my turret, took off my chute, and sat on it. Mike did the same. The other waist gunner looked at us and asked, "What happens if you guys need your chutes in a hurry?"

"We have a problem," I said, smiling back.

Mike did not acknowledge the question. Instead, he told me, "Last night I called Lou Autry. Lou tells me that he knows Roscoe well, and yet he said he didn't know his last name. Sounds fishy. He said Roscoe had been a cowboy in the past and that he was from Texas and has a scar near one of his eyes."

I felt a slight chill. My nemesis was back. This was too much for coincidence.

Mike went on, "Lou said that he expects to see Roscoe tomorrow and he will try to line him up for Saturday afternoon right after lunch."

"Saturday afternoon I expect to be at Mrs. Martin's house," I protested.

"Hell, Harvey!" Mike said. "It's only one hour away. We can go, you can have your meeting, and we can be back in three hours. We'll leave at twelve, be back at three."

"We're going to have a meeting?" I asked with concern. "Did you set up a meeting? Did you give Lou my name? I told you I just wanted to look at him without meeting him."

"Damn!" exclaimed Pruske. "Why such a fuss? Hell, I know you. I know you're not afraid of him. I'll go with you, and if he makes any trouble I'll bust him for you."

I laughed at the statement. Mike always could make me laugh, but I added, "This guy is a tough bastard. But all right, you've got it set up, so let's go. I really would like to look him in the eye."

When we were thirty minutes from the base, Pruske stood up and started to put on his parachute, saying casually, "I'm going to jump out."

"What?" I exclaimed.

"I'm going to jump out, and I hope you're not such a shit that you're not going with me," he said.

"They'll court martial you! You guys will lose your stripes," the waist gunner gasped.

"What for?" Mike asked. "We smelled smoke. We thought we heard someone say 'abandon ship,' so we did. We'll probably get a medal. And besides, I've never jumped out of a plane, and I've never been on a parachute. I'm going. How about you, Harve? You've gotta go with your ol' pal."

To this day it still seems incredible that I stood up, slipped into my parachute, and followed Pruske to the trap door on the floor where he was now sitting with his legs hanging out. The other waist gunner was staring in disbelief. Suddenly Mike pushed himself out and away from the plane. I immediately took his place with my legs hanging out, grabbed both sides of the opening, dropped down and pushed myself away from the plane, counted to three, and pulled the ripcord.

The jolt was severe when the silk snapped open. If I had not taken care to tighten the straps under my legs I think they would have cut into my crotch. I looked around and found Pruske two hundred yards away, floating down, about to hit the ground. Then he was down safely.

I yelled at him and waved, and he waved back. Sixty seconds later, I was on the ground, landing without difficulty. I gathered my chute as quickly as possible and started walking through the timberland and brush in the direction Pruske had landed. In just a few minutes, I spotted him walking unevenly toward me wearing only one boot. I laughed at him and yelled, "Where did you lose your boot? Some girl's husband after you again?"

"Very funny," he replied. "When the chute opened, the snap was terrific. One of my boots flew off and landed in the thick brush. No way for me to find it. But I did spot a road just to the left of us, about a mile . . . Wasn't that a terrific thrill?"

"I've got to admit it was great," I replied. "I hope we don't get busted when we get back to the base."

Just as we reached the road, a truck was coming by and the friendly driver stopped for us. We learned he was going right by the base and we hopped in. He dropped us at the front gate, we walked through it, and no one said a word. We walked to the supply room and gave them our chutes — which looked like bundles of muddy bedsheets — and no one said a word. As we were walking to our barracks, we passed by the other crew members from our plane. They merely nodded at us. We entered our barracks, and no one said a word. We looked at each other, and Mike remarked, "I'm glad I wasn't killed because nobody really seems to give a damn."

At which point we both started laughing. We sat on our bunks and howled with laughter. Mike Pruske was a rascal, but I loved him. There was a free spirit about him and I knew I could trust him — as long as there were no women around.

When Saturday came, I told Roy that I wouldn't be going to Mrs. Martin's house until three o'clock and hoped he didn't mind riding the bus into town. I did not want to take Mike to Mrs. Martin's house again for I felt sure that she could not approve of him.

At noon, Mike and I started toward Lou Autry's place, he on his Harley-Davidson, and I on my blue Indian cycle. I was surprised to learn that a bar as large as Lou Autry's would be stuck back five miles in a small clearing in the woods. When we rode up, there was a pickup truck and a Model A on the red clay parking lot.

The big rectangular wooden building sat four feet off the ground on exposed cedar posts. There was a long front porch full of benches and stools. There was only one door opening onto the porch, and the front wall had four small windows too high to allow you to look in, giving the impression that indoors would be quite dark.

As we rode up, the place sat in complete silence. We could not hear any sound coming from inside the building. We both dismounted and stood there, looking into the woods and the hills that surrounded the place. Our cycles had made too much noise for our arrival not to have been noticed. A glance at Mike told me that he too sensed we were being watched.

"What do you think?" I asked. "How does it feel?"

"Spooky," Mike answered. "Let's go inside. I feel like I am in a cage out here. By the way, I don't see the red cycle."

We walked up the steps and pulled open the front door. It was a relief to find three ordinary-looking men sitting at a table at the far end of the room drinking beer and talking quietly. Lou Autry, a big fat man with a cigar in his mouth and spectacles on his nose, was sitting on a rocker at the far end of the bar. We walked up to him and Mike said, "Hi, Lou. How are things?"

"Real good," he answered. "Real good."

"Do you need any stuff? I could make a run later on," said Mike.

"No thanks." Lou wheezed as he talked, and the cigar bobbed in his mouth. "I'm well stocked right now. Prob'ly won't need anything for a week. Did you see Roscoe outside?"

"There was no one outside," Mike told him. "The place seemed dead. We didn't think there was anyone inside either."

Lou continued rocking as he looked up at us and said, "No more than fifteen minutes ago he was here. He said he was going to wait for you guys outside. But he's a strange one. I never know what to expect. I've never seen him smile and don't think I ever will."

We thanked him and walked out to the porch. We sat on a bench at the end near our cycles and waited without speaking for thirty minutes. Finally Mike asked, "What do you think? Do you suppose it's the guy you know? Do you think he's been here?"

"Yes," I replied. "He's been here. When we first came up, he was watching us, and I do think it's the Roscoe that I know, but I can't be sure unless I see him."

Just then Autry came out. He stood at the top of the steps smoking his cigar, with a cardboard fan in one hand that he would occasionally wave in front of his fat face. He wore wide suspenders which he had slipped off his shoulders and they dangled below his hips. He moved ponderously, as though it was a struggle to keep his big belly from pulling him forward.

Looking around, he spotted us on the bench, and wheezed, "That Roscoe boy! He said he was leaving this country in two or three weeks. He said he heard that the Georgia and North Carolina highway patrols were making bets as to who was going to bag him. He said it was getting a little bit too hot. Been here too long. Going somewhere else."

We figured we had waited long enough, so we climbed on our bikes and started up the gravel road leading from Autry's place. Rounding a curve, we found the road blocked with brush and three men stood in our path. Two were stocky medium-height fellows in coveralls, and the third was tall, wearing khaki pants and a lumberjack shirt.

Pruske turned toward me and said, "I think we have a fight on our hands."

Somehow the situation angered me. I could smell Roscoe's hand in this. I said, "Well, let's get to it." We got off our cycles.

One of the stocky men walked toward me, and I hit him on the side of the face before he knew what happened. Surprised, he reeled back. I turned to the other man and threw a hook to his midsection, followed with a right to his jaw. He dropped to his knees. The first man had returned. I jabbed him with a stiff straight left, and hit him again with a hard right on the side of his jaw. This time he fell flat on his face.

I turned toward Pruske. He was grappling on the ground with the tall man. I walked up to them, grabbed the man by the hair with my left hand, pulled him back and hit him on his cheek near his eye and drew blood. He let go of Pruske, grabbed his face, stood up, and ran away.

Mike Pruske looked more shocked than the man who fled.

"Damn, Harvey! Why didn't you tell me you could fight like that? I sure would have felt safer all this time."

"Pruske, you're a pain in the rear," I said. "Let's move this brush and get out of here."

"Do you think Roscoe put them up to this?" Mike asked as we cleared a path.

"Maybe. I plan to ask him if I see him," I replied.

When we arrived at Gainesville, I headed toward Mrs. Martin's home, and Mike turned a different direction. We waved at each other, and then I heard him yell, "You're my best friend, Harvey Reese. The very, very best!" And he was gone.

# Chapter 16

I returned to the base earlier than usual that Sunday afternoon and went immediately to the public phone to place a call to Vanessa in Savannah. A girl's voice answered and said there was no one named Vanessa at that number.

But when I gave her my name, there was a pause. I heard whispering. Then Vanessa's excited voice said, "Harvey! Why haven't you called me? I have so much to tell you. Can you come to Savannah?"

"Sure," I said. "Next Saturday."

"Marvelous," she said. "Harvey, I have wonderful news, but it can wait. Oh Harvey, I love you." She gave me Virginia's address and asked me to arrive by noon if possible.

Saturday morning I left the base on my cycle at seven. Savannah was slightly over 200 miles, a four-hour ride. At 12:30 I pulled up in front of Virginia's home — a large, expensive house in an affluent neighborhood. I learned later that Mr. Stein, Virginia's father, owned a large department store in Savannah.

As I got off my cycle, Vanessa ran down the long walk from the house. She was wearing a white, short-sleeved picnic dress that made her look very provocative. I did not remember her being so pretty. She ran up and embraced me, putting her head on my chest and squeezing me as if we had known each other for years.

She stepped back, smiling, with her large hazel eyes sparkling, and said, "I love you, Harvey Reese. Guess what! I'm getting married!" She saw my expression and added, "You're surprised, I can tell."

"Yes," I stuttered, "but I'm happy for you."

Only now did I realize that Vanessa had not come alone to greet me. She turned to take the hand of the other girl and introduce her. "This is my dear friend, Virginia Stein."

Virginia was a large girl, slightly overweight, but attractive. "Hello. I never met a knight in shining armor," she said, challengingly.

"Maybe someday we both will," I said, laughing.

"Bravo," she said, and shook my hand heartily. And then she whispered, "You know you saved her life."

Vanessa turned to me and announced, "We're going on a picnic. It's a lovely spot by a lake, and later, at three, Edward, my fiancé, will join us. Edward Delaney is his name."


Our picnic was indeed at a beautiful park. The lake was full of blooming water lilies, with ducks and white swans gliding by. Marigolds and gladiolas bordered the walks, and the grounds were dotted with blossoming magnolia trees. We sat on a large blanket on the grass in the shade of a graceful weeping willow and ate hot dogs, potato salad, lemonade, and apple pie.

After lunch, Virginia announced she was off for a walk, obviously to give us a chance to talk in private. I stretched out on my back, looking up through the lacy tree at the clear blue sky. Though my mind was alert to hear Vanessa's story, my body took advantage of the storybook setting to relax on this warm afternoon.

Vanessa was too excited to relax. She sat beside me with her legs curled under her wide skirt, and in her charming Southern accent began her story.

"Harvey, I've just been bustin' to tell you all that has happened since I left Atlanta. I've really gone from misery to joy in these last weeks, and it was meeting you that turned things around for me. But I'm getting ahead of myself." She took a deep breath and smoothed her skirt. "Well, Virginia met me at the bus stop when I arrived in Savannah. Mother had already called Mrs. Stein, who very convincingly told Mother I was not here, which was easy since Mrs. Stein did not know I was coming. Virginia and I had to tell her mother all that had happened, and she has really been wonderful to me. I always did like her, and Mr. Stein is really like a daddy to me. And I cannot tell you enough about my marvelous Virginia. But let me go on." I hadn't moved a muscle to stop her, and she kept on bubbling with her happy story.

"Two days after I arrived, I felt like myself again, and mostly because of you. I don't think you can ever know what you did for me. I feel like you are someone I have known all my life. Harvey . . ." She paused for a moment and look straight into my eyes with an expression that spoke such tender things. Then she continued. "Last weekend I slept late. When I went downstairs, Virginia told me that Edward's plane had just landed and he would arrive in an hour. Dear, sweet, Edward."

She dropped her eyes to the ring on her engagement finger. "Edward is my second cousin on my father's side of the family. He is thirty-two now, ten years older than me. I have known him and loved him all my life. I fell in love with him when I was twelve. He was so good looking, and very sophisticated. When I told him I loved him, he laughed and said, 'Tell me again in ten years.' Two years later, I learned Edward was engaged to Elizabeth Ann Anderson, one of the richest but most pretentious and self-centered females I have ever known. It nearly broke my heart.

"The engagement lasted for eighteen months, but Edward finally saw through her and broke it off. Five years later, he became a trader on Wall Street. He makes tons of money now, lives in New York City, and only comes to Atlanta occasionally. When I was twenty, still in college, Edward asked me to attend a charity ball. We had a wonderful time. When he took me home, he suddenly asked me to marry him. I thought he was teasing, so I laughed and said, 'Ask me again in two years, after I graduate from college.' He laughed and said, 'Okay.' Since then he has called me often, but we haven't spoken of romance.

"Last week Virginia . . . without my permission . . . called Edward and told him what had happened to me. I never would have called, myself. He flew down immediately, but when he arrived, I ran upstairs, locked myself in my room, and refused to see him. I just couldn't bear the thought of his pity."

Now she leaned forward and took my hand in hers. "Harvey, guess what? He broke my door down, rushed to me, took me in his arms, kissed me, and said he loved me. It was like a novel — 'Gone With the Wind,' or something. It was beautiful. I knew he meant it. His eyes told me so. He kissed me again and again and said we would marry in New York in two weeks. He wanted to kill my step-father and his son, but I made him promise to forget them forever and never to mention their names to me again. When I broke down and cried, he finally agreed. I remember he said, 'All right, darling, our lives will begin from this day.' We'll be leaving for New York tomorrow. Virginia is going with us to be the maid of honor. Now, please, tell me what you think of all this? Isn't it absolutely marvelous?"

I sat up and squeezed her hands. "I am delighted! I really am very happy for you. You know, you have been in my thoughts every moment since I left you in Atlanta. I really did believe happiness would come to you, but I never dreamed that it was just around the corner. I am anxious to meet your Edward. If you love him, I know I will like him." It was strange that Vanessa was in effect asking for my approval, and that I somehow felt that I had the right to give my endorsement.

"Hey!" Virginia called to us from the path. "Look over there. Edward is coming."

After the way Vanessa had talked about him, I guess I had expected Edward to be an Adonis or at least Clark Gable, so I was surprised to see a slightly overweight man with horn-rimmed glasses, but I liked his looks. His suit was tailored and expensive, and his walk easy and confident, his features clean-cut, and his expression intelligent but pleasant. He came directly to Vanessa, kissed her, and then held her in a long embrace that touched me.

Vanessa said, "Darling, this is my gallant Harvey Reese."

Edward stepped toward me, shook my hand, and smiled with sincerity and friendship. He said, "Sir, I'm in your debt forever."

"Nonsense," I replied.

"No, I mean it literally. You were there when she was desperate, and you came to her aid in a most kind and generous way. Because you are a gentleman, you were able to turn her despair to hope. May I consider you my friend, in every sense of the word?"

"Yes," I said. "You honor me."

He sat on the blanket between Vanessa and me and told us that all the arrangements had been made for the wedding. "Harvey," he said, "we would like you to be the best man. It would make Vanessa most happy."

I smiled but shook my head. "There is no way for me to get leave. Thank you. I really appreciate your sincere gesture. I wish I could be at your wedding, but my thoughts and best wishes will be with you."

That night we had dinner at the Steins'. Mrs. Stein insisted that I spend the night, more I believe because I was a military man in the middle of the war than because I was a friend of Vanessa's. That was the kind of hospitality soldiers were finding throughout the country.

The next morning after breakfast, Mr. Stein and I drove Vanessa, Edward, and Virginia to the airport. At departure time, Edward pulled me aside and said, "Harvey, please don't object," and he handed me fifty dollars to repay my loan to Vanessa. Then he added, "Let's really stay in touch and be friends." I agreed with enthusiasm.

Then Vanessa came over to say goodbye. I was hoping she would not kiss me in front of Edward and was relieved when she embraced me instead, but she clung to me for at least two minutes. She finally stepped back with a tear in the corner of her eye and said, "My darling Harvey," and repeated again, "My sweet, darling Harvey." She turned, took Edward by the arm, walked to the plane, up the stairs and through the door, with Virginia close behind. I waited till the plane took off.

On the way back to the base, I was flying on my magnificent Indian motorcycle at perhaps 75 miles per hour. Mark's death still lingered somewhat, but Vanessa was happy now. Yes, Vanessa. How wonderful it was to help her. As I sped forward I reached back with my left hand and pulled out my white scarf from the saddlebag and tied it around my neck so the ends hung loose. I felt invincible with my white scarf blowing in the wind.

# Chapter 17

When I walked into the barracks, Mike was sitting on his bunk. He looked up as if he had been waiting for me and came over before I could put down my bag.

"Harvey, come outside a minute. I've got something to show you." He took me over to his bike and pointed to the rear tire that was shredded, with large gashes on both sides of the tire.

"It looks like someone took a knife to it," I said.

"You're right. I was parked in front of the Midway Cafe having lunch. When I came out, I found it like this. Had to pay ten dollars to a guy with a truck to bring it to the base. I can't imagine who would want to do a thing like that. And to top it off, when I got here there was a message from Lou Autry. I called him and he's changed his mind. He wants me to make a run for him this week. I checked with the sergeant and he told me that I could take off Wednesday afternoon at four, as long as I get back by nine o'clock that night. I'm broke. I've got to take the job so I can afford to buy a new tire. Will you loan me your Indian to make the run?"

"Sure. That's okay with me," I answered.

"Really appreciate it, buddy."

I didn't see Mike when he left Wednesday, but that evening about ten o'clock I realized that he had not returned. I worried a bit, since the sergeant had been so specific that he had to report in by nine. Ten minutes later Roy walked in and told me that Pruske had had a motorcycle accident and was taken to the base hospital and that he was still in surgery.

Without a word, I rushed out of the barracks and ran all the way to the hospital. I dashed in to the desk and asked the nurse on duty about Michael Pruske. She looked at the chart and then very unemotionally told me, "He's in surgery. Don't know when he'll be out."

"Can't you tell me anything else?" I asked.

She studied her chart again, looked up at me, and added, "No, it's not very bad. He'll be all right. But he did lose most of his right hand. No need for you to wait because they're not going to let you see him tonight. Unless you want to wait and talk to the doctor. Might be another hour, though."

I stepped back three feet. It felt like someone had just punched me in the midsection. I turned, went to a chair in the corner, and sat down. Lowering my head, I silently said a prayer for my friend, imploring God's mercy and God's love. At least, I thought to myself, he wasn't killed. Then under my breath I cursed my motorcycle.

Twenty minutes later, a doctor came down the hallway and I jumped up to stop him with a question. "Sir. Michael Pruske . . . he was in surgery. He's a good friend. Can you tell me anything?"

"Sure, soldier," he replied. "I assisted Dr. Rosen — a very fine surgeon, I might add. Your friend still has his right thumb and forefinger, and with some luck he'll have pretty good use of those two fingers. The other three fingers and half the palm of his hand down to the heel are gone. Lucky he didn't bleed to death. Nobody thought of putting a tourniquet on his arm. All they did was wrap it in a towel where they couldn't even check how much bleeding was occurring. You can't see him tonight. He also has a pretty bad bump on his head and he's in minor shock. I'm sure he has a slight concussion. However, he was conscious before the operation and he did speak to us."

The doctor turned to leave, stopped, looked back at me and asked, "Are you Roscoe?"

"No," I replied. "My name is Reese."

"Well, who in the hell is Roscoe? That's all he kept saying. Roscoe, Roscoe, Roscoe."

I went back to my bunk and hardly slept, tossed most of the night, and woke in the morning completely exhausted. Roy practically had to dress me and then drag me to the plane for a priority mission that would take us eight hours. When we finally landed, I threw my chute at Roy and asked him to please check it in, and ran to the hospital. Again they refused to let me see Mike, telling me that he had suffered a mild concussion and the doctor had ordered no visitors.

I was free Friday afternoon and sat in the waiting room from one o'clock to four. Finally a bald, short, slim doctor approached and asked me, "Are you Reese?"

"Yes sir."

He sat down in the chair beside mine and leaned forward. "Pruske has been asking for you, and I'm going to give you permission to go see him in just a minute. But first, let me tell you about his injuries. He has a slight fracture of the skull and has experienced a mild concussion. We have to keep him down for at least another week, but I'm not very concerned about that. His vital signs are excellent. My concern is his right hand. You see, his hand was not cut off cleanly. It was ripped off, leaving jagged bones and flesh. We had to cut the ends of the bones to remove the splinters and trim the flesh so it could heal."

I wondered if the doctor noticed my flinch. As he went on, I realized that I had my two hands tightly clasped as I leaned forward with elbows on knees.

"In three weeks, when he can travel, we are going to send him to Walter Reed Hospital. We have already made the arrangements. They have a doctor on staff who specializes in hands. If anyone can help him, it'll be that doctor. Who knows . . . they might teach him to use what he's got left of it more efficiently than ever. One thing is certain: He must accept a medical discharge. There is no way for him to remain in the Army. I've explained this to him, and the fact that he must be discharged seems to have disturbed him more than his actual injury. His biggest struggle will no doubt be with himself, but you might be able to help his morale, if nothing else."

When I walked into Mike's room, he immediately sat up in

---

141

bed and said, "Where the hell have you been? I've been waiting for two days."

"They wouldn't let me in," I replied. "They said your eggs were scrambled and you know how the Army functions."

"I know. The Army doesn't love cycles, that's for sure. I had a hell of a headache for a couple of days, but it's gone now. But listen, I've got some great news. I'm going to be able to get out of the service. No more rules and restrictions, no orders to go to bed, no orders to get up, terrible food in the mess hall . . . not any more. I'm going to be free! I only wish you could go with me."

His voice trailed off. He wasn't very convincing, but I did my best to appear to accept everything he was telling me. Then his mood changed and he was serious as he continued.

"Listen, my friend. You really do have an enemy. I think Roscoe did this to me. I think he thought I was you. I was on the main highway, heading for Hazelwood, and on that long stretch going through that real thick wooded area I was going fast — and then suddenly, fifty feet in front of me, this thin cable about an eighth of an inch thick popped up and was stretched across the highway chest high. I slammed on the brakes and slid toward it without a prayer of stopping. I stuck my right hand out, lowered myself, and I guess I got under it except for my hand. The cable pulled me off the bike, and I was lucky to land on the side of the road where the ground wasn't too hard. I have skins and bruises all over my body. Your bike kept going and crashed into a tree. I was knocked out and didn't come to until they were wheeling me into the hospital.

"I think Roscoe thought I was you, Harve. I think I was set up and I think Old Man Autry was involved. You remember he told us he had enough supplies. Then he calls me up and says he needs some after all. I just didn't put it together at the time. When they asked me to make the run, I think they thought we worked together, and I believe that cable was meant for you. That's why they cut my tire, hoping you would go alone. When Roscoe saw it was only one of us, and it was a bright blue Indian cycle, he decided he had you. I explained to the doctors what I thought had happened. They sent someone back there to investigate, but there was nothing there. They said the cable was gone, there was no blood on the concrete, and, Harvey, they said that the other part of my hand was gone." Mike was leaning forward urgently now. "That sonofabitch

142

has part of my hand. I don't want him to have any part of me. I want my hand back."

There was a slight sob in his voice before he fell silent. The nurse came in and said that I had to leave. I was relieved. I reached down, took hold of Michael's left hand and squeezed it, and told him I would be back next day.

They had taken my motorcycle to the motor pool and left it in charge of a Sergeant Rigsby. The moment I saw my cycle, I knew there was no way to repair it.

Sergeant Rigsby came up and asked, "Do you authorize me to dispose of that pile of junk?"

"Be my guest," I answered. "Give it a decent burial."

Saturday morning I took Mike's cycle to town on a borrowed pickup and replaced the back tire. I left Roy at the Martins' house, told him I would return in a couple of hours, and on Mike's Harley-Davidson went straight to Lou Autry's place.

The door was locked but Lou's car was parked in front. I kicked the door open, breaking the lock, and walked directly over to where Lou was sitting on his rocking chair. He looked shocked to see me.

"You fat bastard!" I shouted. "You're going to give me a few straight answers or I'm going to punch that big fat belly of yours and then shove your face in the toilet."

He was alone in the place. His face turned white with fear, and there was a placating gentleness in his tone as he asked, "What do you want to know, son?"

He tried to stand, but I shoved him back into his chair. "I think you helped Roscoe set up my friend Michael Pruske. I'm looking for Roscoe, and you'd better give me some correct information or I promise you I'm coming back."

"Listen, son," he said in his slow Southern drawl. "Roscoe's been making most of my deliveries, but he come by and said he was leaving the country — going west somewhere — and wouldn't be working for me no more. He told me to call Pruske for future deliveries. That's the truth."

Lou sat there looking up at me helpless and frightened. I felt some compassion for him. I lowered my voice and said, "Okay, but if you do see him again, tell him I'm looking for him and that I consider him a damned coward." I turned and left.

I went to the still where Mike and I had made pick-ups, but there too they told me that Roscoe had left the state. They gave me directions to another still where they thought Roscoe spent much of his time, but there a bearded old man told me emphatically that Roscoe had gone out west.


Three weeks later, Michael Pruske had his orders to go to Walter Reed Hospital in Washington, D.C., traveling by train. On the way to the Gainesville train station, Mike rode behind me on his Harley-Davidson, holding onto me with his left arm while his right arm and hand were elevated in a cast that started at his neck. On the platform we stood and waited for the train to come in.

"Well, you dumb Polack," I said. "You've got your wish. You're out of the Air Corps. I hope it goes well at Walter Reed."

"Harvey, you are unique! You've got everybody fooled, the only one of our bunch with four stripes, but I know that you are a redneck from Texas. That's about as low as they come," he answered. Changing his tone, he added, "I've never had a brother, but I do now. I love you as my brother. And here, let me give you this." He handed me the executed title to his Harley-Davidson. "It's yours. And I'm not giving it to you because I wrecked your Indian. After all, Roscoe did that. I'm giving it to you because I want you to have it, and if you say no, I'm going to hit you with my left hand square on your mouth."

"But Mike, you'll be able to use it later on. Why don't I just keep it for you until you're ready? Okay?"

"No," he said. "I'm through with cycles. You can't even have a decent date on one. I'm going to get myself a convertible and start enjoying life."

The train had pulled in, and the conductor yelled, "All aboard!"

"Michael Pruske, I don't want you to leave before you know you're my best friend, and you will always be in my prayers," I said. "And I'm glad no one can hear us. They might think we're strange." We both laughed, a little embarrassed at our emotions.

The conductor yelled again, "All aboard!"

We looked at each other for a long moment. Then we gave each other a strong hug, though his cast made it a little difficult. He turned, stepped up on the train, and stood watching me from the steps as the train pulled out. His eyes became red and full of tears, but he didn't say another word.

I waited while the train disappeared far down the track, and then kept on standing there on the platform, wondering if I would ever see Michael Pruske again.

# Chapter 18

Saturday was a beautiful day, and as Roy and I started out on the Harley-Davidson we were looking forward to a pleasant time with the girls. I was still missing my old buddy Pruske, and figured a visit with Mrs. Martin was just what I needed.

While we stopped to gas up the cycle, Roy mentioned that on the previous weekend Sandra had showed him bruises on her arm and back where her father had struck her. He did not see Mrs. Martin, but Lily said she had a cut lip, a black eye, and probably a couple of broken ribs because she winced with pain every time she took a deep breath.

The report upset me. "I don't think anybody should allow that type of abuse," I told Roy. "I think they should call the police and put the old man in jail, at least until he is sober."

"They did call the cops," Roy said, "and they arrested him. When it came time to file the charges, Mrs. Martin wouldn't file. Sandra says it's always the same story. Her mother goes into this long explanation about how she expects her husband to change soon, and that it's very important the children always respect him. Then she says it would solve nothing to put him in jail, and that after all, he's leaving with a load of produce for three weeks, and they certainly need the income. She always rationalizes the situation by pointing out the immediate practical side."

"I wonder what's going to happen one of these days when those two boys get big enough to do something about that damn bully?" I said.

"Well, cheer up for now," Roy told me. "We're going on a picnic today to a place called Bald Mountain Rock. Sandra and Lily are fixing a picnic lunch." He grinned at me as I started off to pay the attendant for the gas. "Don't worry, I'll make sure that you and Sandra have plenty of time alone together. Later we're going to a movie — Errol Flynn, I think. Tonight you can sleep in the living room. I asked Mrs. Martin and she was real happy about it."

Better than the local YMCA where I generally stayed, I thought to myself.

When we walked into the house, Mrs. Martin was sitting in the living room crocheting. As soon as she saw me, she called me over to sit beside her. I was appalled at the sight of her face. Both eyes were black, the left one was bloodshot to the point of obscuring all the white around the pupil. Her lip was cut, and the right corner swollen out of proportion. It made her look grotesque. However, when she talked to me she was so gracious that I soon forgot to notice her injuries.

She took my right hand in both of hers and held it, and spoke to me quietly.

"Harvey, my son, pay no attention to the way I look at the present time. Mr. Martin assaulted me, but I forgive him. My difficulty is trying to forgive him for inflicting unjust punishment on Sandra. They asked me to file charges on him, but that would solve nothing. The solution is to keep Sandra away from Mr. Martin. He does not abuse the boys. His resentment seems to be against me and then against Sandra. He generally is a good person, but when he drinks he's unpredictable." She gave a sigh that tore at my heart.

"I do not see an end to this horror," she said. "I'm telling you because I think you're special, and that you will understand, and perhaps . . ." Her little smile was pathetic as she tried to sound hopeful, despite her swollen lip and bruised eyes. ". . . Perhaps even suggest something."

I could think of nothing to suggest. "I don't know how I can help," I said, "but I am at your service and I'll help you in any way that you may ask."

I was quite sincere in my desire to offer assistance for I was still filled with admiration for the gentle, charming manner of this gracious lady of culture.

At the picnic, we roasted weiners and marshmallows, we climbed Bald Mountain Rock which was not very high, and we played hide-and-seek (which was a farce Roy dreamed up to let Sandra and me go off and hide, holding hands, where I might steal an innocent kiss). At the movies, we held hands, ate popcorn, and talked and giggled so much that people sitting next to us moved away, which caused us to giggle even more.

Usually I found Sandra charming and childlike, but sometimes she would change moods and affect adult habits — smoke cigarettes, use mild profanities, and insist on having a drink. She was her own person most of the time, not seeming to be the child of either Mr. or Mrs. Martin. It was as if the true person had not yet emerged, and I found her a bit mysterious. When she would say something of substance or provocative it would startle me. But when I would question her statement or dwell on some of her inner thoughts, she would revert to the little girl again right in front of my eyes. Sobeit, I thought to myself, she's sort of cute that way.

The next day at mail call, I received a card from Edward and Vanessa from Acapulco. They said it would be impossible to be any happier. The card lifted my spirits.

For the next two months the pattern was generally the same. Roy and I would go to the Martins' home for the girls; we would go on picnics, go to the movies, fly kites, build model airplanes, and enjoy Mrs. Martin's wonderful cooking. We did not see Will Martin very often. Old Will generally traveled on the weekends so that he could make market on Monday morning, usually on the West Coast. When he did come home it was only every third week and he would just stay for a couple of days at the most. The week he was expected, you could sense the tension, see the worried looks and the distress on Mrs. Martin's face.

During my weekend visits, Mrs. Martin and I would spend hours together, talking about every subject under the sun. My admiration and love for her continued to grow, and on more than one occasion I wrote to my parents about this gentle person.

At our base, the rumors started that we would be shipping out in two weeks. Excitement was in the air. Preparations for departure began and we knew the orders would be posted soon. I was notified of my promotion to tech sergeant, the ranking noncom in our squadron, and was gratified that most of the men were pleased.

Then came the Friday evening when I knew what had happened the minute Roy and I walked into the Martins' house. Sandra came down the stairs as soon as she heard me arrive, and she had a big bruise on her cheek and her lip was cut and swollen out of proportion.

"Oh Sandra!" I said with sympathy, and reached out, drew her to me, and held her for a moment.

Ominously, under her breath, she spoke. "If he ever touches me again, I'll kill the son of a bitch."

When Mrs. Martin walked in, her steps were slow and measured and it was obvious that she was in real pain. I stepped forward, took her by the arm, and helped her into the living room where we sat together on the large sofa.

Mrs. Martin asked, "Have the children gone upstairs?"

I nodded yes. Sandra had gone up with Roy and Lily.

"It's the worst news you can imagine, Harvey, my son," she told me. "Will Martin is not going to be on the road any more. They gave him his third citation for driving intoxicated, so he has lost his license permanently. He has a new job as dispatcher for one of the produce dealers at the farmer's market here in Gainesville. He'll be staying home every night from now on."

She looked expectantly at me, but I had no comment. She took both of my hands and drew me closer to her, and said, "Please Harvey, for God's sake, take Sandra away from all this."

I drew back slightly and said, "What? I beg your pardon?" I was not sure what she was asking . . . or perhaps I just wasn't sure how to respond to what she was suggesting.

"You do love Sandra?" she asked.

"Yes, I love her. But please understand, I'm not in love with her."

---

"I do understand. And she will understand for now," she said. "Please take her away from this horror. You will be doing the greatest service anyone has ever done for me. I believe if she is gone, Mr. Martin will change. I believe the antagonism will disappear. Please. Please. Do this for her. Do this for me. Do this for us."

"Mrs. Martin," I said. "I'm not in love with her. I cannot just take her with me. I'm sure you are aware of the Mann Act. If I take her, I'll have to marry her. And some day it will have to change. Do you understand? You say she will understand for now. But will she understand in the future when she will have to go through a big adjustment? Are you sure *you* understand?" I asked pointedly. "It cannot last forever. Someday it must change. How will it affect her then?"

"I understand," she answered. "Perhaps you will learn to love her."

My mind was racing, seeking other possibilities or solutions.

"Mrs. Martin," I said, "Could you send her to New York to work or to relatives away from here? She could start a new life."

"There is no family except in this area. Mr. Martin would never allow it. New York — she is too immature. She would be violated. Probably be forced into prostitution. I have thought much about it . . . there is no other solution. I fear something terrible and violent is going to happen." At that moment there was terror in her voice.

I stood up and said, "I will be back. I must think."

Once out of town I was soon speeding on my cycle along a small country road in an area thick with trees. I found a clearing next to a small creek and stopped. Dismounting, I sat on the grass next to the creek and watched the small stream of water rushing between big rocks.

My thoughts returned to Mrs. Martin. I realized that she was very dear to me. Then I questioned, do I really have to marry Sandra? What an extreme solution. Sandra will learn she is not who I seek. Is this fair to her? What about the future? I thought of my mother's promise regarding the quest. How would my decision here affect that future love she promised? I must simply have faith that it would come to be, sometime, somehow. Then I remembered Mrs. Martin's premonition of something terrible and violent to come.

Two hours later I entered the living room and found Mrs. Martin still sitting on the sofa where I had left her. I sat next to her and began, "Mrs. Martin, I will not learn to love Sandra in the way you hope. I am searching for someone else. Do you really believe you can explain this to Sandra?"

She closed her eyes as if to question herself. Then she looked directly at me and nodded slowly and firmly.

I looked at this fine lady in such great distress, turning to me for a glimmer of hope, and found I could not turn away. For part of what my mother taught me was that I was strong and that I must give help to those who needed it. There seemed to be no other solution.

My decision was made. "With your permission, Mrs. Martin, I will ask Sandra to marry me. We will have to get married next week, because week after next we will be shipping out."

She began to cry softly with relief, and then slowly she started sobbing, till finally she was crying so loudly and from such depths that I was at a loss to comfort her. All I could do was hold her in my arms until the emotion had passed.

# PART 4

# The
# Search

# Chapter 19

Early in 1946 I was discharged from the Air Corps, and I headed home to San Antonio with my wife.

I was in turmoil. For the first time in my life I was having difficulty knowing where I was going. I desperately tried to be a husband to Sandra, going through the motions, doing what I thought husbands should do . . . regularly questioning my integrity and my honor, asking, what is just and fair? . . . wondering about my mother, my quest, and my fleeting lofty goals.

When I kissed Sandra, I was torn between the restraints I thought I should exercise, knowing that someday our relationship would change, and the response that I felt was fair to her as a husband now. I was not at all sure that Mrs. Martin had told her of my true feelings and that my actions had been prompted by the emergency of the moment and the situation. But I had promised myself that it was up to Sandra to bring up the subject.

I often said to myself, "You must not hurt Sandra in any way. You must show love and consideration, and somehow, for the time being, be a husband in every sense of the word." Then, in disgust,

I would add, "You must talk to her about the conversation with her mother, you coward, you cannot let this go on." Everyday I would hope: Maybe tomorrow she will bring it up. But you must wait. Be patient, let her get stronger, more independent, more mature. And, although we were always considerate and courteous with each other, we both were aware that a barrier existed.

Gradually I began to notice a change in her. Her personality became harsher, with a sort of forced gaiety. She enjoyed drinking on a daily basis and would not listen to suggestions about moderation. Her use of profanity increased. She now had close friendships with other women who became bridge buddies. The drinking did not cause drunkenness, but rather a dramatic change of personality, intense and severe. It was strange and also fascinating, but it did not eliminate my turmoil and torment.

I became more active in sports, playing golf and tennis twice a week, and I was recruited by a semi-pro baseball team and became their number one pitcher. I concentrated on the business my father had started two years before the war, selling plant food in paper sacks. It was an all-purpose fertilizer that he purchased in bulk, and then his fifteen employees would package it by hand in one- and five-pound sacks. The plant food was good for most house plants. He called the company the Green Stem Plant Food Company. During the war, he had difficulty obtaining the fertilizer, which was made by one of the giant chemical corporations. Most of those companies were dedicated to the production of munitions, and fertilizer was manufactured only on a limited basis. During the war years, my father had developed some health problems. On more than one occasion, he wrote me that he thought of closing the plant. I persuaded him to wait until I was out of the service.

After I had been home long enough to thoroughly analyze our operation, I developed a game plan for expansion. I went to the bank and presented my plan and was pleasantly surprised at the ease with which I obtained a $10,000 loan. We changed the packaging completely, went to sealed glass containers with very colorful labels, and expanded from a one-product line to a fifteen-product line with specialty plant foods. There were foods specifically for gardenias, roses, geraniums, and a number of other flowers. The basic product was the same, with a few ingredients added as required for a specific plant — iron and copperas for gardenias, for example. By specializing, the products could be priced higher, allowing us to triple our gross profit.

When I first became involved, the company was selling only in the local area. Two years later, our volume had increased from $10,000 to over $200,000 per month, and the number of employees from 15 to 80. Automatic filling and labeling equipment were part of our assembly line. I was recalling and putting to use much that I had learned from my beloved mentor, Walter Maurer. The first year, we opened the El Paso, Dallas, Houston, and Arizona markets and the following year expanded to Los Angeles, Chicago, New York, and New Orleans. I appointed brokerage firms to represent us in each market.

In every city, the top man of each company became a close personal friend. By 1948 we had a $200,000 line of credit at the bank and were preparing to introduce a complete new line of twenty-one products, styled and designed to be sold in grocery supermarkets.

Marketing was the key to our growth. To insure success, it was necessary for me to visit the Los Angeles, Chicago, and New Orleans markets at least once a month. Some trips were for three days; others required a week, and because of the situation with Sandra, I welcomed the frequent absences from home. I always allowed an extra day for social activities with my broker and his wife.

Late in 1948, Sandra gave birth to twins, a girl, Sue Ann, and a boy, Robert. These two angels became the central focus of my life.

Then one night a strange conversation occurred that set me free to continue my quest. I had come in from a baseball game and hurried to the nursery to see the babies. The maid was with them, and she told me my wife was getting dressed to go out and my supper was waiting to be served. After I had played with the children a while, I went to Sandra's dressing room and found her finishing her make-up and almost ready to leave.

"Will you be late?" I asked.

"What do you care?" she said, as she emptied the contents of a brown purse into a blue one which matched her shoes. "Are you going to wait up for me?"

"Do you think I should? You know, I worry about you." I wasn't sure what this new indifference meant. I could tell from her tone that she had been drinking because it always triggered belligerence.

"I really don't care, one way or the other. I'm going to see some friends and we may go on somewhere from there. I'll be home when I get here. The maid will see to your supper and the kids."

She picked up some gloves and the purse and sailed out the door, saying, "Bye-bye, Harvey," in the affected haughty accent she sometimes put on. I heard the gears of her car clash and the wheels spin as she backed out of the driveway and sped down the street.

I stood there staring sadly out the window. There was information in the tone of her voice which conveyed much more than her words. Somehow she managed to get across to me a new attitude, a new adjustment to our relationship. It was not something she intended to discuss with me, for she was not open to arbitration. The financial comfort of our life she had quickly taken for granted, and she assumed that domestic help would always be available and that her independence was hers alone, to do with as she pleased.

It was a new relationship, separate in spirit, with a final split inevitable. She was clearly saying, in effect, "Go on your foolish quest, it matters not to me. Just don't tell me about it. I will live my life as I wish!" She suddenly seemed strong and forceful.

My reaction was to turn to others. The welfare of my employees had always been important to me, and now I extended it to their families and to many others. I worked closely with young men in trouble, and found that I could make a difference in their lives.

# Chapter 20

Two years later, my life had taken on a new shape, and I was enjoying it — except for that vague feeling of something still to come, something promised, something glorious . . . that continued to elude me.

This day, in the perpetually idyllic setting of Southern California, I was feeling quite relaxed in a lounge chair courtside at the L.A. Tennis Club. Next to me sat Joyce Madison, sipping on a tall Tom Collins. Occasionally I would glance toward the court at the two players doing fierce combat in their deliberately-chic tennis outfits, but most of my attention was directed toward Joyce.

She's gorgeous, I thought to myself as I studied her: stylish blonde hair glistening in the sunlight, her beautiful blue eyes large and doelike, finely molded features that were classic, and a soft smile on her mouth which gave her an angelic look. Her long, slim legs below the short tennis skirt drew attention from everyone who passed, especially the men. Her rounded, supple hips slanted up sharply to a very small waist and the full bust seemed sculptured beneath the snug-fitting sleeveless tennis top. Even in sports clothes Joyce had an air of elegance which I found rare.

Each glance from a passing admirer gave me a twinge of jealousy. At the age of twenty-three, she was poised and sophisticated, and she had mannerisms which endeared her to me. Yet, after eight months of a close romantic relationship, I could not honestly say that I was in love with her.

Even today, after all my business successes and fortunate investments of these last four years, it still seemed almost incredible that I was sitting next to one of the richest young women in Los Angeles. She was surely one of the most gorgeous and probably the least pretentious, despite the fact that her family was "old money" of long standing.

For a quarter of an hour we had not spoken. We would look at each other intensely, oblivious of those around us. When our eyes met, her face reflected love and adoration. And then, suddenly uncomfortable, I would shift my gaze — more because I was unable to respond to the full measure of her uninhibited commitment than because we might have observers. I was aware that she wanted a pledge of consummated love between us, but at this time I was simply not ready to go that far.

Before we fell silent, we had been discussing our relationship, and the unpleasant incident at the front gate with James Becker, her former fiancé. Joyce had broken off the engagement two months before she met me, but James was nevertheless convinced that I was somehow to blame for his misfortune. Joyce had explained that she gradually realized James was a self-centered, egotistical, selfish fellow, and she believed he was incapable of really loving anyone. She believed his real distress over the broken engagement came from loss of face and embarrassment, rather than her rejection of him.

Becker glared at me whenever we met — which seemed to be very often. If we went to the symphony, he was there just a few rows away. At the opera he was sitting at the other end of the same row. At the Shubert, at a Broadway play, he was there on the same night. We would see him at our favorite nightclubs, often at dinner, at McHenry's Tail of the Cock, Perino's, or at the Beverly Hotel.

Joyce was sure that her mother was the informant. Mrs. Madison was not pleased with our relationship and she was very much aware that I was married and had two children. Every time we met Becker it was the same — he would smile at Joyce and glare at me. I had not told Joyce that last week someone took a shot at me in the parking lot of my hotel. James Becker, I suspected. It was a poor attempt from a car driven at high speed. Missed by ten feet. I figured that the gunman was not a professional and was too afraid of what he was doing to be accurate.

Today as Joyce and I had walked in the front gate of the Club, Becker had stepped directly into my path.

"Just a minute, Harvey Reese," he said, "I want to talk to you."

I stopped and looked at him curiously, then I put my hand on his chest and shoved him hard against the fence, simply pushing him out of the way. My contempt was unpremeditated, but I made no attempt to hide it. He was shocked. The hurricane fence rattled, and the surprise turned to an ill-concealed fear. I smiled at him as Joyce and I went through the gate.

When we were out of his hearing, she touched my hand and said, "James never forgets anything. Be warned, my love."

I put my arm around her waist and gave her a friendly pinch.


Now Joyce suddenly pushed her highball glass aside and faced me squarely. As she swung her legs under the table her knees came against mine. She looked at me intently and asked, "Harvey, are we ever going to get married? Do you plan a divorce soon?"

She had not been this direct before, and I was sorry I could not respond in the same tone.

"I'm not sure, my love," I replied. "I'm just not sure."

She gave a little stifled sigh that hurt my heart. Then dropping her eyes, she asked casually, "Do we have to go out with Frank and Melinda tonight?"

"Yes," I replied, "and you gave me your blessing when I asked you about it. It's important to Frank. I don't want to hurt him."

Frank Montez had been my broker and distributor on the West Coast for the past two years, and by now had become a very close friend.

"Listen, my dear," she said, taking my hand in hers. "I love

Frank. I think he's a fine man. He's fifty-five and you're twenty-seven, and your close friendship surprises me, but I think it's nice. It's Melinda that bothers me. I don't think he ought to marry her. That bleached hair . . . she's plucked her eyebrows to less than a pencil line. She dresses like a prostitute. She's only thirty and she's been married three times. And I've noticed that every time she gets near you she leans on you with her big boobs. Frank's a gentleman, and I don't understand how he can be attracted to that woman. By the way, is he Mexican?"

"He says he is, and if he thinks it, then it's true. Actually, his mother was half Italian and his father's mother came from Spain. But if you understand Mexicans, you will understand why Frank is truly a Mexican and a *caballero* of the first class."

"A *caballero*?" she asked.

"It means more than a gentleman. It denotes honor and nobility of character. Joyce, there is a side to this I haven't explained before. Two years ago, just a short time after we began to work together, Frank's wife died of cancer. For six months he was devastated. He was so depressed he could hardly do his work and I was quite worried about him. Then Pancho Andreas, his compadre — his very good friend and your tennis pro here at the Club — insisted that Frank be admitted to membership, and the board evidently thought enough of Pancho to accept his recommendation. Shortly after that, he met Melinda, and Frank had a rebirth. The fact that she's ostentatious and a bit vulgar doesn't matter to me. What does matter is that he is vital again, enthusiastic, and full of hope . . . and I love you for your tolerance and your patience."

"Well," Joyce said, "I love you for loving Frank."

With that quick understanding and acceptance which was one of the particularly nice things about her, she put aside her criticism.

"He's so good looking," she said. "Frank reminds me of Cesar Romero except I think he's better looking. Were you joking when you said we were going to Mexican nightclubs and honky-tonks?"

"No, it's for real. Frank loves Mexican music, loves Mexican food, loves to dance to Mexican music, and so do I. We'll have fun. And I'll avoid Melinda's tits."

Joyce laughed and said, "I would hope so."


The evening was a great success. The food at La Malaguena

was exceptional Mexican cuisine. Frank was driving his new white Cadillac convertible. We went to three different places. We drank margaritas and danced, and when we changed partners I could not avoid Melinda's tits. When we returned to the table, Joyce merely said, "Ah ha," with her right eyebrow arched.

At one of the clubs, Frank went on stage and sang with the Mexican band. He was rather good and everyone applauded and yelled for more. I was glad to see him so happy. Melinda played her role perfectly, looking at Frank adoringly, leaning on him, kissing his neck when they danced, and late in the evening announcing to our surprise that their marriage would take place in three weeks.

It was one in the morning before we turned into the long circular drive to the Madison estate. Although I had been there a number of times, the elegant mansion never failed to impress me.

"Go ahead, kids," Frank said, as he stopped at the front steps. "Have a drink and I'll take Melinda home and be back in about an hour and a half."

I looked toward Joyce for her approval and decided she had probably worked this out with Frank ahead of time.

The moment we walked in the front door it was obvious we were the only ones in this sixteen-room mansion. There were no lights on except in the foyer, and the rooms rang with silence. We went upstairs to the library which had a bar in one end and a huge fireplace.

"What would you like, Harvey?" she asked.

"Oh, whatever you're having will be fine."

She poured a couple of brandies into snifters and set them on the bar. "I'll be back in a minute. Get comfortable." She went out, closing the door behind her.

I picked up one of the snifters and began to prowl the bookshelves. Fifteen minutes later, I was sitting on a big leather sofa, engrossed in a book on antique weapons, when a small door near the fireplace opened and Joyce came in. Now she was wearing a flowing orchid negligee which was almost transparent, and the full beauty of her lovely body was all too evident.

She glided to where I was sitting and knelt in front of me. Taking my face in both hands, she kissed my lips tenderly but I felt the passion that was building in her. She could turn a tender, gentle touch into something sensuous in a way that I found intriguing.

She stood, took me by the hand, and led me through the small door. Just down the short hallway she opened a white door and led me into her bedroom.

The room was large and luxurious and very feminine, decorated in shades of yellow and white. She drew me to her bed and sat down, and I sat next to her. Then she lay back, I turned, leaned over her and kissed her for a long moment. When I stopped to study her beautiful face, she pushed me aside gently so she could take off her negligee. Now she wore only a very short, transparent, flimsy little gown.

She lay back again. I leaned over her and kissed her. This time her lips were hungrily sensuous and passionate. Panic came over me and I sat up.

Looking up at me with a troubled expression, she asked, "Harvey, what's wrong? Don't you love me?"

"Of course I love you, darling. But somehow this is not right. Something is wrong . . . something that nags at me." I could not look at her as I spoke.

She gave that pathetic little sigh again that shot a pain through my heart.

"I'm not the one you are looking for, am I?" she asked. "A few months ago you did believe that I was the one. But for the last two months I have known. I knew you were no longer sure. I had to find out. But let me add, I will take you even with conditions. Harvey, please look at me."

Her gentle hand on my chin turned my eyes toward her. I looked at that angelic face. A tear was rolling down her cheek and I suddenly thought to myself, what the hell! I took off my coat, lay next to her and put my arm around her waist, then leaned down and kissed her almost violently. She responded passionately and the full length of our bodies pressed together with urgency.

But a shock went through me — almost as though something grabbed my shoulders and pulled me back. I stopped and sat up.

"Joyce, my darling, no! I mustn't! I can't!" The thought flashed through my mind that I could not allow the honor of my life to be dominated by the passion of this moment.

I stood up and without another word went to the door and left her room.

As I was going down the long elegant staircase, my thoughts

went to my mother, and I wondered if I really ever would find my love. Perhaps it was just a creation of my imagination. Maybe I was not capable of loving one woman above all else. Maybe I had grown up and must face realities and stop living in a dream world. A boy's life must be put aside someday. It was hard to accept the fact that I had refused what Joyce had offered. Perhaps I did not know who I was. The riddle! If I could answer the riddle! Ten years ago my mother said I was not ready. Was I ready now? The riddle of the five illusions: Who are you? Where do you go? Whom do you challenge? Whom do you fear? What do you seek?

Oh hell! Maybe this was all nonsense.


I was waiting on the front steps of the Madison Estate when Frank drove up two hours later. As we headed for my hotel I was silent, and Frank said nothing until we reached the parking lot.

"My friend," he said, as he cut off the motor, "you are troubled. Do you want to talk about it?"

We sat in his convertible in the moonlight and I told him something of my dilemma.

Finally, he told me, "Harvey, I know you are an honorable man. I know that you are married, but you have explained that you must search. I don't exactly understand, but I know that your actions always reflect integrity. I'm not sure of your relationship with Joyce — in some ways, you both act as if you are married, but sometimes you look at her as if you're not sure who she is. I know she loves you dearly. I believe you are a true *caballero*. I believe you fight the good fight always, never a low blow. But my friend, maybe what you seek does not exist. I only bring it up because I am your friend and I worry that you sometimes look unhappy."

"Thanks, Frank. Thank you for your friendship and your loyalty. But please, there's nothing to worry about, and surely no reason to worry about Joyce. I don't believe I am capable of hurting her. But I'm afraid it is true — Joyce is not the one I am seeking. I don't intend to see her again, Frank. The problem is mine. Maybe you're right. My so-called search may be an impractical task."

He looked at me inquiringly, but realized that I did not want to pursue the matter any further.

Leaning back, he lit a cigarette and said, "Pancho Andreas is a very close friend of mine. So is Bill Thompson. But Harvey, I consider you my best friend. My plans are to marry Melinda in six weeks." He chuckled. "I know she said three, but I can't wind things down in just three weeks so we can take time off for a honeymoon. If you can return in six weeks, I would be honored to have you as my best man. We have both made considerable money in California, but that has nothing to do with the way I feel about you. Are you my compadre, Harvey Reese?"

"Forever, Frank Montez, forever!" I returned, and then we embraced. I got out of the convertible and watched him drive away singing a Mexican country song.

I turned toward the hotel and came to a hedge where two men stepped in front of me. One asked the other, *"Listo?"* ("Ready?")

The stance they took was belligerent.

*"Que paso, hombre?"* ("What's the matter, man?") I asked.

They were surprised. The small one asked, *"Eres Mexicano?"* ("Are you Mexican?")

*"Ya mero,"* ("Almost,") I answered.

The small one turned to the big one and said, "What are we doing this for? That *gringo* can't ask us to go against one of our own."

I quickly asked, "James Becker?"

They looked at me, surprised. "Yes," said the big one. "We work for a friend of his. He said you insulted him."

"Listen, *muchachos,*" I returned. "You're not going to let that *gringo* make you take arms against a compadre, are you?"

"Hell no!" said the little one. "But he gave us fifty dollars each."

"Good," I said. "If I run into him, I'll tell him you beat the hell out of me."

They both laughed heartily and said, *"Bueno,* let's go," and they disappeared into the darkness.

# Chapter 21

**M**anuel Davila, one of my plant foremen, met me at ten the next evening curbside at the San Antonio airport. I threw my bag in the back and jumped into the front seat next to him.

"Manuel, I'm happy to see you. Did that last big order get out to California?"

"Yes sir," he replied. "And the shipment to Chicago will be going out tomorrow. Everything is going well and we have gotten in orders that will keep us busy for the next three weeks."

We had built a good reputation for fulfilling delivery commitments which I was determined to maintain. My next trip would be to Chicago, right away, and for at least two days.

"Good. Anything else to report?" I asked.

"Yes, afraid so," he said. "I have some bad news. Your Uncle Jonathan is quite sick. Your father has been to see him and said that your uncle has asked for you and that you should get to Luling as soon as possible."

This was a shock. I now realized that I had always thought of Uncle Jonathan as eternally robust. It was hard to believe he could be seriously ill. My impulse was to rush to Luling that moment, but I would arrive after midnight.

"Thanks, Manuel," I said, mentally rearranging my schedule as I talked. "I'll go tomorrow morning. You'd better take me home. I want to leave for Luling before sunrise. Tell Diane to cancel my appointment at the bank and reschedule it for Friday." Diane Walker was my personal secretary, and she ran the office well in my absence.

When I reached home, I found Sandra and a bunch of her girlfriends in the den. They had two tables of bridge going at opposite ends of the big room. In the center, a large buffet was covered with food — several dips and chafing dishes, three kinds of cheese, cold cuts, a huge fruit platter, and two hot casserole dishes. The ladies didn't seem to have started on their feast yet.

There were various remarks of "Hi, Harvey, you back for a while?" and Sandra gave me a slight kiss and asked, "May I fix you a plate? Everything is delicious!"

"Thanks," I said. "I am hungry."

"How about a drink?"

"Okay, a martini."

As she poured it, she added, "I thought you were getting back tomorrow. I don't like you surprising me."

"Finished sooner than I expected," I said. "I'm glad. Gives me a chance to see your friends."

She called to the women at the far table, "You all about through with that hand? Let's eat before it gets cold." Then, in a strident tone, she called, "Maria! *Pronto!* Come serve dinner. Come, come, move!" Her voice was so harsh it embarrassed me. Maria was a gentle soul and did not need that kind of urging.

Sandra filled a plate for me and set it on the corner of the far table where I ate with four ladies I hardly knew. The conversation was lively; many highballs had evidently been consumed already. Sandra's friends were interesting people. Most of them were married but somehow independent of the responsibilities of their marriage. I could see the model for her own attitude.

As soon as I finished eating, I made my excuses to retire and told Sandra I was going to see the children.

She was still nibbling on some tostados and dips as she told me good night. "Don't wait up for me. We'll be rather late," she added.

"I won't," I assured her. "I have just learned that Uncle Jonathan is quite sick and I'll be leaving early tomorrow to go to Luling and see him. Have a good game."

The next morning, I got to Luling about ten o'clock and went directly to Jonathan's home, only to learn that he had been moved to the ranch, which was nearly forty miles from Luling.

As I drove down the dirt road toward the ranch house, a hundred memories splashed through my mind about this great ranch and my wonderful uncle. At the house, there were three cowboys sitting out front, with a lost look on each face. It was strange not to see Juan Delgado here, but I remembered he had gone back to Mexico two years ago. When I stepped out of my new Oldsmobile, the men nodded, somehow indicating they knew who I was despite the look of the city dude. I was wearing a suit, and felt out of place. Wishing I had come in my pickup, I took off my coat and tie and threw them into the front seat before I went into the house.

Jonathan was propped up in his bed. Angie, his wife, was in the kitchen area, and there was a young girl sitting next to my uncle, holding his hand. I guessed her to be about eleven years old. When Jonathan saw me, his face lit up but I was shocked at how pale and drawn he looked. He made an effort to sit up, but it was obvious he was in too much pain.

He turned to Angie and said, "Would you take Becky outside? I want to speak to Harvey alone."

Jonathan waited till the door closed behind them before he said, "My boy, I am dead. Seems my appendix ruptured, and I didn't realize it. Had a hell of a stomach-ache for four days. They operated, but too late. The poison had spread everywhere." His voice was weak and I had a hard time connecting this pale, suffering man in the bed with my vital, hearty uncle. "They had hoses in my stomach and my nose, but I understood that I was not going to make it. So I made them take out all those damn hoses. They've got me full of dope . . . makes me sleep a lot. Lucky I'm awake now. It won't be long before they give me more dope. Harvey, Angie knows

168

that I want to be buried on the ranch and that you will tell her where. I want to be near the big oak. I want you to go there and pick the spot. Somewhere on the east side of that big oak tree. Will you do that for me, my boy?"

I took his hand in mine and said, "I'll pick the best damn spot you could imagine."

He managed a slight smile and squeezed my hand, then softly he continued. "I'm sure you noticed Becky sitting by me when you came in. She is the only regret I have for leaving this world. I love her dearly. She's Roscoe's sister, you know — or maybe I should say niece."

"No!" I exclaimed. "I did not know."

"Yes, she is the child of Amy, Roscoe's sister. Remember all that sad story? When Amy died, I took the baby home with me. Named her Becky. She is my special treasure. I have kept on paying the taxes on the Rafferty Ranch for her sake. Promise me you'll help her when I'm gone."

I nodded. This was so like my uncle. In the past he had adopted two other children. One was a four-year-old sickly boy who died of pneumonia a year later. The other was a harelipped youngster of sixteen who graduated from college with a petroleum engineering degree. I was surprised at this information about Amy and Becky but too concerned about my uncle's condition to ask him any questions, so I sat quietly and let him go on.

"Roscoe is back in South Texas, a foreman at some ranch. You know he left the state for twelve years, but now I hear he's back. I've been trying to get word to him. He doesn't know that he has a new sister. Strange boy, that Roscoe. I understand he spent two years in the penitentiary in Missouri, and he's only been back in Texas for a year. But I only heard about him three months ago at a cattle auction in Cotulla. An old hand of mine told me that he wasn't sure what ranch he's on now.

"Enough of Roscoe. Harvey, I understand you are a big success. Big home with maids, two cars, flying all over the country, dressed up all the time, golf at the country club . . . Just a minute, I'm having a pain . . ." For a moment he had sounded stronger, but now he lay silent, and I could see what the pain was doing to him as he fought against crying out. I just sat there next to him and squeezed his hand.

Finally he gave a deep, shaky sigh. "It's gone now," he said. "That's the way they shoot through my body sometimes. What I was wanting to say was that you must not get too domesticated, my boy. Don't let all those things you're buying break your spirit. I've seen good men drown that way. Money corrupts. Gives you power. Power can steal your soul."

Now the pain was back, and he whispered something I could not hear. He beckoned me closer. I put my ear close to his mouth and heard him clearly say, "Don't forget, Harvey, don't forget. Wild turkeys can fly. They can fly . . . can fly . . ." He stopped. There was a tear at the corner of his eye.

"Go now, quick," he said. "Go find my spot. Come back and tell me."

My eyes filled with tears. I got up and turned away from him, walked to the door, and stood there for a moment while I rubbed my eyes dry. Outside, I walked up to the tall, toughest-looking of the cowboys sitting on the bench outside, and said, "May I borrow your horse?"

He nodded. "The Appaloosa there — it's already saddled."

I ran toward the Appaloosa, and with a running leap I was on his back. I hit him with both heels and he took off like a shot and was galloping at full speed before we cleared the corral. In ten minutes I was at the big oak.

I leaped off the saddle as the Appaloosa came to a sliding halt. I walked around the tree, trying to determine in which direction the sun would set at the different seasons of the year. Finally I picked a spot twenty feet from the trunk on the southeast side. A slight bluff, it seemed to be under the protection of the big oak, with two large pecan trees nearby. This would suit him fine, I thought. He'll like it here.

I made the trip back to the ranch house at full gallop, eager to make the report to my uncle, but within a hundred feet of my destination I could see the tall cowboy who owned the Appaloosa standing with his hat in his hand and his head bowed. I knew Uncle Jonathan was gone.

I pulled the Appaloosa to a halt, and I lowered my head and prayed, "Lord, have mercy on Jonathan, Thy servant. Let this beautiful soul take flight and be with Thee this day."

I stayed at the ranch for three days after Jonathan was buried, much of the time just walking the ranch, sitting by the Blanco River, occasionally climbing a hill, looking across the valleys, and absorbing the beauty of the Hill Country of Texas. Late in the afternoons I would follow the path from the back side of the big corral through the grove of lush woods to the flowing spring and the three small lakes, my magical spot where my uncle and I had visited together. I would watch the waters cascade down the varicolored stones and remember Jonathan, who still seemed bigger than life here at this special place.

In the mornings, I would wander out to the big oak tree and sit by his grave, remembering the good times, remembering the good hunt, remembering the fine man . . . and there I prayed.


A week later, when I finally returned to the office, I could not seem to concentrate. I found myself staring out the window the entire day, thinking of Uncle Jonathan, enduring that grieving process we seem bound to go through when we lose someone we have dearly loved — wishing we had been with them more and regretting every missed opportunity.

On my second morning back, Diane came to me and proved once again how valuable she was to me in my business life, as well as how sincerely she cared about my personal welfare.

She sat down across from me and said, "I hope I am not speaking out of turn. I know what your uncle meant to you, but everyone in the plant is concerned about you. Manuel said he would not approach you unless you called him. Allen Kline in Chicago has phoned ten times in the last five days. May I at least tell Manuel you'll speak to him in a day or so?" She took me by surprise, but it had the right effect.

"Thanks, Diane," I said. "Wait twenty minutes and send Manuel in."

"What about Chicago?" she asked. "When should I call Mr. Kline?"

"Make a plane reservation for tomorrow and let him know I'm coming. Also make me a hotel reservation, the Palmer House will do."

When Manuel came in, I stood, reached out and shook his

hand. "Sit down," I told him. "Manuel, my friend, I want to thank you for the responsible way you are handling your job. I haven't been much help lately. It's a real comfort to know I can rely on you to take care of things here when I am absent."

"May I express my sympathy for your great loss," he said.

"Thank you," I replied. "Now it's time I get back to work. Please bring me up to date on the company."

His report was all good news. We would meet our shipping commitments, production on the new line was going as scheduled, and all the orders on the old product line would also be shipped as promised. Before he left my office, I thanked him again and promised to call regularly.

When Diane returned, I asked her to make out a two thousand dollar check, payable to the bank in Luling, for a savings account for "Becky Rafferty, a minor." I spelled the name for her, and she prepared the check without comment.

As I drove home that night, I remembered Uncle Jonathan, but no longer with sorrow. I felt an overwhelming sense of joy and gratitude for having had the privilege of knowing him and loving him.


The next day, in Chicago, Allen Kline, my distributor, and I made five calls and every one resulted in huge orders, beyond my expectations — a grand total of six carloads. That night I went to my favorite spot to eat dinner, the London House on Shoreline Drive. The food was excellent, the atmosphere sophisticated, and there were handsome furnishings, fine leather upholstery in the booths, and outstanding service.

The London House was not very large, and therefore the entertainment had to be intimate. It featured the best jazz groups in the country — small groups of four and six, composed of excellent musicians on each instrument.

Joe, the maitre d', usually kept a center booth open in case a celebrity walked in without reservations. This special booth was always available to me if I phoned ahead. When I arrived, Joe would say, in an eloquent Italian accent, "Mr. Reese, I've been waiting for you. Your reservations are ready. Center booth as usual."

I would tip him discreetly but generously, and sit in the large booth that was designed for four. I had probably dined at the London House at least two dozen times, and only on two or three occasions had I ever brought anyone with me.

Tonight I sat alone in the center of the booth, facing the band. Jay Kingsley, a world renowned jazz singer, was performing, accompanied only by piano, bass, and drums. My favorite waiter, Adam, served me. After looking at the menu briefly, I ordered a dry martini, to be followed by steak Diane, new potatoes, asparagus hollandaise, and for dessert their famous candy crunch cake.

While the band took a break, I sipped on my martini, and my thoughts went back home to San Antonio. My two children had become the center of my attention there. I was overwhelmed by the love that I felt for these two little people. I thought of Sandra and it saddened me. Her looks were stunning — tall, a striking figure, reddish dark hair, bright blue eyes, and now an air of confidence that added to her glamour. Yet her life of bridge and cocktails seemed empty and pathetic to me. I felt somehow guilty, but I had nothing to offer to improve the situation. I believed she looked happier than ever before — perhaps because an understanding now seemed to exist between us.

Jay Kingsley returned to the stand with his accompanists and started with the jazz version of "Tangerine," followed by Cole Porter's "Begin the Beguine." Adam served my meal, and as I started to eat, a most attractive young lady walked up to my booth and said, "Do you mind if I sit here with you? I notice that you are alone and I would like to see and hear the band up close."

She had dark auburn hair that was pulled back into a knot, and very dark brown eyes that danced with expression. A most attractive face, with large lips that seemed to have a constant smile at one corner. Five foot four, I would estimate, without her very high heels. Slim, but very well proportioned, wearing a tight blue skirt, a white blouse with long sleeves and a high collar, and a tailored jacket that matched the skirt.

A very pretty girl, I thought to myself, but . . . "I'm really not interested in having company," I replied, "and if I did, I am capable of selecting my own companion. I'm sure there are lots of men here . . ."

Her look stopped me. Then she broke into laughter and said, "You think I'm a hooker, don't you?"

"Well . . ."

"Listen, mister, I'm a theatrical booking agent, and I'm interested in Mr. Kingsley professionally. That's it! I would like to book him for a club in Evanston. You have the center booth, you are alone, there's plenty of room — I really thought you wouldn't mind. If I have to, I'll say please. But look at me. I'm very pretty, I've got good looking legs, beautifully proportioned hips, I'm intelligent, I am a good conversationalist, I love a good laugh, and I am just a working girl trying to survive. But not *that* kind of working girl. Since you refused the bad girl, how about letting the good girl sit right next to you and not bother you? I won't even speak unless you speak to me first. By the way, my name is Mary Alice Sanders."

Her manner was so beguiling and her eyes flashed with such enthusiasm that it made me smile. Just then, Joe, the maitre d', walked by and she grabbed him by the arm and said, "Joe, please tell this gentleman what I do so that he won't have any bad ideas about me."

Joe leaned forward and said quietly, "Mr. Reese, she's a booking agent, and I apologize. She slipped past my desk and came right to you. Her husband was a good friend, and I sort of like her too, but if you say so, out she goes."

"No, no, Joe. It's fine. Let her sit here. But, Mrs. Sanders, I insist that you join me with dessert or something. I don't want anybody watching to think that I won't even feed you."

She laughed as Joe walked away. I continued, "There's one more condition. My name is Harvey Reese, I'm from Texas, and I'm leaving Chicago tomorrow, but I'll return in three weeks. You must promise to have dinner with me when I come back."

She turned and looked at me quite surprised, hesitated, and then said, "Sure, cowboy. I'll be glad to. I wouldn't agree, except that you rejected me and I don't want to be the same kind of cad."

"May I take you home?" I asked.

"No. I really must talk to Mr. Kingsley. Here's my card. Let me put my home phone number on the back. You call me, tell me when you're coming, and we'll have dinner."

When Adam brought the candy crunch cake, he brought a piece for Mary Alice also, as I had requested. She ate it as she listened intently to Jay Kingsley, only occasionally looking toward me and smiling. Finally, after an hour the band broke and started off the stage.

Mary Alice jumped up and said, "Bye. Call me when you get back in three weeks. I've got to go talk to Mr. Kingsley," and she followed him through the back door. I asked for my check and left.

# Chapter 22

In San Antonio three days later, there was a call from California while I was out of the office, with a request that I call back as soon as possible. I knew the number — it was Frank Montez, my broker. I was surprised, for it was 9:30 in the morning, 7:30 in California, and Frank never called me that early.

When I reached him, he said, "Harvey, you've got to get to California today. I have an emergency and I don't know anybody else who could help me. You're the only one I trust in this matter. Please come to California."

"Can't you tell me a little more?" I asked.

"No, compadre, not on the phone. Come. Come today. I need you tonight."

I left on the one o'clock flight and arrived in Los Angeles at three — or five o'clock San Antonio time. Frank was at the gate to greet me. We took a seat on the first bench we found in the airport, and I could see that he was very serious, which was unlike him.

He began, "Harvey, I've told you before that my father died when I was twelve years old. It was my Uncle Ignacio who loved and raised me, sent me to college as if I was his own son, never refused any request that I ever made of him. I loved him as I loved my father, and now he needs me. His wife, Ophelia, used to abuse him terribly after he got old. She would tongue-lash him constantly, always critical of whatever he did or said. Finally, five years ago, she died. He had two daughters. They took over when Aunt Ophelia died, and they were even worse. They were like jailers, screaming at him and never letting him leave the house. On one occasion when I was visiting, one of them actually slapped him. You see, my uncle was eighty-six last year; however, he never lost his mental faculties. He was always sharp, and he knew what was happening to him.

"Three years ago, one of his daughters died and they buried her next to her mother. At the cemetery, my uncle made me swear that I would never allow his body to be laid next to those two women. I promised. It meant everything to him. He also begged me to drive him home that day. I had to argue this out with my cousin, his daughter, and she finally agreed only because she did not feel at liberty to fight with me in front of the entire family.

"On the way home, my uncle asked me to drive him to the desert, and directed me to turn onto a dirt road that led to the foot of a mountain. When we were under the shadow of the mountain he asked me to stop the car, and he said, 'I want to be buried here.' I told him I could not promise that, but I did promise that he would not be buried next to my Aunt Ophelia.

"Harvey, my uncle is lying in state at Brandon Funeral Home at this very moment. He died yesterday afternoon during his nap. The funeral is scheduled for ten o'clock tomorrow morning. Tonight there will be a rosary at eight. Bill Brandon, the owner of the funeral home, is one of my very good friends. He has agreed to help me keep my promise, although he seems scared to death. He's afraid of losing his license.

"I have insisted to my Cousin Ruth, Uncle Ignacio's daughter, that after the rosary the casket should be closed and sealed permanently. It took awhile to talk her into it, but she has agreed. The plan is to switch caskets tonight after the rosary. Two of my nephews were going to hold an all-night vigil, but they understand that

I considered my Uncle Ignacio as my father and that I wish to be alone with him all night, holding the vigil alone. Bill and I have an exact duplicate of his coffin ready to make the switch.

"St. Joseph's Cemetery is huge. It covers several blocks. My Aunt Ophelia is at one end and my father is buried far off at the other. I own two plots next to my father's grave, and we will bury my uncle next to my father. They loved each other. The empty casket will be buried next to Ophelia."

"The pallbearers will notice that the casket is too light," I suggested.

"No," he said, "My Aunt Ophelia loved pinto beans, so we are going to put a hundred-pound sack of pinto beans in the casket that will be buried next to her. That ought to make her happy!"

His explanation cracked me up, and I began to laugh. Frank looked at me disapprovingly for a couple of minutes, but then he couldn't resist the humor in his own joke and he joined in.

Growing serious again, he explained, "Bill Brandon knows the guard at the cemetery, who has agreed to unlock the gate, then go have a few beers and not return for a couple of hours. Bill is very nervous about the whole thing and wants no one else involved, but I've convinced him about our close friendship, and he has agreed to let you help. He's not even going to use a hearse. I've borrowed a van, and that's the way we are going to transport my uncle's casket. And then, Harvey, my compadre," he added in a happier tone, flashing his captivating smile, "tomorrow, as soon as the funeral is over, I'm going to the courthouse and get married. Melinda has agreed."

"I thought you weren't going to get married for three more weeks."

"Harvey, life is too short and too unpredictable. I'll get married tomorrow, and you are the only person who is going to be there with us — unless you wish to invite Joyce."

"No," I said. "I don't even want her to know that I'm in L.A. I have to return to San Antonio as soon as possible. I have too many loose ends . . . too many things are pending that I haven't completed. Besides, I believe it's best to leave Joyce alone, for her sake as well as mine."

Frank casually added, "Remember James Becker? He has moved to New York. Doesn't bother Joyce anymore."

I was glad to hear it, but it didn't have any bearing on my decision to cease our relationship.

That night after the rosary, Frank and I sat together and waited patiently for everyone to leave. Ruth Montez, Uncle Ignacio's daughter, was the last one to leave, with Frank's nephews. As she walked down the aisle, Frank approached her and said, "With your permission, I will now have the casket sealed." She nodded and left.

A half hour passed as we sat in the chapel waiting for Bill Brandon. Frank began to worry. "Bill should have been here thirty minutes ago."

Finally Brandon walked in, looking ill at ease. He was greeted by the only other attendant that was on duty. We heard Bill tell the man to go stay in the front office and not to leave until he was told because a very important long distance call was expected. The young man agreed, and left the chapel.

Frank, Bill, and I went into the back room. Another casket, made of red mahogany exactly like the one in the chapel, was open and sitting on a cart with large casters. Frank and I went out to the van to get the hundred-pound sack of pinto beans.

As we carried the sack indoors, Frank remarked, "These are the best grade of pinto beans you can buy."

I started snickering and Frank followed suit, but Brandon met us in the doorway and seemed genuinely offended at our ill-timed levity, so we sobered up. We put the beans in the casket and sealed it.

Brandon looked out into the chapel to make sure no one was there. We quickly rolled the casket with the beans into the chapel and put it in Uncle Ignacio's place, then rolled the casket with Uncle Ignacio out to the van and the switch was complete. I joined Frank in the van and we followed Brandon, who was driving a black Cadillac. The cemetery was five miles away. When we arrived at the gate, Brandon went to speak to the guard, and when he returned, he was so nervous he could hardly speak but did manage to mutter, "They've changed the guard tonight. How much money do you guys have?"

"I've got one hundred," Frank said.

I had five hundred in my pocket, but I didn't think that much would be needed. "Here's another hundred," I said.

"Good," Bill said. "Please give it to me." He took the money, went back to the gate and talked to the guard for ten minutes. Finally we saw the guard taking the lock and chain from the gate. Then he went over to a small Ford and drove away.

Brandon drove his Cadillac through the gate and we followed in the van. Frank parked as close to graveside as possible, but the three of us still had to carry the heavy casket over a hundred feet to the graveside. Frank and I were pleasantly surprised to find that the grave had already been dug.

Brandon noticed the question on our faces, and said, "I had four wetbacks digging here all afternoon. I came by four times, but nobody seemed to notice that they weren't from the regular work force. I paid them and told them to take off. Your job is going to be to cover it up, which is much easier than digging. Tomorrow I'll get my landscape people to pack it down as much as possible and cover it with grass."

We lowered the casket into the grave. There were two sacks of dirt in the van, about fifty pounds apiece. Beside the grave, Frank cut them open with a pocketknife and started spreading the dirt on top of the casket. He looked up at me and explained, "This soil comes from the spot where Uncle Ignacio hoped to be buried."

Frank knelt down and I knelt next to him. He prayed softly. I could not hear the words, but his tone was so sorrowful that it made me weep. I put my arm around my friend's shoulder and my heart was torn by every muffled sob that came from him.

When the emotional moment was over and Frank regained his control, we each took a shovel and started filling the grave. Brandon had been pacing up and down, waiting nervously. When we were through, the mortician came toward Frank and took his hand and said, speaking in the graceful formality of the Spanish language, "May I comfort you in your hour of sorrow?" The two friends embraced, and that scene touched me deeply. I had not been sure I liked Bill at first. He seemed a bit stuffy and proper. But his sincere sympathy for Frank's sorrow made me like him better.

When Frank and I returned to the van, he sat silently for a moment, then turned, looked at me, and said, "We are all facing death. We must hurry, and waste no time."

The next morning, the funeral went without incident. The casket with the pinto beans was laid to rest, next to Ophelia. The large crowd at the funeral was there mainly because of Frank, for most of them had not even known Uncle Ignacio.

Frank was approached by one of his friends, who said, "At least your uncle is lying next to his loved one."

Frank replied, without blinking an eye, "Yes, Uncle Ignacio has been laid to rest next to his loved one, and Aunt Ophelia is lying next to her loved ones. I'm sure they are all going to be very happy together."

I had to bite my tongue or I would have broken out laughing.

After the funeral, Frank and I drove to his office and I waited in the car while he went in to pick up Melinda and to change from the dark suit he had worn for the funeral. When he emerged, he was smiling happily and his gray eyes were glistening in anticipation; his wavy dark hair added to his dashing good looks. Now he wore brown and white wing-tip shoes, tailored off-white slacks, a light blue silk shirt, and a beautifully-tailored ivory tweed sport coat with a blue and white striped scarf at his neck. He truly was a handsome man.

Melinda came out wearing bright red pumps with four-inch heels and a tight red skirt with a split on the side. Her white blouse with bright red polka dots plunged in the center to expose quite a bit of her bust. She wore brilliant red lipstick and too much rouge. A bit overdone, I thought, but who gives a damn? Look at Frank. He's so happy, nothing else really matters.

At the county courthouse, the marriage ceremony was rather short. Frank kissed Melinda and we walked outside. Standing on the sidewalk in the center of Los Angeles, Melinda suddenly announced, "Well, Harvey. You can kiss the bride!"

She grabbed me and planted a kiss on my mouth that embarrassed me. I looked toward Frank, but he was smiling, expressing no objection. He said, "Harvey, this is the happiest day of my life. I've married this wonderful woman. I loved my Uncle Ignacio, but he's over his torment and at peace, and my prayers are that you, too, Harvey, will find happiness soon. Come on. Let's get to the car. We will take you to the airport."

"No, sir," I said. "I'll take a taxi. I have my overnight bag with me. I can find the airport. I want you to start your honeymoon and happiness now."

Frank took my hand. We looked at each other for a moment and then embraced with great emotion. Without another word, he turned, put his arm around Melinda, and they walked off. I stood there watching them, hoping that Frank would always be this happy, and yet, at this moment happiness seemed so fragile to me.

Six weeks later, Frank was committed to a nursing home for the physically and mentally disabled. Shortly after his return from his honeymoon, he had merged his company with the Kirk Heimer Brokerage Company. The day after the merger, he was driving on the Santa Monica Freeway and was sideswiped by a young man of seventeen driving a pickup. Frank's Cadillac spun around and he was thrown out. His head hit the concrete, causing massive brain damage. He was in surgery for three hours.

I did not hear about the accident for two weeks. Melinda either did not want me to know or just did not bother to tell me, and Kirk Heimer hadn't known of my close personal association with Frank.

The day after I finally heard the awful story, I went to see Frank. He was conscious but he didn't recognize me. It was so painful for me that I did not return to see him for another six months. When I did, I found him like a little child, playing with crayolas, scribbling on colored paper without purpose or pattern. His doctor told me there was no hope that Frank would recover. The brain damage was permanent.

I sat on the bench next to my friend at the worktable, and I spoke to him. He continued to scribble and only occasionally would he look up, with blankness in his eyes, without expression, and then return to his scribbling on the colored paper. The attendant said that Melinda had not been there for more than three months. I put my arm around Frank's shoulder, and he started rocking back and forth, and I rocked with him.

I could not bear to leave his side for another two hours. I finally said goodbye as if he was leaving on a long trip, embracing him two or three times, holding him in my arms for long minutes. He just stood there, with his arms hanging at his sides, without any expression.

As I left the nursing home, I said to myself, farewell, my friend, farewell.

Every week I phoned the nursing home to learn about Frank. The nurse at the other end of the line always gave the same report, "There is no change." I could never bring myself to visit him again. He died three years later. I have never forgotten his words, "We are all facing death. We must hurry, and waste no time."

# Chapter 23

The following week, I went to my office to prepare for a trip to New Orleans. I would be there for a week, and my broker, Dale Edwards, and his wife, Louise, had invited me to stay at their home. Usually I preferred a hotel, which allowed me the freedom to do as I wished and come and go at any hour. But on this trip, since Dale and I were going to work the Louisiana territory together, it seemed logical to use his house as a base of operations.

When I reached the office I found it difficult to concentrate. I sat behind my big black-walnut desk and stared at the two piles of papers that needed my personal attention. My eyes roved over the other objects in front of me. They were like a summary of my life. The desk itself had come from Mexico and I remembered the craftsman who had made it to my order. On it now were souvenirs from the war, a small Golden Gloves memento, a tennis ball with the signatures of Frank and Pancho, my father's pocketknife, Uncle Jesse's bullet clip, the keys from Michael Pruske's motorcycle, a portrait of Sandra and my two children, Uncle Jonathan's western hatband, a harmonica, a watergun, a kazoo, and several other toys that I enjoyed fooling around with.

Then my glance moved to the walls which were covered with at least twenty photographs of friends and family. My eyes stopped at Uncle Jonathan's picture and then at Frank's. I thought of the deaths of those two fine men, and about Joyce whom I had put in the past. I thought of my search, my quest, and felt a sort of futility, of disillusion and melancholy. There was the situation at home, the "arrangement" which had dissolved into something that felt dishonest. I kept thinking I would settle that problem when I found the Special Person I was seeking, but perhaps this was just procrastination. Certainly my home was not happy, but I wasn't in it much, and the resolution was going to be painful for Sandra as well as for me. It seemed to me that everyone's story can be told at least two ways — one, for instance, in sympathetic tone with explanation of any faults or errors, and the other in lurid terms to make the same character caught in the same incidents seem indulgent and selfish. Right now I wondered if my own life wasn't perhaps neither of these but just a farce.

These feelings were strange to me. I had been lonely at times in the past but never depressed. And depression was not really the word for my mood now. Discontent, yes, melancholy, and a disillusionment that seemed to be based on betrayal. Betrayal? What made me think that? By whom? My mother? Surely not. But was there really someone special just for me? Were my mother's high ideals only appropriate for a youth of seventeen? And did I truly have to help everyone who asked for help? There was a lack of practicality about the attitude she had posed for me. After all, for many people Don Quixote was just a fool on a nag tilting at windmills. The term "quixotic" meant idealistic but impractical. I had looked it up once to find that its synonym was "imaginary," which startled me.

I got up and stood at the window, watching thin clouds drifting slowly toward the north, feeling almost overwhelmed by the unanswerable questions which bewildered my mind. Then I was brought back to reality by the appearance of Diane in my door.

"Homer Smith is here to see you," she reported. "Said he has an appointment. O.K.?"

"Oh, uh, right. Ask him to come in."

Homer and I had played high school football together and had remained close friends. After the war he started a washateria which was successful and he soon opened two more. A few months ago he had told me he was having a cash-flow problem and needed additional capital, and he wondered if I would like to invest $15,000. He promised a good return on my money. At that time I let him have $4,000 and told him to check with me later. Now he had called and asked if he could come see me, saying he was in a jam.

He walked into my office smiling, shook my hand, and sat down, looking awkward and embarrassed. Homer was a stocky fellow with the broad shoulders of a lineman, but now at twenty-eight he was beginning to show a bulge above the belt which might be too much beer or perhaps just not enough exercise. I had always liked his good-humored grin and in high school we had made big plans about how we were going to lick the world.

He asked about my family and I inquired about his. Then he said, "Harvey, I desperately need seven thousand dollars. I've already told you about the financial difficulties I've been having with my washaterias. Two of them are doing fine, but the third one I opened in a very expensive shopping mall, and it has lost lots of money. The lease payments are too high and I didn't have enough cash flow to make the equipment payments last month. I think I can survive if I can hang on for three or four more months. I have found someone that I believe will sub-lease the mall location, and I think I can sell the equipment to a company in Houston. I will only have to discount it fifteen percent. To survive, I need about $7,000. The bank has refused me. I didn't know who else to turn to, Harvey, and that's why I'm here."

My feeling of disillusion and loneliness was still strong in me as I answered him. "Homer, you need seven thousand. I need seven thousand. Many people need seven thousand. Do you know how much money I have loaned to friends in the last year? Over $18,000."

Homer asked, "Have you been hurt?"

"What's that got to do with it?" I snapped back. "Did you know I just wrote to my girlfriend in Los Angeles? I gave her up. She wasn't the one. It is something about honor. It doesn't make sense. I don't know what I'm looking for. I think I'm living in a fantasy."

Homer had a puzzled look on his face. I realized he didn't know what I was talking about. I wasn't sure I did.

---

"Anyway, Homer, this time I've got to say no. I thought I had an obligation to anyone who asked me for help. Maybe I don't. Maybe I was misled. Anyway, no."

He looked at me for a long moment and then changed the subject. "I understand you are playing semi-pro baseball for the Spanish American League. I heard your team won the championship last year, and that you pitched a three-hitter."

"No," I said, "it was a five-hitter, but I did shut them out. I enjoy playing ball. I enjoy staying in shape. Are you staying in shape these days?" I did not like the conversation. That last remark was stupid; I could see he was not spending any time on his body. I felt I was toying with Homer and his whole future. He looked as uncomfortable as I felt.

"No," he said, "I really haven't had much time. Well, Harvey, thanks for seeing me." He reached out, took my hand and shook it, then turned and said, "I'll be seeing you."

He walked out and I was left there feeling empty. I could hardly believe what I had said to him, but worse, at this moment I did not understand myself. For despite the deep melancholy, I felt the power of my money. Homer's destiny had been within my power because of money. I could have helped him . . . and yet helping him seemed a contribution to an unrealistic dream.

Diane walked in and announced, "Your plane leaves in an hour. You'd better hurry." Then, with a knowing smile on her face, she added in a teasing tone, "By the way, Mr. Reese, you're an awful soft touch. How much did it cost you this time?"

"Not a penny," I said angrily. "And what the hell business is it of yours?" I got up and walked out, leaving her in shock.

On the flight to New Orleans, I was wishing I had not agreed to stay with Dale and Louise. Perhaps the real reason I had accepted their invitation was because Annette Dupont lived in the house next door, and she was the most beautiful girl I had ever met.

Annette's story was unusual. It seemed that two years earlier, when she was eighteen, her father came home one afternoon and told his wife he was departing for Europe on a one-way ticket. He explained that he had withdrawn $25,000 from their savings account, leaving a balance of $65,000 for their three children.

"I'm taking off this afternoon, and I want you to go with me," he said.

"What about the children?" his wife had asked. Annette's two brothers were fifteen and fourteen years old at the time.

"They're big enough to take care of themselves," Mr. Dupont answered incredibly. "You must make a choice — the children or me."

Dale learned later that the reason for this seemingly irrational proposal was that Dupont had just seriously wounded a man in a knife fight and he was fleeing from the police and from the other man's vengeance. Mrs. Dupont went into her bedroom, packed a bag, and wrote a note to Annette that read,

Your father and I have decided to go live a life of our own. You are eighteen years old. You will have to take care of yourself. Your brothers are old enough to be of help to you. Love, Mother.

Then Mr. and Mrs. Dupont walked out the door, and got into a waiting taxi, directing it to take them to the airport. And no one had heard of them since.

Dale and Louise, working through a judge who was a close friend, spent three months getting a court order which would allow Annette to draw money from the savings account for her and her brothers to live on. They found that the house was theirs, free and clear. This year, the older brother would graduate from high school and the younger boy would be a junior. Annette, through Dale's help, had found a secretarial job at a local bank. In effect, Dale and Louise had almost adopted the family.

Dale, a big, good-natured fellow, was a perfect match for Louise. She was short, a bit plump, but with a cute Irish face, a puckish sense of humor, and a kind heart. Both were in their middle thirties.

Annette was very immature and child-like when her parents left. With the help of Louise, she had matured rapidly and to good effect, making the transition from bobby socks to high heels, from pleated skirts to form-fitting sheaths which revealed her tall, good-looking figure. She had learned to wear her lush black hair in becoming styles and to use just enough make-up to enhance her natural beauty. Her face was perfect in every feature — more perfect than any of the stars in Hollywood. Annette was absolutely the most beautiful woman that I had ever seen. She was reserved and did not speak often, and this attribute gave her an air of sophistication which belied her innocence. Everywhere she went people stared at her.

A year ago, Louise had arranged my first date with Annette, and since then it had been understood that the four of us would go out together whenever I came into town. Only on rare occasions did Annette and I go out alone, and then I made it clear it was only as good friends.

But whether we were alone or with a crowd of people, she always seemed somehow to impart a sense of loneliness. This air — almost an attitude of alienation — did not seem to have anything to do with the departure of her mother and father. She identified with the loneliness that she sensed in me, and she talked about it and would ask me about my feelings to see if my loneliness matched her own. I told her I would someday find the one who would end my loneliness, that it was a promise given to me many years ago.

"If you find that I'm the girl, please let me know," she once said laughingly.

On that occasion I grabbed her, kissed her, and said with a chuckle, "Don't you tease me!"

She smiled and said, "But do let me know. I don't want to wait forever."


Dale Edwards met me at the gate at the New Orleans airport. He stepped forward with his hand stuck out and the warm, wide grin on his face that always made me feel so welcome. In his deep Louisiana drawl he said, "Annette told me this morning she's dying to see you. For a gal that generally plays it silent, that's a lot."

"Fantastic," I said, as I shook his hand. "How are Louise and the kids?"

He answered, "They are a wild bunch, but all of them are fine."

"Dale, I understand we are leaving tomorrow morning for Baton Rouge. If we cover Lafayette, Opelousas, and then down to Lake Charles, how many days will we be gone?"

"Three nights, but tonight we're going out and eat fancy.

Commander's Palace. Then we're going to the Lousiana Wholesale Brokers Annual Ball. Very formal. That's why I asked you to bring your tux. Three hundred dollars a couple. The money goes to charity. I want to see you romancing Annette a little bit, my boy, you hear?"

When we walked into the Edwards' home, Louise came from the kitchen hurriedly in her evening dress, followed by her four sons, ages seven, five, four, and two — a cute bunch of kids.

"So nice to see you again," she said. "We will be ready to go in thirty minutes. It's already seven thirty, and we don't want to be late. Dale, take Harvey up to his room. Let him freshen up and change into his tux. I'm going next door and help Annette."

Louise's cheerful enthusiasm and her natural courtesy made me happy to be there. I hurriedly changed and as I started down the stairs I saw Annette and Louise standing in the middle of the living room. Annette was a vision of loveliness, wearing a strapless white evening dress that hugged her body from the bust to the waist and then flared to the ground. Her jet-black hair was swept up in soft, crowning curls, making her pale shoulders appear exceptionally naked. She was wearing long earrings and her dark eyes were soft and glowing. Her full lips always had a slight taunting smile. My knees seemed to buckle. I felt like a high school kid on his first date.

I appreciated Dale's foresight in ordering corsages for our dates. At the foot of the stairs, he handed me a box for Annette — a beautiful yellow orchid that I nervously tried to pin to her gown. I had to ask Louise for help, and the two ladies giggled at my ineptness.

After a wonderful dinner at Commander's Palace, we went to the Roosevelt Hotel. As we walked into the Grand Ballroom, I realized that all eyes in the room were upon Annette. The big band had just finished playing "Moonlight Serenade." For a moment I felt self-conscious, but then a wave of pride took hold and I proudly escorted her to our table. An attractive middle-aged woman winked at me as we passed and I winked back.

Before I had taken my seat, the band started to play "Deep Purple." Annette took my hand and led me to the dance floor and melted into my arms. I was delighted at how well we danced together. My style was to glide smoothly and make quick graceful turns, holding my partner firmly around the waist, cheek to cheek. There wasn't a step or a spin I made that she wasn't with me in perfect unison. With the side of her forehead against the corner of my mouth, I was intoxicated with her perfume, her softness, her femininity. I would turn my lips slightly occasionally and give her a light kiss. Her response was to press closer to me and to squeeze my hand.

Dale and Louise looked very happy and very approving, as if our romance was of their making. I only danced with Louise one time. Annette and I danced for two hours. When we returned to our table at the beginning of an intermission, we found Dale's car keys and a note that simply said, "We've gone home in a taxi. Take the car. We will leave the front door unlocked for you."

Annette and I drove around New Orleans for an hour, with my arm around her, using my left hand to steer the car as I had ten years earlier when I was in high school. Her head was on my shoulder and the scent of her perfume flooded the car. We parked by the Mississippi River on this clear moonlit night, and the world stood still. Each deep breath aroused my passion. The night was endless and tomorrow did not exist.

I kissed her gently. She caught her breath, then leaned back and looked into my eyes.

"My darling," I asked, "are you all right?"

Her soft, dark eyes were half closed as she whispered, "Forever, I love you."

As I reached to put my arm around her, my hand accidentally rubbed against her bust. She took my hand and held it on her breast. With that soft, sleepy look still in her eyes, she smiled and for the first time I was aware of the passion within her. I slipped my hand around her body, pulled her toward me, and kissed her, this time more firmly than before. She pressed her breasts against me. Her breathing had become short and rapid, her mouth wet, soft, and seeking. I tried to pull back but she would not release me, so I accepted her emotion and kissed her hungrily and passionately. Yet I felt this kind of passion had no place on this night.

I gently but firmly pulled back a little. "My love, not tonight."

She smiled and said, "Whatever and whenever you say."

I was astounded at her words and actions. I had never known her to be forward. Now every action seemed suggestive, every kiss, every movement — holding my hand, the way she looked at me, her passion and desire — and yet neither vulgar nor insensitive. I was convinced that she had never acted like this with anyone else. It seemed as if she had discovered a mystery within herself, as if innocence was about to be shed, discarded willingly and without reservation . . . longing for love and commitment, with no evil intent, not ominously but rather a willing next step on the ladder of life.

On that night, Annette was not one girl . . . she was all girls, all my deepest desires. Her beauty overwhelmed me and caressed me and made it all into a dream. The memories of that night are jumbled between reality and fantasy. May it always remain so.

When I kissed her goodnight at the front door, her body melted against mine, pressing hard against me, her hips, her breasts . . . like on the dance floor. The hunger, the passion nearly overcame my determination. Our kisses seemed endless and forever.

Her mouth went past my lips and she whispered in my ear, "Want to come in? Please?"

I kissed her again and once more I had to fight my own body's response to her desire . . . her innocent desire, for I knew it was still untried and I must not take advantage of it.

"My darling, I must say goodnight. Until tomorrow."

She hesitated for a moment, then smiled, turned, and slipped through the door. I waited until I heard the door lock. As I turned away, I saw the moonlight filtering through the tall trees, flooding both front lawns. I walked very slowly across the grass. I wanted to capture that night in my heart, not in my conscious memory.

When I reached the edge of the Edwards' porch, I noticed a shadow to the left of the steps. It was Michael, Annette's seventeen-year-old brother.

"Sir," he demanded, "were you being honorable with my sister?"

He was holding an open knife in his right hand. I walked up to him, and said, "Michael, I could be no other way with your sister."

I took the knife from his hand, closed the blade into the handle, and handed it to him. "Never confront a man with a knife unless you intend to use it. You could get killed. Michael, I would never do anything to hurt your sister, but I'm proud of you. Don't stop protecting her. Tonight I kissed her, but I will do nothing to dishonor her."

I reached out, squeezed his shoulder, and said good night. Going up the stairs to my room, I felt a sudden anger toward young Michael. He had brought me back to earth. In doing so, he marred the magic of that night. Annette's eyes, her lips, her fragrance, the moonlight, the river had vanished for the moment.


On the fourth day, Dale and I were driving from Lake Charles back to New Orleans. The purchase orders and the business were even better than we had hoped for. Knowing that we would pass by the airport before entering New Orleans, I asked Dale to pull into the airport.

"I'll catch the next flight for Chicago," I said.

"You're leaving now?" Dale asked in surprise. "We haven't worked New Orleans yet."

"You can handle that."

"Harvey, what's wrong? You've hardly mentioned Annette for the last three days. When I bring her up, you change the subject. She is a wonderful girl. Nothing bad happened, did it? But whatever, I'll support you all the way. You know that."

"No, no. Nothing bad," I replied. "She is wonderful and beautiful. But there is something missing between us. It's probably my fault. She seems to be something beautiful and wonderful to hold and to kiss, but not to talk to. After I leave her, I feel like I have been to a movie, that it wasn't real. I don't know, Dale, it might be me. I'm going to fly to Chicago tonight and try to see a girl I met not long ago. She will probably think I'm crazy, but I have to find out more than I know now. For the last year or so, I have felt panic. I have a situation at home that I must resolve. I can hardly believe my quest would last this long."

"Your quest?" Dale asked.

"I'm sorry," I replied. "That's just an expression I use sometimes. You see, my mother and I . . . ." I hesitated, noticing Dale's confused expression. "Forgive me, Dale. I speak of things of long ago. Sorry. I know I'm not making sense. Just take me to the airport. I'm going to Chicago."

# Chapter 24

I arrived at Chicago's O'Hare Airport at nine that night. Hurrying through the lobby, I picked up my bag, caught a taxi, and headed for the Palmer House Hotel. I checked in and went straight to my room. After a quick shower and shave, I called the London House and asked for Joe, the maitre d'.

"Joe," I began, "the last time I was in your place, Mary Alice Sanders gave me her card with her home phone number, but I did not bring the card with me. Could you give me her number?"

"Mr. Reese," he replied, "Miss Sanders is here tonight." I felt a surge of excitement.

"Is she alone?" I asked hopefully.

"Yes, sir. We have a new jazz group tonight, the Eddie Gordon quartet. They are excellent, and she is here trying to book them. May I suggest that you hurry over. There is a party of four at your favorite booth who are just leaving. By the time you get here it will be available to you."

"Joe, can you tell me something about Mary Alice?"

"I'll be glad to discuss the matter when you arrive, but right now, Mr. Reese, we are quite busy and I must attend to my customers. Please hurry over. I will be waiting."

The hotel elevator was right across from my room. Going down, I felt like it was moving at a snail's pace. I almost ran across the lobby and up the long corridor that led to the front door where I jumped into the first taxi in the line and exclaimed to the driver, "Here's an extra five. Get me to the London House fast!"

At the restaurant Joe was waiting to greet me. "Mary Alice Sanders is in your booth," he said. "How's that for service?"

"Did you tell her that I was coming?"

"No. The booth was vacated and she took it without permission. Mary Alice can be most aggressive sometimes," he added with a tolerant smile. "You asked me about her. Let me tell you. Bob Sanders, her husband, was a most successful theatrical agent for a number of years. I'm not sure exactly what his final illness was. It has been a year, or maybe a year and a half since he died. About six months ago, Mary Alice announced that she was going to continue with his business. I know she has been working very hard. I don't know how successful she has been so far, but I think she'll make it. May I now take you to your table?"

I went to the booth and stood looking down at her as she concentrated on the band, oblivious of my presence. She was as attractive as I had remembered, and I was remembering, too, how we first met. Clearing my throat, I asked, "Do you mind if I sit here with you? I would like to be near the band."

She looked up and I think for a moment, in the subdued light of the restaurant, she didn't recognize me. Then with a twinkle in her eye, she picked up the game and said, "I would love to have company. Tell me, good-looking, how much do you charge?"

We both laughed. She slid over and I sat next to her.

"This time, will you join me for dinner?" I asked.

"I will be delighted."

Adam, our waiter, asked, "The usual, Mr. Reese? Steak Diane?"

"Yes. But this time, for two. Pick a bottle of champagne for us — a good bottle."

The conversation during dinner was delightful. It was interesting, intelligent, and I found Mary Alice could converse on any subject. We were delighted to learn we shared similar philosophies on most subjects. She smiled, laughed, and joked. Well into the second bottle of champagne, I reached over and held her hand. She looked straight into my eyes and squeezed my hand. It seemed as if we had known each other for many years.

She took a deep breath, sighed, and said, "I did not believe I would ever feel comfortable with anyone like this again."

The band had stopped playing. "What about making your contact with Mr. Gordon?"

"Oh, I did that before you arrived. I've already booked him."

"It's one o'clock. May I take you home?"

"I would be delighted to have you take me home, Cowboy," she said. "And I might add, I think I'm a little bit tipsy so please, dear sir, please do not take advantage of this poor defenseless girl."

I smiled, helped her out of the booth, and said, "Never, my love."

We walked the block to the parking garage where we found her car. I asked for her keys and she asked, "Do you intend to drive?"

I replied, "Yes. Always."

She hesitated, and then said, "Marvelous! Drive me home. I live in Evanston."

When we arrived, she invited me in to have a nightcap. Her house was small, just two bedrooms, but very stylish and furnished elegantly and expensively. As soon as we went in, she kicked off her shoes and said, "Come into the kitchen. I want you to help me."

In the kitchen she turned on the lights. I walked directly behind her, turned off the lights, reached for her arm, brought her toward me, and kissed her.

In a whisper she said, "You don't really want another drink, do you?"

"No."

She took me by the hand and led me back into the living room, stopped by a lighted lamp and turned it off, leaving only a small light glowing in the hallway. We walked to the sofa. She sat down and pulled me down beside her.

I must have kissed her for five minutes before she pushed away and said, "Hold up, Cowboy, hold up. I'm confused. I don't know what's happening."

"Listen, Mary Alice," I said. "I'm also confused. I seem to be on a merry-go-round, but it's possible that with you I can get off that merry-go-round. I feel — no, I believe — there's great hope that you might be someone I've been searching for. It's been a long time . . . you might be . . ." I was almost babbling in my effort to sort out my thoughts and explain them to her. She stopped me by planting her lips on mine again. The kiss seemed endless and passionate.

But finally she pushed me away and stood up. "Cowboy, I want you to go. I'm confused. I want to think about this. When I lost my husband, I thought that was it. I did not believe I would ever fall in love again. I'm not saying I love you. I'm saying I'm mixed up. You make me want you in so many different ways. I wish you would leave now, but will you come back tomorrow?"

"No, I cannot tomorrow. I've got to go back to Texas. I made a commitment. I'm on a baseball team and in two weeks we're playing for the championship." She was looking at me like I was crazy. "I've got to work on my conditioning. It's not fair to the rest of the team."

Still puzzled, she asked, "Are you a professional baseball player?"

"No," I said with a laugh. "I'm a businessman. I distribute products on a national scale, a good-sized operation here in Chicago, in fact. Baseball is just a sport that I love. Right now, here with you, it seems unimportant, but the game is just two weeks away and I am the starting pitcher. I can't let my teammates down. Look, at the end of next week, I'll come back and be with you for a couple of days. Please tell me we've got a date. I'll fly in Saturday morning and be here by noon. Let's see . . . today's Friday — that will give me about seven days. I'll spend two days with you next weekend, then go back, and with one more week I should be ready."

Her expression had been changing as she understood my dilemma. "Sounds marvelous," she said. "I need a week to think." She took my hand, led me to the door, and gave me her car keys. "Take my car. Leave it in the parking garage, that same one, and I'll pick it up tomorrow. My neighbor will give me a ride to town."

At the front door, I kissed her again, pressing my body against hers. She gently pushed me away, patting my cheek affectionately, and went back inside. I was most conscious of the big smile on my face. As I walked to the car, I suddenly had the urge to jump and yell Wahoo! I thought to myself, maybe I have found her after all. Mary Alice. What a beautiful name. There ought to be a song about Mary Alice. Maybe there is.


By the time I got back to the garage it was 2:30 in the morning. The parking garage was multi-level and at this hour seemed completely deserted. There was plenty of room to park Mary Alice's car on the first level, but since we had picked it up on the third, I wanted to leave it exactly where it had been so she would have no trouble finding it.

I turned the sharp curve leading up to the third level and saw a man staggering down the ramp hanging onto the rail. As I came alongside him, he looked up and I could see that he was badly beaten. His face was covered with blood, the sleeve of his suit was torn, and one of his trouser legs was ripped, exposing a bloody knee. I slowed down almost to a crawl as I came even with him. He looked up but didn't say a word, took two more steps, and fell.

I stopped and lowered the window and asked, "Can I help you in any way?"

"No," he replied. "Leave me alone. Besides, they might still be about."

I drove on up the ramp to the third level and parked Mary Alice's car in the space where we had picked it up. Getting out, I opened the trunk and took out the jack handle, then put the keys on the floor of the car, locked it, and hurried down the ramp to the second level. The injured man was still on his knees, trying vainly to stand up. I put my hand around his waist and my head under his arm and brought him to his feet.

He said, "There are some men hereabouts that ran off when you drove up. They will probably return and you will be involved. Please leave me and go away."

"They won't have an easy time of it," I replied, and showed him the tire tool.

I almost had to carry him to the street level, but he was a small man and it was not too difficult. Once on the street, a taxi appeared and I hailed it and helped him in.

"Get out of here fast," I told the cabbie. As we sped off, I looked back through the rear window and saw two men emerging from the garage, watching us depart. "Take us to the nearest police station," I said.

"No, no!" protested the man. "Please, just take me home," he told the driver. "The Woodway Apartments on Manchester Street. It's only about fifteen minutes away." Then he turned to me and almost in a whisper he said, "I know those men, and I deserve what I got. But the worst thing that can happen is publicity."

"If you know them and you don't go to the police, they will do it again," I said.

"Please, let me explain." He took a deep breath and, hanging his head in an attitude of complete defeat, he told me, "I'm a priest."

"What!" I exclaimed.

"Yes, a priest. And I owe some gambling debts. I made promises I could not keep."

"But then why aren't we taking you to a church?"

"I have an apartment. If you take me there, I will try to explain."

The Woodway Apartments were shabby and dirty. His apartment consisted of a small sitting room with connecting kitchen and an even smaller bedroom. I had to help him take his coat off. His assailants had twisted his left arm and the shoulder was sprained. With alcohol and cotton, I cleaned the gaping wound on his forehead and an abrasion on his cheekbone. Both knees were skinned badly. They had evidently slung him to the ground. He was a small man, five foot six, I estimated, with clean-cut features, slick black hair that he combed straight back, and deep-set brown eyes that stared when he spoke. His age, I later learned, was thirty-one.

"My name is Sullivan," he began, "and I have only been a priest for two years. Before I went into the seminary, I gambled considerably. I was not aware that I had a problem and there is no way to tell an Irishman that gambling is wrong. I thought I could conquer the obsession. But after I became a priest, I had many hours to myself. I tried to pray and meditate and somehow master the boredom and despair that I felt but I could not, and I started to gamble again. I would borrow money from my fellow priests, and I asked for money from my family who could ill afford to give it to me and had already been more than generous. I spoke to the Bishop and he urged me to take a leave of absence for six months in an effort to find myself and master the problem. That's what I'm supposed to be doing now, but instead, for two months I have gambled more and become indebted to some professionals. After many unsuccessful efforts to collect from me, tonight they picked me up at the corner and took me to that parking garage, not expecting to be interrupted. I don't know how far they would have gone if you had not come by. Perhaps they would have ended my misery by killing me."

Father Sullivan put his head in his hands, and his attitude was so abject and pathetic that I thought his tale must be over, but there was more.

"And now," he went on, "for the past month a woman lives with me. She is a good woman who could not find work and had no place to live. She tried to be a prostitute but it revolted her. She cares for me and I for her. I believe I am not worthy to be a priest again. But I am so miserable that I wish I could die."

He spoke with such remorse that he touched me. And then suddenly he looked straight at me and demanded, "What should I do? What can I do? You are the first person I have told, other than the Bishop. You must help me. Tell me what to do."

I was stunned, for up to that moment I fear I had been judging him and possibly condemning him. Now somehow he made the problem mine. I had an impulse to turn and just leave the room — but I could not.

He was sitting on a wooden stool at a small breakfast table, and I was standing over him dressing his wounds when he asked me to help him. I sat down facing him directly and without hesitation said to him, "All right, I'm going to tell you exactly what you must do." But I must confess that I did not really know what I was about to say. "First I must ask, do you still wish to be a priest?"

"More than anything in the world," he answered.

"Think now. Are you completely sure that you want to continue to be a priest?" I insisted.

"My heart and soul hunger to be of service to God, but my body and my mind fail me so."

Suddenly the door opened and a swarthy woman entered. I thought she might be a gypsy because of her dress. She must have been thirty-five or so, tall and rather attractive. She looked at me and then looked at him.

*"Quien es?"* she asked him. ("Who is this?")

*"Este hombre es amigo,"* ("A friend") Father Sullivan assured her.

At first she showed slight fear, presuming that I had inflicted the priest's injuries. But then realizing this was not so, she went to the other end of the small room and sat looking at us.

I asked him, "About the woman, do you have to keep her? How great are your desires?"

"No, I can do without her, I promise you, but I don't want to hurt her."

"May I speak to her?" I asked. He nodded.

I walked over to the woman and said in Spanish, "It is better if you are not with this priest. It is not good for you nor for him."

She shook her head and said, "We don't do things, he only screwed me one time, and then only because I asked him many times. But he will not do it no more. He is not my lover. If I had two hundred dollars, I would go back to Cuba."

Without hesitation, I took two hundred and fifty dollars out of my pocket and handed it to her. She stood and picked up a small bag in the corner. Going to a chest of drawers, she took the contents of the center drawer, put them in her case, and went over to the priest. Kneeling in front of him, she asked, "Padre, would you bless me?"

He made the sign of the cross over her head and then gently placed his hand on her head for a moment. She got up, went to the door, and left.

I went back to my chair and saw that the priest was staring at me in amazement. I spoke to him then, slowly and deliberately, and the words just came . . . they flowed without hesitation and with conviction, and I listened to my voice as surprised as he.

"Most men never have an opportunity to serve their fellow man. You do. Do not throw it away." And I said to him the very words my mother had said to me. I told him the world has music for those who listen. I spoke of honor, and the search for truth, and integrity . . . to reject no one, and to unfurl his wings and begin his voyage through the infinite worlds of God . . . a search for good among so much bad. "You will find God's love waiting," I told him.

Suddenly a bridge was there for us, and we were now brothers who loved one another. We embraced, and since that day the moment has remained a precious memory for me, for I felt this was what my mother had wanted me to do, and her very words had helped me to help this man find his way. New hope had also returned for me. My mother's words, the promise, the quest — and now Mary Alice, who seemed so lovely, pure, and chaste.

The next day, I went with Father Sullivan to a bar on the southside and paid his bookie $1,200. Then I had the taxi drive us to his parish. He got out and stood on the sidewalk with his small bag at his side, looking into my eyes. Not a word was spoken. None was needed. As we drove away, he raised his hand and blessed me.

# Chapter 25

Back in San Antonio, I spent the next week going to the office every morning and working out with the team each afternoon, but I was not very happy with my progress. It seemed to me that I did not have as much strength as I had the year before.

After each workout, I would go into the locker room and just sit there, exhausted. Teammates kept asking me, "Are you okay?"

Not wanting to shake their confidence, I usually answered, "Don't worry. I'll be ready."

I confided in no one except Charley Kirk, our trainer. When I described my feelings of weakness and exhaustion, he said, "You're just not in shape. You'll be ready for the game. Don't worry about it."

I was not convinced.

On Saturday I landed in Chicago at noon, rented a car, and went directly to Mary Alice's house. When she opened the door, I was surprised to find her in a robe, her auburn hair hanging long and loose about her shoulders.

"I worked last night, up very late," she explained. "Have you eaten? I'm fixing breakfast."

"As a matter of fact, all I've had is a cup of coffee."

"Good. I'll make us a great breakfast. My personal pancakes, sausage from a very special delicatessen — nothing like it — and eggs with a cream sauce you won't believe." As she spoke, I watched her closely. She seemed so beautiful to me.

"May I kiss you?" I asked.

She walked toward me. "You certainly may," she said, and wrapped her arms around my neck. It was a long, delicious kiss.

She broke off and said, "Come into the kitchen. I don't want my sausage to burn."

During breakfast, she kept up a constant chatter, with the enthusiasm I had come to think of as typical of her. She explained how she was beginning to succeed as a booking agent, despite the warnings of her friends that a woman would never be able to make it.

Suddenly she stopped and reached toward me, putting her hand against my cheek, and asked, "Darling, do you feel bad? You look tired."

"Yes," I said. "That's the word. I feel a bit tired, sometimes exhausted. I guess I've been working too hard. I'll be all right. Let's finish breakfast. I have a lot to say to you."

After breakfast, she ordered, "Go into the bedroom. I want you to lie down. I'll be there in a few minutes. I want to lie next to you."

I showed my surprise at the remark. She added, "Nothing like that. I just want to lie down next to you and kiss you. Okay?"

I took off my shoes and my jacket and lay on the bed on top of the covers. It felt good to stretch out. I must have fallen asleep because I wasn't aware when Mary Alice came to lie beside me. When I opened my eyes she was there, still wearing her robe. I drew her next to me and kissed her. Then over and over again I would draw back from her for a moment and look at her face, she would open her eyes and her smile was as much from those beautiful eyes as from her lips; then I would kiss her again, each time for a little longer.

At last she put her fingers on my lips and said, "Let's talk. I want to talk, please."

"Okay." I lay on my side, watching the wonderful way her mouth moved as she formed her words.

"The last time we were together, you said that I might be 'the one.' I don't know exactly what you meant, and I want you to tell me. But first, let me tell you that I believe you are that special one for me. Am I the same for you? Is that what you meant?"

I said, "A wonderful lady told me that I would know when I discovered the special person who would be like no one else in the world for me. I would know by a touch or by a kiss. Since the day I met you, you have given me new hope. Something happened in New Orleans that made me want to rush to you."

She stopped me and asked again, "Am I the one you are looking for?"

"I'm not sure," I replied. "That's why I had to hurry here — to be with you and hopefully . . ."

She interrupted and said, "Well, I do think I'm the one, but I'm afraid you might not know it. I want to tell you what I think, how I feel about you, and how we can enjoy our love together. First, let me tell you I am terribly in love with you, and that is something of a miracle to me. But I am not like other people, and I don't want to be like other people. I don't believe life should be dull; rather, it should be lived in complete freedom and without shame. I would always want you to feel free. I want our love to be strong, so that nothing can disturb it or harm it or affect it. I want to feel free to go out with other men if I choose and for you to feel free to date other women if you want. It won't bother me."

Her statement made me sit up immediately, and a kind of chill began to come over my body, but she didn't seem to notice and continued. "Joe tells me that you are married."

"Yes," I answered. "It will take me some time, but that will change."

"Fine, when you do. That's okay. In the meantime, it just doesn't matter. I have my career here in Chicago and you have yours in Texas. When time permits, I will come visit you in Texas, and when you have free time, you come to me. I want to be with you as much as possible, but if I'm lonesome and we're not together, I want the freedom to go out with other men if I have a need. There will be no inhibitions and no guilt in our relationship."

"Hold up!" I said. "Hold up a moment. Let me stop you. I

can't believe what I am hearing. You wouldn't care if I went to bed with another woman?"

"It might bother me slightly, but I think I can handle it."

"Well, I couldn't handle it! If you were mine, I wouldn't stand for it for a minute. And there is the question of honor. I couldn't live with myself."

"Are you a moralist?" she asked.

"What the hell does that mean?" I returned angrily. "We're not talking about titles. We're talking about dignity. We're talking about allowing the human spirit to live with honor and integrity."

As I spoke to her, I found I was striking my breast with my own fist.

"You can talk this way?" she asked, a bit sarcastically. "You, that are married?"

I stood and said, "I could have explained that to you. It was something that happened a long time ago, a situation in which I felt I had no choice. This is another matter, in which I do have a choice. I must leave."

I slipped into my loafers, grabbed my coat, and started toward the bedroom door. I heard her say, "Harvey, just a minute, please. Please, don't open the door."

I waited a moment, then I turned and she was standing beside the bed, her robe dropped to the floor around her feet. She stood completely nude, with her arms reaching toward me.

Again she said, with a voice full of pleading, "Harvey, please."

I walked back and stood in front of her. She took my right hand and placed it on her left breast. I slid my left arm around her waist and kissed her. Her body pressed against me. For a moment, nothing mattered. But then her words, her proposition, returned to me. I stiffened and drew back. I reached down and picked up her robe and placed it around her shoulders. The robe hung open, still revealing her lovely body.

"I wish you well. The best, always," I said. I turned and headed toward the front door.

She followed. At the door she touched my shoulder and said, "I'm in love with you. Are you really going to leave?"

"Yes," I said. "Thanks for breakfast." I leaned forward, gave her a light kiss, and went out the door to the rented car waiting at the curb.

I heard her say faintly, "Cowboy, I hope you find what you're looking for."

As I drove to O'Hare, the disillusionment I had felt when I spoke to Homer Smith returned to me. But now a more profound sadness was present. With my teeth clenched, I said to myself, you have been living in a dream world. Wake up. Face realities!

The following week I trained hard on Monday, Tuesday, and Wednesday. Each day I ran four laps, threw a hundred pitches — fast balls, as hard as I could — and then twenty-five change-ups and ten or fifteen sliders. Each day, when I first started throwing, the first thirty pitches had good speed and good control, but then the feeling of exhaustion began to affect my speed and my control and they would get progressively worse. After the workouts, I would go into the locker room and Charley Kirk would give me a rubdown.

Thursday morning, I was at my desk dictating letters when Diane interrupted me, saying that the Reverend Neely was waiting to see me. Reverend Neely was a black minister who had a very small congregation and a little wooden church in a depressed black area. About once a month he would come to see me at my office. He would only stay a couple of minutes, just long enough for me to give him twenty or thirty dollars — whatever small bills I had in my pocket. He would bless me and leave.

I asked Diane to show him in.

"What can I do for you, Reverend?" I asked.

"Well, Mr. Harvey, as you know, we're struggling. We're helping many folks and we pray for you all the time. Just wondering if you could help me the way you always do?"

A kind of suppressed rage flooded my mind. Here it was again. The obligation. The demands. All the claims people made on me while my own dreams escaped me. I shook my head, as much to clear it and try to speak calmly as to tell him no.

"Sorry, Reverend, not today. Can't help you today."

The look on his face was that of disbelief. He knew he could always count on me.

"But, Mr. Harvey . . ."

"Look, Reverend," I interrupted. "Why me? Why not the guy

down the street? Why not your own congregation? *They* are supposed to support your church, not strangers. Why don't you get them to give more? Why have you made me your sucker?"

The minister stood as erect as he could, with as much dignity as he could muster, and said, "Mr. Harvey, you are not a stranger to me. My flock are poor, but they are good folk, and I wouldn't make you a sucker. I'd pray the Lord would strike me dead first. If you do not want me to come here any more, I will not. But I will always pray for you."

Diane was standing at the door during our conversation, and when he walked out, she said to me, "What's happened to you? I don't understand."

"Nothing's happened. Am I different from other men?"

She shook her head sadly. "I guess you're not . . . but I thought you were."

After she left, I sat in my chair, trying to justify my act — trying to convince myself that I had been living in an idealized world, that life was not just one big noble act, and that I must struggle and fight to live with the realities of life.

With that thought I felt my body shudder.


The game was scheduled for Saturday. I decided that on Thursday and Friday I should only work out lightly in an effort to stay loose and relaxed and conserve my strength. On Thursday, when Charley came in for my rubdown he said that Edgar Bostich, the sportswriter, wanted to talk to me.

As soon as I trotted out on the field, Bostich walked over to me and introduced himself. "I saw you pitch last year. I thought you pitched good enough to be in any league. Your fast ball and your control were amazing. If you pitch that good on Saturday, I'm going to write a feature story on you — the businessman that could have been a big leaguer."

I laughed and said, "You sure anybody cares?"

"If I write it, they will. Give it all ya' got. I'll be behind home plate."

Saturday we were established as the home team, so we were the first to take the field. I took my warm-up pitches and noticed that the stands were full. I loved the excitement of a big game, and as usual I had butterflies until the first pitch. I saw Bostich sitting behind the screen, directly behind home plate. He waved at me.

In the first inning, I had good speed and good control — struck out one man and the other two hit ground balls to short. It was an easy inning for me. In the second inning, I walked two men, struck out one, gave up a hit that brought in a run. The third inning was a disaster. I had lost my fast ball. I had no control. Gave up three runs, and when I left the game, the bases were loaded. I felt completely spent.

I went directly to the locker room and fell onto the rubdown table. I thought I was alone, but then I discovered that Bostich had followed me in. He stood next to the table and said, "I thought I ought to tell you. No one else might. I think you are sick. No one can lose as much as you did from one year to another unless something is wrong. How do you feel?"

"Exhausted! I'm sore all over," I replied.

"How long have you felt like that?" he asked.

"For about two weeks, but not as bad as this. I really don't understand it."

"Listen," he continued, "you better get yourself to a doctor. I guess I won't write that story. A pity."


That night in my sleep I must have had a high fever. When I woke in the morning the sheets were wet. My body felt clammy. It was a struggle to sit up on the edge of the bed. It was even more of a struggle to dress and get to the car. I knew I needed help.

The drive to my doctor's office was almost impossible. It was a strain to turn the wheel or to press the brakes. The parking lot attendant had to help me out of the car and into Dr. Heath's office, then the doctor had to help me into one of his consulting rooms and onto the examination table. He asked me to lift my left leg. I could not. He asked me to lift my head. I could not.

Without emotion, he said, "I think you have poliomyelitis . . ." Polio! I remembered vaguely that only two days ago Jerry Pizzini, my neighbor, had called to tell me his small son, Bobby, was in Santa Rosa Hospital with polio. There was a lot of it around that year. The papers in big towns ran box scores on the front page counting new cases. But I thought it had nothing to do with me.

# PART 5

# The
# Dream

# Chapter 26

O n the third day, still in isolation in my iron lung, I was aware of a nurse coming in to take my temperature. She leaned over and whispered in my ear, "Don't give up. Fight hard, you can make it," and quickly left. And although delirious to the point of madness, I recall vividly the thoughts and fantasies that emerged from the mysterious recesses of my mind: my mother, my father, my wonderful uncles, Jonathan and Jesse; Roscoe; my girlfriends, Joyce, Mary Alice, and beautiful Annette; Mrs. Martin; my good friend Frank Montez; and my army buddies Mark Evans and Michael Pruske.

And my brother Paul. Twice in my delirium he saved my life. In both fantasies we were children. Once he pulled me out of a whirlpool in a Hill Country river that would have taken me under. Another time he stood between me and a wall of fire that was trying to fall upon me. These incidents had never occurred, but it was clear that my brother loved me and would have risked his life for me.

Uncle Jonathan's cowhands, Wade, Jeff, Joe, and especially

Juan Delgado . . . my delirium included Dr. Montemayor and his cousin, Ernesto Martinez, the great matador, and his magnificent wife. In one incident, I jumped in and saved the matador from being killed. Paco, Conchita, and I found El Rio de los Santos and we lived there happily the rest of our days in peace amid great beauty.

To this day, I remember every thought during that mysterious period. But especially, there was my mother. She would come and go and then return again whenever one of the others would leave my thoughts, speaking to me softly and gently about honor and my quest, reassuring me that my love — my fellow traveler through time — would be discovered.

"You are different," she said. "But to be different, you must *know* that you are different. Man is a traveler, a voyager. He takes but one voyage through life. The world is your vehicle. Space is your route, your journey. It is important that your conscious mind knows that you are searching.

"There must be a quest. Without a quest, there is no journey. Only the searcher is a voyager, and if the searcher's quest is lofty, pure, and honorable, then life will not be base, nor a waste. It will be worthy of man, and the world will be beautiful. There is beauty and music in the world for those who listen."

During the night of the third day, she spoke to me again, and reminded me that Don Quixote found his Dulcinea. She told me not to lose heart, but rather pick up the gauntlet and accept the challenges that life offers.

"Have patience," she told me. "Your deadliest foes are within you — fear, vanity, and the loss of faith. Kill them! Do not let them dwell therein. Be someone special, courageous, and sincere."

On that night, I looked at the past, and the past looked at me . . . and I had resumed my quest.


When I awoke on the fourth day, I actually felt good. The good feeling was soon overshadowed by a slight panic when I realized that I was in a very particular prison. Not in a room eight by ten, as a convict, but in a round drum that endlessly pumped air and exhaled air. Only my head stuck out, sealed off at the neck.

I called out, but no one answered. Finally a nurse came — and had to stand at my side so that I could see her. This was the only way to speak face to face with anyone. I could also see behind me through the mirror that was attached to my iron lung at a forty-five degree angle above my head. I must lie flat. I could not turn my body to the left nor to the right, only my head. There were openings on the side of the iron lung, covered with rubber and with slits for the nurses to reach in to help with my needs. The Man in the Iron Mask, I thought, but worse. He could at least walk about. There was no way for me to know whether I had been sentenced for life.

The nurse asked if I wanted a drink and added, "Great hope for you. Your fever lasted for three and a half days. It is difficult to tell how much damage the fever has done to your nervous system, but some people have fever for four, five, or even six days, and many of them die. Don't give up hope. I think you are fortunate. And besides, we have Colonel James Shield on the staff here at Brooke General and he's one of the best men in this field. Now that your fever is gone, the Colonel will be coming in to see you."

At one o'clock, Colonel Shields, followed by four other doctors and two nurses, came in and greeted me. "Well, young man, you've had a go of it! But it looks like you are going to make it." He put his hands through the side slits and I felt them move on my body. "Now I'm pressing on your abdomen. Try to breathe against the pressure of my hand . . . Go ahead, breathe one more time . . . Good. There seemed to be slight movement . . . Let's see if we can wean you from this iron lung.

"Now, move your left leg . . . Well, that one lacks response." His hands were moving over my body, checking my responses and diagnosing the damage caused by the disease. "Your left arm seems very weak. Don't know how bad yet. You seem to have damage all over your body. Let's not worry about that now. Let's worry about getting you out of the iron lung first."

As he spoke, my hopes rose. At that moment, the only thing I cared about was trying to get out of my prison.

The next day I was rolled to another ward and my machine had to be disconnected from the electrical outlet for the transfer, and I found myself fighting for breath. The move was made as fast as possible, and as soon as I arrived at the new location my iron lung was plugged in. It was a wonderful relief to feel it resume the job of breathing for me.

My new quarters held three other iron lungs, two women across the room and a young GI a few feet from my new station. As the moving crew departed, an orderly appeared beside me.

"I am James Craig — Sergeant James Craig," he said. "I'm in charge here, and I'll be taking care of you." He was a tall, good-looking black man of about thirty-five. "They tell me that we might work you out of this lung." He gave me a big smile and seemed to exude a kind of strength and confidence which I sorely needed right then. "I've gotten many out."

In a quiet voice I asked, "How bad is the fellow next to me?"

Sergeant Craig leaned over with his mouth close to my ear. "Young Jack Dwyer. I'm afraid he'll never get out. Both his diaphragms are completely paralyzed."

"How about me? Level with me, please," I asked.

"Look, I'm not kidding you. Let me show you." He unlocked the iron lung and slid out the bed on which I was lying. He pulled me out about three feet. I was immediately apprehensive. It is impossible to truly describe to someone else how fast you can become dependent on breathing assistance of this kind. You are quickly convinced you will not be able to breathe on your own at all, and a unique kind of terror overwhelms you.

Craig saw my apprehension, leaned over my face, and said, "Now, Reese. Very calmly, breathe, slowly."

I did, and I learned that I could. Although I was struggling, joy overwhelmed me. I was doing it on my own.

"See! I told you," he said, with a big smile on his face. "Now let's keep you out for three minutes."

After two minutes, I asked him to please put me back, that I was becoming exhausted. He agreed, and slipped me back into the iron lung. When I was back in its security, I said, "Thank you. Thank you very very much." And added, "How does one scratch his nose?"

Smiling, he replied, "You ask Craig. He will scratch it for you."

He was still talking in a low tone as he began to tell me about Jack Dwyer, my wardmate. "Jack's a great kid. Only nineteen years old. He's from Minnesota. Been in the lung for five weeks, so

215

he's gotten used to it. He's a big cut-up. You're going to enjoy him. A great sense of humor. I love that kid. I love him very much. He has deep religious convictions. He will surprise you. Let me introduce you."

He turned toward the other lung and raised his voice. "Jack, this is Reese. He's a civilian but he's a vet — did his time in W.W. Two. You all should get acquainted." And having performed the introductions, Craig left us for a while.

Jack's iron lung was parallel to mine and our heads were side by side, eight feet apart. We turned to look at each other. He said, "Hi, Reese. How are you feeling?"

"Not bad, considering," I replied.

"I saw Craig pull you out of the lung," he said. "You did great. I haven't been able to do that yet, but I'm still hopeful. How bad did it hit you in other places?" he asked.

"I'm not sure," I answered. "I seem to be able to move my hands and my right arm somewhat. I can move both of my feet a little, but I can't move my left leg at all. How 'bout you, Jack?"

"Hell, man. You're lucky," he said. "I haven't been able to move anything from my neck down. But they told me not to give up, and I'm not. I'm going to work hard."

"Work hard?" I asked.

"Yeah, with the physical therapists. They are special trained nurses that reach in through the openings on the side of the iron lung and work your hands and legs, and try to bring back your muscles. They're great. They work with you for two hours in the morning and two more in the afternoon. You'll have a particular nurse assigned to be your therapist. They've already been here today."

He seemed suddenly tired, perhaps from talking so much. Now he added more slowly, "What time is it?"

"I don't know," I said. "Where do you find out?"

"The clock is to our left, over the door. Since they moved you in, your lung blocks my view. Can you see it?"

"Five thirty," I said.

"Good. They'll be bringing our dinner soon." He was quiet, and I listened to a couple of mechanical whooshes before he went on. "I'm not on solid food yet. Mostly liquids. But they make great soups and they've got all kinds of juices. Have they given you any solid food yet?" he asked.

"I don't think I've eaten anything in four days," I said.

"Oh, yeah, that's right. If you've just come out of isolation, you would not have eaten. Bet you're starving," he laughed. I could not believe he could joke, considering the situation. I admired his spunk.

Sergeant Craig came back and told us, "Supper's coming. But first, Reese, let me introduce you to the two ladies across the hall." He raised his voice so they could hear him. "The lady over there is Mrs. Starkey. Her husband is a colonel, so you have to be properly respectful. Our other lady is Corporal Julie McMahan. I think she will be graduating very soon. She's already staying out of the iron lung all night now — she sleeps on that bed next to it."

Julie said, "Hi," looking up into her mirror to find me.

I said, "Nice to know you ladies."

Mrs. Starkey merely blinked her eyes twice. Later that night when the others were asleep, Sergeant Craig explained that Mrs. Starkey had spinal meningitis and was paralyzed from the neck down. She had been in the iron lung for over a month and just this morning they had detected pneumonia in her right lung. Every few minutes she would make an effort to cough, very feebly and faintly. Nurses were checking her every fifteen minutes.

My supper consisted of liquids, and everything was sucked through a straw — soups and juices and even melted Jello. Lights-out came early. I slept fairly well, but was awakened a number of times by Mrs. Starkey's vain effort to cough. The nurses kept coming in with flashlights every few minutes to check her. Finally, about three in the morning, the endless pumping of my iron lung put me to sleep.

At six o'clock I was awakened by the activity around Mrs. Starkey's iron lung. Then abruptly all the activity stopped, and I could hear Julie McMahan's sobbing. I turned toward Jack. His eyes filled with tears as he said, "Mrs. Starkey died." In a few more minutes they wheeled her iron lung out of the room.

I was convinced that this day would be solemn and sad, but after breakfast I was surprised at the busy bustle that started when the physical therapists arrived. Jack and Julie were attended by their usual therapists.

A slightly stout, hippy, large-busted, tanned, smiling nurse came up to me and said, "I'm Lieutenant Kovac. I will be your therapist for the rest of your stay here at Brooke General." She was a handsome woman in her mid-twenties, and although stout she had a very small waist and a thoroughly feminine manner. She patted me on the cheek and said, "Okay, let's get started."

She reached into my iron lung, grabbed my hand, and said, "Squeeze," which I did, though it was embarrassingly feeble. "Well," she said, "that's a beginning. Now let me check your legs and your abdomen."

She removed the only cover that I had inside the lung, which was just a small towel. I immediately said, "Do you mind if I stay covered?"

She withdrew her arms and stepped up closer to my head and said, "We're not going to let modesty stand between us, are we? Look, Reese, you need a lot of help. We don't know how bad your muscle condition is at this point. Whatever muscles have been spared, you'd better let me work them, including your cheeks that you lie on. Every muscle counts. I'm a good therapist. I think I can evaluate what you have left and make the most of it. So come on, sweetheart, be a dear and let me work with you. Forget that I'm a woman, although I can't promise that I want to forget you are a man. Let me do my job and help you get the hell out of here. Okay?"

"Okay," I responded. "And by the way," I added, "I think I'm in love with you." We both laughed.

Her visits the rest of the time I was at Brooke were the highlights of my day. She was wonderful. She made me feel — even in that condition — a bit macho . . . always congratulating me heartily when a new muscle responded, no matter how weak. Colonel Shields told me that Lieutenant Kovac was by far the best physical therapist on their staff.

Later that day there was excitement in our ward when we learned that Julie McMahan was graduating and going downstairs to the women's physical therapy ward, leaving her iron lung behind. All the nurses, doctors, and wardmen were on hand as we bid farewell to Julie. Staff and patients alike were thrilled to share in her progress as she made this big step toward recovery.

Now it was just Jack and me in the ward.

Paul, Sandra, and other members of my family were allowed to see me the following day, but only for short periods, and they were told that it would be best to keep future visits short and far apart. When they objected, I agreed with the doctors, explaining that I had a job to do and it would be better if I concentrated on my recovery and nothing else.

I asked permission for visits with Manuel and Diane. Aware that I had business responsibilities, the chief nurse approved. I told my two faithful employees what I expected from them during my absence, and they both said they could handle it.

For the next week the routine was always the same — breakfast, lunch, and dinner on a precise schedule, and the physical therapist appearing promptly at her time. By the end of the week, I was able to stay out of the iron lung for as long as two hours.

Jack and I had become good friends. It was the football season, and he was cheering for the University of Minnesota, a team that was not doing very well. He explained that the following Saturday, Minnesota would play Michigan for The Little Brown Jug, and he was hoping for a big upset — that did not occur. When I joked about it, I realized that he had taken it very seriously and was depressed. I did my best to cheer him up, as did Sergeant Craig. By this time, it was apparent to me that Sergeant Craig really did have a special affection for Jack.

When Craig was on duty he insisted on feeding us, instead of leaving it to the regular wardmen. He would feed Jack first, while I waited patiently. Then he would come and feed me. One evening during dinner, he asked if I expected any visitors that evening. I said, "No, not that I know of."

He explained that for the last two days there had been a tough-looking character hanging around the courtyard below. "When the MPs questioned him, he said he was a friend of yours and was trying to see you, but since he wasn't a relative, they wouldn't let him in."

I asked Craig if he knew his name. He said, "No. Every time he was questioned, he would saunter off, grumbling."

"What does he look like?" I asked.

"A mean-looking bastard, with a scar on the corner of his right eye."

I had never felt such helplessness before. "Craig," I whispered, "he is my deadly enemy, and here I am, unable to defend myself. This man has already tried to kill me twice."

Craig had been watching me very intently. He said, "I believe you. When I described him your face went white. Look, Reese, he always comes here late in the afternoon. He won't get to you, I promise you. If he comes here tomorrow, I'm going downstairs and confront him. I don't want you to worry about it. You can't do anything about it now. You leave it to Craig. What's his name?"

"Roscoe Rafferty." Craig's words reassured me somewhat, but I still felt insecure. There were times when Jack and I were in the ward alone. What could I do if Roscoe Rafferty entered while we were alone?


That evening during supper, Jack and I talked about football, mostly about his Minnesota team. An hour after supper a heavy rain began to beat against the windows. Craig came in and said, "I'm tucking you guys in. I want you to go to sleep now."

After Craig left and the lights were out, Jack's voice came in the dark with a kind of urgency I had not heard from him before. "Are you afraid?" he asked.

"Of what?"

"The rain."

"No. I love to sleep in the rain, especially during a thunderstorm like we're having."

"But Reese," he said. "Have you thought about the possibilities during a thunderstorm?"

"What possibilities?"

"The electricity can go out. We can lose all power, and if that happens, our iron lungs stop working."

I had to confess the thought had never entered my mind. "These iron lungs are designed to be pumped manually, aren't they?" I asked.

"That's right," replied Jack. "But when the power goes out, there's a lot of other emergencies in the hospital."

"I'm sure that Craig would come right in," I said, trying to reassure him — and perhaps myself as well.

"I hope so, Harvey, but it panics me. It might take only a minute and a half for me to die."

I realized that Jack could not sleep. I slept sporadically, waking every hour or so, but my apprehension was mostly about Roscoe, not the thunderstorm. The driving rain continued most of the night. Every time I woke I spoke to Jack, trying to reassure him. Finally, about five in the morning, the storm subsided. I could hear Jack breathing deeply, finally asleep. I said a prayer of thanksgiving for him.

The next afternoon, Craig came into the ward about four o'clock. As he went by Jack, he stroked his hair in a gentle manner that touched me. He came over to me and said, "Reese, that Roscoe fellow was downstairs again. I asked him to leave, but he said he wouldn't until he spoke to you. He tried to step around me, but I blocked his path. Then he made a mistake — he shoved me. I hit him with a right as hard as I could."

He held out his hand. "Look at my knuckles. I skinned them. He's pretty tough, though. I thought he would go down, but he didn't. He hit me with a left on the side of my face, but he didn't know that I used to box as a pro. I hit him with another left and right, and he stumbled back and fell to one knee. He got up, glared at me, and walked away. He looked back once, with murder on his face. I think I've convinced him he cannot bother you. I also spoke to the MPs — they have a station right across the street — and told them about Roscoe. They said they'd keep an eye out for him and arrest him if he tried to enter the building again."

A week later I was able to stay out of the iron lung most of the day, and I started trying to feed myself, with some assistance. Lieutenant Kovac would put me on the bed next to my iron lung when administering therapy. The fact that I was making good progress in front of Jack disturbed me, because it was pretty obvious that he was not improving. However, he seemed very happy and enthusiastic with the rate of my recovery.

During that week, Jack developed a cough. They assured him that there was no danger, since they were giving him penicillin twice a day. Saturday afternoon we listened to the radio, hoping to learn the results of the Minnesota game against Ohio. Jack was disappointed to learn that Minnesota had lost badly.

After supper, Craig and another medic lifted me and placed me in the iron lung again for the evening. About an hour after lights out, Jack called just as I was dozing off.

"Reese," he asked, "are you awake?"

"Yes. Why aren't you asleep?"

"I don't want to go to sleep. I've got something to tell you. Is it okay, or am I keeping you from your sleep?"

"No. Not at all. I don't really like to go to sleep this early. What's on your mind?"

"Reese," he began, "I'm going to die tonight. I won't be here in the morning. And I had to talk to someone. I had to tell someone my thoughts."

"What?" I exclaimed. "Don't be silly. Jack, you are progressing. I don't want you to think that way. Listen . . ."

But he stopped me and said, "Please listen to me. Please let me talk."

"Okay," I replied.

"We don't own our bodies. We don't own ourselves. The body is lent to us by God. Yet we are part of the universe. Our bodies are not possessed by us, only our souls. If we are at peace, as I am right now, then we are in harmony with God. We are just a small part of this great universe that God has created, but we *are* a part of it, and we will always exist and we will always exist as part of it.

"Tonight I can see into my heart, and there I find love for all my fellow men, and I feel one with God. Don't cry for me, Harvey Reese, when I am gone. I am one with God. Tell James Craig that I love him. I am tired now. I'm going to go to sleep. Goodbye, Reese."

His voice had trailed off almost to a whisper, but in the silence of our ward every word was audible to me. I stayed awake until Craig came in to check us. He went to Jack, saw that he was asleep, then came to me. I started to tell him what Jack had said, but then I felt that it might be a betrayal.

Craig said, "I will be on duty all night. I'll come in every now and then and check you fellows. I'll be right outside the door."

I was awakened about six in the morning by the sound of crying. I turned my head toward Jack. Craig was holding him in his arms, embracing him and sobbing. Craig kept saying, "No, Jack. Not now. No, Jack."

Finally Major Savage came in, put her arm around Craig, and walked him out of the ward. Jack lay peacefully on the bed of his iron lung that had been pulled out. He had only a small towel across the mid-section of his body, as I did. Two medics came in, picked him up from his bed, and laid him on a stretcher, covered him, and rolled him out of the ward.

I was now alone, all alone in the large ward, with only the endless pumping of my iron lung for company. For the first and only time I asked myself why did this happen to me. But the thought came to me that that was a pointless question, and it was one that I never asked again.

# Chapter 27

Two days later, I was able to stay out of the iron lung all night. Craig had decided that I should try, and although I was apprehensive, I agreed. It was remarkable that the doctors would give a sergeant that much latitude in treatment, but they respected his long years of experience with patients with respiratory problems and quite often would ask his opinion. During the doctors' visit on the day of my attempt, Craig revealed our plans. They said, "If you think he's ready, go ahead."

Knowing my uneasiness, Craig actually sat on a chair all night leaning against the wall next to my bed, assuring me that I could call him at any time with only a whisper. Four days later, the doctors told me that since I was not struggling to breathe — and, in effect, was breathing almost normally — I was ready to move to the physical therapy ward.

That same day I learned that two new patients were in isolation, both in iron lungs. They would be moved into this ward within two or three days. So the silent struggle goes on, I thought to myself.

My new ward was on the ground floor and already held eleven patients, all of them veterans of the Korean War. Some had lost one or both legs, others were minus arms, one had been hit in the spine and was paralyzed from the waist down. At the far end of the ward was a man who had no face; he was blind and could not speak, nor could he hear. He communicated by drawing letters with his finger on the hand of the nurse or the medic who took care of him. Another soldier had been shot in the hip and had extensive damage; he was trying to learn to walk with a new hip made of steel. Many of the men were learning to use artificial limbs.

There was only one other polio victim — a man who had arms like a weightlifter but was paralyzed from the waist down. He was in the bed next to me, and his name was Bill Patterson. On my other side was Oscar Masters, who had lost both legs, one at the knee and one almost from the hip.

Across the aisle directly in front of me was Robert Logan, who had been awarded the Congressional Medal of Honor. Logan had lost his right arm and had scars on the right side of his face. He had fallen into a deep depression, despite plastic surgery which had done wonders so that the scars were hardly noticeable. There seemed no way of convincing him that he looked all right. He was constantly requesting that the curtains be pulled around his bed, and spent most of his time just lying on his side staring steadily at the wall.

Chris Jones, a very large black man on the bed next to Logan, had lost both his legs, but not in combat. While he was changing a tire on a big Army truck, the jack had slipped and crushed his legs. One was removed right below the knee and the other just above the knee. Oscar Masters and Chris, who had been in this ward four months and three months respectively, were both doing very well using artificial legs. In fact, Oscar could actually drill with other soldiers. Chris walked pretty well but he still needed the support of crutches. Their days were spent practicing on their artificial limbs, or working with the end of the leg where it had been cut off. They would massage the stump, rub it, slap it, pinch it — anything to toughen it. The idea was to make it tough enough to eliminate pain when using the artificial limbs.

Both Oscar and Chris had accomplished the toughening task well, and they had been in the ward long enough to begin to overcome much of the depression which seemed to be the number one enemy of the newly handicapped. Most victims learned to handle the worst of it, but the majority of them would continue to have bouts of depression for the rest of their lives.

Robert Logan, the Medal of Honor winner, had been in the ward for three months. His wounds had occurred when he was throwing a hand grenade and it exploded and blew off his right arm. With the grenade above his shoulder in the throwing position, his helmet had protected him considerably, so that the only scarring was on the right side of his face.

After the plastic surgery, his fiancee came to the hospital to see him. She assured him that everything was the same and that as soon as he was discharged from the hospital they would get married. A week later, he got a Dear John letter from her, begging forgiveness for her inability to cope with the situation and telling him that for the time being their engagement was off. He was already depressed; after the letter he merely sank deeper. A month later a friend came to visit and let it slip that his girlfriend had gotten married. That was two months ago, and Logan had hardly spoken since except to mumble once to his physical therapist that he was not a man, that he was just a part of a man, and then he refused to be measured for an artificial arm. He would accept his meals but only because his doctor made it clear that if he did not eat he would be moved into another ward and be fed intravenously. So he stayed in our ward, but they had to spoon-feed him as if he were a baby.

Bill Patterson, the paralyzed polio victim on the bed next to me, explained how everybody was depressed on this ward except him. Yet for the next three weeks I would hear him crying every night beneath his sheets, trying desperately to muffle the sound.

That night after lights out, I lay on my bed and wondered about myself. I was not depressed. I had not been depressed. And I did not believe that I would ever be depressed. Only on one occasion in the past had I questioned what had happened to me — and why. I could not take credit for overcoming depression because I never suffered from it. Since coming to the hospital I had had a birthday, and now at twenty-nine I was the oldest patient in the physical therapy ward. On occasions I was even referred to as the Old Man. But I really did not believe my seniority was the explanation for my firm mental balance. When I took the time to wonder about it, my thoughts instantly reverted to my mother, but I was not sure why.

My first morning on the ward, immediately after breakfast, Lieutenant Kovac came in and said, "Now that you are out of that damn iron lung, we're going to really move forward. Reese, I expect one hundred percent cooperation. We're going to work three hours in the morning and three more in the afternoon. If you get too exhausted, I want you to tell me. Otherwise, we're going to *go!*"

She was always cheerful and encouraging. We became fast friends. Every day she would tell me the latest gossip, the progress of every patient, both physical and mental, the latest escapades of the nurses and the physical therapists, and the latest on patients' families, their loves, and their wives. Knowing these facts about the men was another tool to use in the psychological adjustment that was standard with most handicapped patients.

Lieutenant Kovac was a delight. She could make me smile and laugh, and it was always with enthusiasm that I waited for her arrival. "Now, Reese," she would say, "I'm going to work with every muscle in your body. I'm going to handle you rather personally. Don't you get horny on me. You understand?"

"Yes, ma'am. I understand," I said. "And by the way, I love Polacks."

"At ease!" she answered. "You are talking to a lieutenant in the United States Army."

"And you're talking to a United States civilian, the highest rank of all!"

During the first month my therapy was done on my bed; thereafter they would put me on a stretcher and take me to a private room that had only a mat on the floor. PFC Eddie Cole, the medic in our ward, would wheel me in, pick me up in his arms, and lay me on the mat on the floor. As he left, he always announced, "Be back in a couple of hours. Get strong, Reese. Don't want to carry you around forever."

Lieutenant Kovac would get on her knees and lift one of my legs at a time, stretching the muscles. It was very important to keep the muscles stretched and relaxed. Sometimes the stretching was quite painful. She would flex the legs back and forth fifty times each. Then she would sit me up and slide behind me. She would pull up her nurse's uniform skirt, spread her legs, and pull me up against her bosom. In this position, she was able to work my arms as if they were hers.

I was very conscious of lying between her legs with my back against her breasts. I was also aware that she was conscious of this fact, and she would tease, "You like them, Reese?"

"They're nice," I would answer.

She would laugh and squeeze me against them a little bit more and say, "I told you, don't get horny on me."

"How do I avoid it?" I asked.

"Don't think about me as a woman. Think about me as a professional doing her job. But it is also my job to give you an incentive. The day you can stand up all by yourself and you can reach out with your right hand, I will let you squeeze my tit. Agreed?" she said.

"Oh boy. Some sweet day. I will count the days, Lieutenant Kovac."

"But for now, Reese, let's be professional."

"Okay," I said, "but could you squeeze me just one more time, please?"

I noticed that Lieutenant Kovac did not allow anyone else in the ward to take any liberties with her. I concluded that her philosophy was to build confidence in her patient, not only physically and mentally but that — considering the fragile nature of man's vanity — his self-esteem needed special attention, especially in relation to women. Some of the depression of many newly-handicapped men could be traced directly to apprehension about future sexual contact with women. I was fortunate that I had no such depressions, but I was not about to tell the Lieutenant that her special attentions were unnecesssary. She allowed her patient limited physical contact as a reward or incentive for special efforts during the tough therapy sessions. There was a thin line that we both knew existed, and we both — in a tongue-in-cheek manner — accepted the principle that good effort from the new strong man should be rewarded. If Lieutenant Kovac had decided that squeezing a tit was the trophy to be awarded after my first steps, I sure wasn't going to reject it.

In my sixth week in Ward C, I was told that I could have com-

228

pany. Eddie Cole offered to call people for me. "You must have lots of folks you want to see, since this is your home town. Where do you want to start?"

I gave him the name and phone number of Manuel and told him to ask Manuel to bring Diane with a complete status report on the business. "That's all for now," I told him. "I've got to find out what has been happening at my company. When I have that in hand, then I will see other people."

A half hour later, Major Savage, who was the hospital administrator (known as the Black Widow because of her strict policies), appeared at my beside wearing her best spit-and-polish manner. "Reese," she said, "there are some people who want very much to see you, and you cannot be unkind about it. Your wife calls often. Your brother calls every day. You seem to have friends from coast to coast who keep calling. A lady named Joyce in Los Angeles and Annette in New Orleans phone at least once a week. But Homer Smith and a Reverend Neely show up in the waiting room every other day. Both of them are there now. So I suggest you see them now. I'll send them in one at a time. Which one first?"

Her manner was very stern for someone who was telling me to be kind. I knew she would not take no for an answer, so I said, "Yes, ma'am. Send in Homer Smith first."

Homer walked into the ward with a look of such deep distress that I was touched. I knew I had lost quite a bit of weight, but it hadn't occurred to me how I would look to people who hadn't seen me since all this started. He paused at the door until Eddie pointed to my bed. As Homer came toward me he looked stunned, and by the time he got to my bedside he broke down crying. He reached forward and embraced me. I felt the silence from the others in the ward, but I had neither the strength nor the courage to push him away. There was no doubt about his sincerity.

After a moment, I said, "Homer, it's not as bad as you think. I have considerable general weakness, but I have muscle function everywhere. I do expect to recover." And then with a laugh I added, "I think."

It was apparent that he did not think it funny. "Harvey," he asked, "is there anything I can do for you? Please ask me to do something for you."

"No, Homer. I'm in a wonderful place here. The treatment

that I am receiving is the best. I'm in the best hands available. Thank you, Homer. I know you mean it."

"Oh, I do mean it, Harvey," he replied. "As soon as you are out of the hospital . . ." he hesitated. "You are going to get out?" he questioned.

"Of course." I smiled reassuringly.

He continued, "As soon as you get out, let's get together. Let's be friends the way we were in high school, without any reservations. Please, Harvey, let me be your friend again."

"You've always been my friend, and I do appreciate you coming by. But Homer, I think you'd better go now because I'm not supposed to have long visits yet. And thanks. I hear that you've been coming regularly and asking about me. I do appreciate your concern, but in the future, Homer, let me call you. I promise that I'll call you every couple of weeks and tell you about my progress. I feel that right now I should put all my energies into my recovery. You understand?"

"Sure," he replied. "I understand. But keep your promise and call." He leaned forward again, embraced me, squeezed me, and then abruptly turned and walked out of the room.

No one in the ward made a comment except Bill Patterson next to me, who said, "He's a good friend, and he truly cares about you."

Within minutes Reverend Neely walked in and I heard a comment from the other end of the ward about a 'Hallelujah preacher.' I noted that his shoes were polished, his brown pants had a sharp crease although they were too short, his blue coat — although showing obvious wear — was ironed, and his blue striped tie was neatly tied and very straight. He was holding a worn brown hat in his hand and walked with a slight limp. His face was somber.

As he reached my side he began talking in a mournful tone. "Oh, Mr. Harvey, why did this happen to you? I pray it had happened to me." He raised his eyes and the pitch of his voice as he went on. "Oh Lord, please bring your healing and your blessing upon Mr. Harvey here. This is a good man. This is your servant. Please, oh Lord, let him be healed."

By this time, everybody in the ward was silent and looking toward me. Nurses had stopped, the ward men had frozen, everybody seemed to be transfixed. Reverend Neely turned toward the others and said, "Please join me in a prayer for Mister Harvey. He is a fine and good man."

He fell to his knees and started praying in a booming voice with such sincerity that everybody in the ward lowered their heads. Although I felt very touched, I was embarrassed that everyone seemed to be praying for me. It was a long prayer that I thought would never end. Finally Neely said, "Amen," and fell silent. No one in the ward made a sound. Then the Reverend stood up, leaned over, and took my hand. It was the first time that I recall his ever touching me. But there was no doubt that the touch was pure love.

"Mr. Harvey," he said, "I will not come and bother you any more. I just had to make sure you were all right. Every member of my congregation will pray for your recovery, and you *will* recover. Mr. Harvey, may the Lord bless you."

Then he turned and spoke to everyone else in the ward. "May the Lord bless all of you, and may He heal each one of you." As he walked away I noticed that the back of his coat was torn. My eyes welled with tears. For the next five minutes, everybody whispered in the ward as if holiness had paid a visit. Every day we received visits from priests, ministers, and rabbis, but this visit from my old friend was the spiritual highlight of my stay at Brooke Medical Center, and I had the distinct impression that everyone in that ward was conscious that this was a man of God. The awareness that I was loved by Reverend Neely was wonderful.

The next day Manuel and Diane arrived before lunch. Manuel went to great lengths to explain the concern of everyone at the plant about my illness. Everyone hoped that I would have a quick and speedy recovery. Diane said nothing, just sat on my bed and occasionally looked at me in a way that showed the effort she was making to show very little concern.

The report on the business was most encouraging. Orders kept pouring in, and they were being handled properly. Diane told me our bank balance, the amount of receivables, and the inventory report. The figures could only illustrate that we were prospering. As we came to the end of the report, she said, "I know you have been knocked for a loop, but you'll be back. I have no doubt."

I looked at her for a second and realized that she was trying to speak lightly but that her words were most sincere and heartfelt. I said, "Thanks. I'll try my best." Then I turned to my foreman and said, "Manuel, I want you to bring me or send me one dozen water guns."

"Water guns?" he asked as though he hadn't heard me right.

"Yes, water guns. Like in cap guns, but water guns. Okay?"

His expression at first almost made me laugh, but then I think he remembered the spread of toys on my desk, and he replied soberly, "Yes sir. Since this is Friday, I'll send them Monday. Will that be all right?"

They both stood and smiled, approving of the water guns. Diane said, "You haven't changed a bit. You'll get your water guns. Have fun. But hurry back. We miss you at the office."


On Sunday afternoon, Sandra came to visit — and made a big impression on the men in the ward. Sandra was a good-looking woman, and when she was dressed in high fashion as on this day men did not hide their admiration.

"May I smoke?" she asked me.

I nodded.

She sat on the chair next to my bed and asked, "How are you feeling? You look better than I imagined. I am glad." As she spoke, she looked about the ward, carefully studying the other patients, showing small concern about our conversation. "The girls were over last night for cards and stayed until 2:30 this morning. That's why I could not get here earlier."

I was happy she had gotten back into the routine of card parties with her friends and seemed perfectly happy.

"Do you need anything?" she asked.

"Nothing," I assured her. "I am making good progress and I really haven't time for anything except the therapy that will get me out of here. You will understand that is why I must limit all visits."

"That's okay with me." She lit another cigarette.

"How are the children?" I asked. "I sure do miss them."

"Mischievous."

We sat silently watching the TV in the ward for the next twenty minutes. Then she turned toward me, smiled, and stood up. She leaned over and gave my cheek a light kiss and said, "I best be going. Call me if you need anything."

She turned and left the ward. The eyes of all the men followed her to the door.

# Chapter 28

The next day, during our morning session, Lieutenant Kovac asked if I had ever tried to talk to Robert Logan.

"Only one time," I answered. "We were alone in the ward, and I asked him if he knew the time. He did answer me, but all he said was, 'No, I don't have a watch. Sorry.' As a matter of fact, I was surprised that he said that much. Why?"

She had walked behind me, pulled up her skirt, sat down, and pulled me up against her bosom. She started working my arms as she explained. "Lieutenant Marian Conti is Logan's therapist. For three months she's been working with him and gotten no response. On occasions he announces that he no longer is a man. She told me she's sick of the lack of progress and that tonight she might make a liar out of him."

She was getting even more vigorous with my arms and I was beginning to sweat as she went on. "Lieutenant Conti is divorced, has been married twice. I think I know what she has in mind. I don't approve, but if something unusual happens in the ward tonight I hope the rest of you guys can keep your mouths shut."

"None of my business," I replied. Then I asked, "Are you wearing a bra?"

"No," she replied. "How can you tell? Do you like?"

"I like."

She gave me a big squeeze and said, "Don't forget, Reese, don't get horny on me." We both laughed.

As she left for the day, PFC Cole came in. He struggled trying to put me back on the litter. "You're getting some of your weight back," he said. "Let me see you sit up without help."

"I'll try," I said. I struggled, but I managed to pull up, swinging my legs slowly to the side, and there I was, sitting on the side of the stretcher.

"Do you think you can stand by yourself?" he asked.

"I'd like to try," I answered. "Where is Lieutenant Kovac?"

"She's gone," he said. "You don't have to worry. We won't tell her."

"Okay, let me try."

I slowly slid off the stretcher, and I was standing alone! Eddie had his arm around me just in case, but I was overwhelmed with joy. For three months I had not stood on my own two feet, and now it seemed to me that this was the greatest physical experience of my life.

Eddie must have shared moments like this with others and had an idea what I was feeling, because he said, "Isn't it great! You're on your own, my man. I'm happy for you." He picked me up without warning and put me back on the stretcher. "That's enough for one day," he said. "I think you have just conquered the world."

I was hardly back in my bed in the ward when Lieutenant Kovac reappeared. She was holding a large shopping bag, and she asked me, in a tone that mingled curiosity and amusement, "What in the world are you up to, Reese? What do you intend to do with all these water guns?"

I was a little disconcerted. She wasn't supposed to know about this yet. I had a childish desire to spring my plan as a surprise on everyone.

"How did they get into your hands?" I asked.

"A young man asked if I knew where you were, and when I said yes, he handed me this bag. If he had given it to Major Savage you would have gotten your ass busted."

"She cannot bust me. You keep forgetting I'm a civilian. Look, Lieutenant, some of these guys need . . . something or other. Who knows . . . a good water fight might be just the thing. Why don't you just hand them to Eddie and let him fill them? Just forget you ever saw them."

Without another word she handed the bag to Eddie, smiled, and walked out of the ward. Eddie said, "I'll be right back."

Ten minutes later, he returned with an obviously heavier bag. He handed me one of the guns. I immediately squirted Chris Jones, across the aisle. He screamed and said, "Hell! That's cold! No fair. Give me one."

Eddie started distributing the guns, and before long water was being squirted across the aisles from bed to bed. Everybody in the ward, including Eddie Cole — our big sweet ward man — was shooting each other. It was a free-for-all. The water guns were long distance firing, large water capacity, super-duper models. It wasn't long before everybody was soaked, including our sheets and pajamas.

Without warning, the door swung open and Major Savage walked in and screamed, "At ease, everyone, at ease!"

Now I knew why they called her the Black Widow. She walked up my side of the aisle, staring at each patient with a frown on her face that would have frozen the Rio Grande. At the end of the ward she turned and started back down the other side of the aisle across from me.

I could not help myself. I squirted her on the rear.

Wheeling around, she looked at me with a vicious scowl. She came toward me and pulled the curtains completely around my bed and I could not imagine what I was in for. Then the Black Widow bent down . . . and kissed me on the mouth. In a whisper, she said, "Bless you. They needed this."

I must have gaped because she reached down and pushed my chin up, closing my mouth. She smiled for a second, then resumed her frown.

Pulling the curtain open, she walked down the aisle, and at the door turned and said, "Cole, reload the guns one more time. After that, pick them up. And I expect you to change all the sheets, dry off the patients, and put dry pajamas on everyone."

The whole ward gave a cheer. One lone voice said, "We love you, Major Savage." The rest of us thought he had gone too far.

Only Robert Logan had not participated. The gun was untouched on his bedside table.

That night, half an hour after lights out, I was still lying awake rethinking the whole water-gun fight, enjoying the fact that I loved every one of these GIs. The ward door opened quietly, and Lieutenant Conti walked in with soft steps. She was not beautiful but she was handsome and her figure was above average — certainly someone you would consider an attractive woman.

She walked up to Robert Logan's bed and slowly, quietly, pulled the curtain around his bed. He must have been asleep, because I heard him say in a startled voice, "What are you doing?"

She replied, "Shush. Be very quiet."

A few moments later, you could hear the bed shaking slightly, then a bit faster, and then almost violently. I know some of the other GIs must have realized what was going on, but no one made a sound. About twenty minutes later, I heard Conti say in a hushed voice, "Here's a kiss for you. You are really quite a man." She pulled the curtain back slightly, just enough so she could leave. Looking neither to the left nor right, she walked straight to the door and was gone. The minute she was out, PFC Cole walked in, sat down on his chair, leaned back against the wall, lowered his head, and fell asleep.

The next morning I was wakened by the rattle of the trays announcing breakfast. Across the aisle Robert Logan was looking at me. He smiled and asked, "Are we going to have another water-gun fight today?"

"I hope so," I said.

"Good. I want to be in on it. Damn, I'm hungry. I've never been this hungry in my whole life."

The ward man arrived who usually helped him eat. "That's okay," Logan told him. "I'll feed myself."

A week later, Logan was fitted for an artificial arm, and from that day forward his progress was remarkable. It takes all kinds of therapy . . .

One day right after breakfast, Eddie Cole came to tell me that

Juan Delgado was asking to see me. Juan Delgado, I thought to myself. Uncle Jonathan's shadow. I hadn't seen him nor even heard his name since before the war.

When he walked into the ward his steps were graceful and confident. I saw that he was still slim, sinewy, and still had that poised and self-assured look I remembered so well — the look which made weak men cringe. At the ranch, he was always the cleanest and best dressed of the men. His invariable costume was khaki pants, polished cowboy boots, a clean shirt daily, with a red bandana around his neck, and a Stetson at a slight angle on his head.

Today he was wearing tan gabardine slacks, western cut with slit pockets, that fit like a glove. His dark brown shirt was form-fitting with mother-of-pearl buttons down the front, and on the cuffs and pockets. His collar was buttoned, but instead of a tie he wore a thin leather strap clasped with an emblem of an eagle carved from buckhorn. His alligator dark burgundy boots were beautiful and obviously handmade. His tan Stetson had a leather band and a feather on one side.

In Spanish he spoke, "Señor, I heard you were sick. I have come to pay my respects and offer you my services."

I enjoyed looking at his handsome face that reflected such strength of character and integrity. I also spoke in Spanish. "Juan, I am very glad to see you. Where have you been all these years?"

"After the war, your uncle was no longer in danger. The man who threatened him died. I went back to Mexico. I married, and last year, in childbirth, my wife and the baby both died. I sold my ranch. It was a little one, but it had good soil and good water. I went back to your uncle's ranch and learned he went to heaven. I loved that man like my father."

Seeing Juan brought a flood of memories. He made me feel close to Uncle Jonathan again, and to my youth. I collected myself enough to offer him the chair beside my bed, but he preferred to stand in that familiar poised way which looked relaxed but was so ready for action.

"They told me about your illness," he said. "I decided to offer you my services. Yesterday I came, late in the afternoon. They said you were eating supper and they would rather not disturb you. I had other things to do, so I decided to come back today. Señor, when I left yesterday, I thought I saw Roscoe. He was sitting on a bench at the corner. When he saw me, he walked away quickly. Señor, would you like me to do something about Roscoe? I could end your troubles forever if you only say the word."

"No, no, nothing like that. I appreciate your offer and concern. Juan, when I get out of the hospital I want you to come see me. I want you to work for me. I want you to be my friend and companion, the way you were to Uncle Jonathan. How old are you, Juan?"

"I am fifty, Señor, but I can do anything that a twenty-year-old man can do."

"I believe that. Don't worry, Juan. I am not giving you charity. There are many things that you can do for me. I need a man I can trust completely. Go back to Mexico, clean up all your affairs, and then come back. I believe in a month or two — maybe three at the most — I will be able to be active again."

"I am at your service forever," he said, "and may the saints always smile upon you."

He strode out of the room, and I lay thinking of that other world I knew so well which seemed so far away — in years as well as miles. Bill Patterson cleared his throat in an invitational way and I realized that he and the other men were probably curious about my unusual visitor and our conversation in Spanish. But I ignored the hint and kept silent. I was enjoying revisiting old scenes; time enough for reality later on.


After breakfast, Lieutenant Kovac came by to tell me she would be thirty minutes late for our therapy session. "Colonel Shields wants to talk with me about your case," she said. "He will probably have a formal conference with you tomorrow. PFC Cole will take you to therapy in a half hour."

"Lieutenant Kovac," I said, "please do not wear a brassiere today."

"What are you talking about, Reese?" she said. "You think I'm crazy?"

I gave her my best smile and said, "Please?"

"Well," she replied, hesitating. "Maybe." And walked away.

Private Cole rolled me to the private therapy room on the litter when it was time. He started to help me down but I stopped him.

"Leave me on the stretcher," I said. "Lieutenant Kovac will help me down."

Cole left as the Lieutenant walked in. She said, "You're not ready."

"Yes I am," I replied. "I want to try to stand." I swung my legs to the side of the stretcher and sat up. She immediately stationed herself close to me. Slowly I slid off the stretcher to a standing position, twelve inches from her. Reaching out my right hand I put it over her left breast and squeezed gently. She was not wearing a bra.

She smiled broadly and said, "Good for you, Reese! I knew you could make it. I felt it in my bones. And by the way, talking about feeling, how *does* it feel?"

"Standing, or your breast?" I asked.

"Both."

"They both feel wonderful," was my answer. Slowly I released her. I took a very short six-inch step toward her, stopped for a moment, then another, and my legs started to buckle.

She reached for me, grabbed me around the waist, and said, "Hold on, Cowboy, hold on." A fleeting thought of Mary Alice flashed through my mind.

Lieutenant Kovac lowered me onto the mat, smiling all the while, and started working with my legs. She said, "Tomorrow you will see Colonel Shields. He will evaluate you and tell you what he thinks about your case. He usually is correct with his diagnosis and evaluation, but in your case, Reese, I think he is going to be wrong. I believe you have just now started your recovery. When you lean against me, against my bosom, and I work your arms, I can feel a vibrant vitality that's lying dormant due to the shock from the polio virus. And that vitality within you is just now beginning to respond. Colonel Shields would not accept my report. I am talking to you truthfully and sincerely. I don't want Colonel Shields to discourage you."

"Lieutenant Kovac," I said, "you're a sweetheart. What's your first name?"

"Dorothy," she said, almost meekly.

"Well, Dorothy, I am about to kiss you on the mouth, lieutenant or no lieutenant." And I did, and she responded.

---

At ten o'clock the next morning, Colonel Shields walked in with two other staff members. I was the only one in the ward; all the other patients were at therapy. My session had been rescheduled because of this meeting.

The Colonel was a tall, distinguished-looking man — reminded me of Walter Pidgeon. He pulled up a chair and sat next to me, crossing his legs and making himself comfortable. He began very casually, talking as if we had all day to pass the time with each other. "Reese, I've looked over your charts. I've gotten reports from everybody and I am pleased with your progress. Major Savage tells me that you are the best morale-builder in the ward, that you joke with the men, you make fun of their handicaps, talk to them about business, of the days when you were a cowboy, and about your experiences in World War II. Major Savage tells me that you called that war 'the good war,' if there is such a thing. For your information, I agree with you. I also was in that war, and it was the good war. This 'police action' in Korea is no good for anyone."

Now his tone changed and he put both feet on the floor solidly and leaned forward with his hands clasped between his knees. "But now let me get to your case. Reese, it is tough but we must face facts. I am afraid that you likely will never walk again. You probably will never be able to function unless you have someone with you. I'm sure you will not be able to drive a car; you'll have to have a driver. At home you will need special help and care. No doubt you can find loved ones to help you in the bathroom, to bathe and assist you. You probably won't be able to travel without great difficulty, so my suggestion is — don't travel. It's not necessary. I would limit my activities as much as possible. Conserve your energies. Don't ever over-extend yourself. I understand you are a business man. You should cut those activities down to a limited amount.

"In other words, Reese, it is better to back off in a protective shell than to expose yourself and get hurt, both physically and mentally. That's my evaluation and my advice to you, based on good medical judgement." He looked at me and I said nothing. He added, "Now Reese, don't go silent on me. If you have anything to say, please, please say it. It's good to get it out."

"Colonel Shields," I began, "they tell me you are the most

knowledgeable man in this field, but in this case, respectfully, I cannot and will not accept your evaluation. But I thank you for your consideration."

There was a moment of silence. He abruptly stood. I expected anger. Instead, he saluted me. He said, "Damn! I hope you are right." He turned and walked out and I never saw him again while I was in the hospital.

A week later, in the middle of the afternoon, Eddie Cole came bustling into the ward and headed toward me with an urgent air. "Reese," he said, "there was a scuffle in the back of the hospital a few minutes ago. Some fellow was trying to come in to see you and he was tackled by that Mexican that came to see you a few days ago. Your Mexican had a knife at the guy's throat. By the time the MPs got there, the Mexican had let him up, apologized to him, and left. I wonder what that fellow said to your Mexican. The guy is carrying a big burlap bag, and now he is downstairs and he still wants to talk to you. He's kind of self-conscious and ill at ease. Says his name's Roscoe Rafferty. What should I do?"

"Cole," I said, "that man has been my enemy in the past. I'm not sure. I can't figure out what's on his mind."

We were interrupted by the entrance of Juan Delgado. Cole turned to Juan and asked, "How did you get in here?"

"Cole, it's okay," I said. "He's a friend. Let me talk to him for a minute. Just stand by." In Spanish I said, "Juan, what's going on?"

"I believe Roscoe is not dangerous to you anymore," he said. "Perhaps you should let him talk to you. I will be right outside the door at the other end. I will be watching carefully. If you need me, I will move in quickly."

"Thanks, Juan. That makes me feel better. Cole, go ahead and bring Rafferty in."

Cole answered, "Okay. Back in a minute."

When Roscoe walked in Cole was directly behind him. At my bedside they both stood, looking awkward and uncomfortable, without saying a word. Roscoe was rather handsome, I thought, except for the scar at the corner of his eye. He was carrying the burlap bag Cole had described, and he dropped it to the floor, then took off his black cowboy hat. He wore jeans and well-worn boots and looked the typical cowpoke.

"Reese," he began awkwardly, "I don't know how to tell you this. I've hated you from the first day I saw you, but I was full of hate in those days. You became something I wanted to destroy. You had people that loved you, and Joe told me that you were your uncle's pet. I guess jealous is what I was."

He was more articulate than I had expected, but even so his words came in slow sentences. It seemed as though they were being forced up from deep in his gut, and came out with pain. He was turning his hat in his hands nervously as he went on. "Recently I learned what you did for Becky, and I learned what your uncle did for Becky — and for me, I guess. Anyhow, we still have our ranch, and I think I owe that to him. I don't understand people like you all, but I want to ask you to forgive me. I guess you know I'm the one that set the cable that cut off your friend's hand in North Carolina. I'm sorry. I don't understand why you were kind to Becky, but from this day on, if you let me, I want to be your friend."

I said nothing, just stared at him. I was still trying to figure out what he was getting at and whether to believe this confession and amazing conversion.

After a moment, he continued, "And if I cannot be that, at least I will not be your enemy." Again he hesitated, perhaps waiting for a response. I still said nothing, and he went on. "I want to return something that belongs to you."

He opened the burlap bag and pulled out a set of deerhorns mounted on a simple polished piece of oak. The horns had twelve points. It was my twelve-point buck from the ranch.

"These horns belong to you," he said. "You made a beautiful shot. You hit him on the neck and broke his back."

He laid the horns on the bed next to me, turned, and started to leave. I spoke after him, and said, "Roscoe, it's all behind us. We'll leave the past to the past."

He turned and smiled slightly. I had never seen Roscoe smile before.

When he had left the ward, Juan Delgado came in and said, "I'll be back in one or two months, *padron*. I will be back and a new era will begin."

For the next two months, the routine was the same — daily physical therapy with occasional sessions in the whirlpool. I was able to sit up in the wheelchair for long periods now, but my arms were still too weak for me to roll myself around. With my right arm, I could feed myself and I could even write a letter if I needed to, but it was a struggle. Eddie Cole and I had become good friends. He would sneak me out of the ward at night about twice a week, and we would go to the base theater to see a movie or go to the beer garden and have a hot dog and a beer.

Bill Patterson, the polio victim on the bed next to me, had taught himself to do tricks on a wheelchair. He had unbelievable strength in his upper body but he never regained any movement or feeling in his legs. Bill was discharged from the hospital a month before I was.

Oscar Masters and Chris Jones had become so proficient in the use of their artificial legs that they were actually allowed to join the Brooke Medical Drill Team. They were both discharged the same week. Robert Logan was invited, along with four other Medal of Honor recipients, to the White House to dine with the President.

And so, gradually our original group broke up, going our separate ways.

# Chapter 29

In the last two months in the hospital, it became routine for Manuel and Diane to come once a week to give me progress reports and to discuss business problems. My brother Paul came to see me every other Sunday. Children were not allowed to visit at Brooke Medical Center, so I had not seen mine a single time since I was admitted. Now, after five and a half months, I was eager to look at their little faces.

On a Friday, five and a half months from the day I entered the hospital, Major Savage told me that I would be leaving the next day. I was wearing a small brace on my left hand, a long brace on my left leg, and a short one on my right. I had not been able to walk more than a single step with braces. They were like chains attached to me, and I was leaving the hospital with considerable apprehension and concern. It seemed to me the decision for my discharge had come very abruptly.

Major Savage handed me a note from Lieutenant Kovac. It simply said, "Goodbye. Good luck. I know you will do fine. My very best. Dorothy Kovac." I wished I could have seen her one more time.

The time had come to evaluate the future, to make some decisions about myself, but I felt I was not ready.

Saturday morning an ambulance took me home. The attendants rolled me into the house and transferred me from the stretcher to a hospital bed that had been set up in the living room. The upper half of the bed was raised at a forty-five degree angle so I could sit up somewhat. For a few moments, there was excitement. My children, Sandra, my brother Paul, and Mrs. Baker, our babysitter and neighbor, were all there to welcome me.

I was introduced to the nurse, Miss Parsons, who had been hired to take care of me for the next three months. Everyone was cheerful and seemed happy. The children climbed into bed with me and I hugged and kissed them. Then suddenly there was silence, as if no one knew what to say next. Mrs. Baker blurted out that I looked terrific, then she looked around awkwardly at the others. Realizing abruptly that they were in the presence of a very handicapped person, they did not know exactly what to say or do about it.

"I am quite tired," I said. "I think I should take a nap now."

They all nodded, their faces showing relief, said goodbye, and left, except for Miss Parsons. She took a chair across the room facing me and sat there motionless; it made me uncomfortable. I was not really sleepy, but everytime my eyes opened there she sat. After ten minutes, she asked if she could go outside and have a smoke. I nodded, thankfully, and she left. I lay on my bed and thought to myself, okay Harvey, the next move is yours. What are you going to do about it?

Just then the nurse came back. "There is a person outside who wants to see you," she said in a disapproving tone. "He says he is Juan Delgado."

"Wonderful," I said. "Please invite him in."

Juan came in, strode directly to my bed, and asked, "Are you ready? Shall we go?"

"Damn right," I answered. "Where are we going?"

"To the ranch. You will need some warm clothes. Where can I get them?"

"There's a closet in the hallway. Get what I need. And please hurry."

Miss Parsons had stayed outside, evidently smoking a cigarette. Juan returned from the hallway with wool pants, a corduroy shirt, warm socks, a jacket, and my cowboy boots and hat. He pulled my pajamas off and dressed me, then he slid me off the bed and I stood shakily on the floor, bracing myself against him. He grabbed my belt at either side and held me firmly, face to face.

In Spanish he said, "Don't worry, Señor, I've got you. Don't be nervous. I will not let you get hurt. I want you to take two steps."

I complied. I was surprised how good my cowboy boots felt. Then I took a third step and my left leg collapsed. He grabbed me and stood me back up. "You will have to learn to lock the left knee," he said.

"They gave me a long metal brace for my leg," I replied.

"You will not need it. It is clumsy. It can trip you. My brother had a similar leg and he merely learned to lock it. I know you have other weaknesses, especially in your left arm, but they will get stronger. Now, Señor, with your permission, I will pick you up and carry you."

He lifted me in his arms and started out of the house. As we went out the back door, Miss Parsons was leaning against the house smoking a cigarette.

"What are you doing?" she screamed. "You can't do this! You cannot take my patient! What are you doing?"

Juan ignored her, opened the door of his pickup, and put me on the seat. He hurried back in to get my jacket and Stetson. By this time the nurse was almost hysterical.

"I'm going to call the police!" she yelled at Juan.

He turned on her with a ferocious growl, and his voice was low and menacing. "Woman, shut your mouth or I will smash your face."

She took two steps backward and flattened herself against the house, horrified, and not another sound came from her.


It was hard to believe that only this morning I had ended months under strict authority — a kind of incarceration — and now I was in a truck driving through the Hill Country. By the time we arrived at the main gate of the ranch I was so full of excitement I could hardly restrain myself from a shout of triumph.

It was three o'clock in the afternoon when we reached the house. I asked Juan, "Who owns the place now?"

"The ranch belongs to Jonathan's daughter. She has leased it to another rancher, but the house and one hundred acres belong to me with the right to hunt anywhere on the ranch for the rest of my life."

He carried me into the house. It smelled wonderful. He had cooked a pot of chili and a bowl of pinto beans earlier that day, fully expecting to bring me to the ranch. He sat me on the bed.

I gave him a big grin and he smiled back and said, "I see that you're happy to be here. Can I help you go to the bathroom?"

"No, Juan, thanks. I'm okay."

"Good, Señor, because we are going to go sit in a hunting blind. We might be there for some time. I wish to show you something."

As we drove through the woods heading for the blind, I became absorbed in the beauty of the country. I had dreamed about it in the hospital, but the dreams had no smells, no sounds, and little color. How great it felt to really be here once more. Damn, I thought to myself, how great it is to be alive! My senses seemed keener than ever. I wondered if my illness and handicap had triggered this new beautiful awareness.

Juan parked the truck in some thick bushes. He picked me up and carried me a short distance to a hunting blind on the side of a hill facing west. I noticed that he was not even breathing hard. Although slim, he was very strong.

The hunting blind was built of old boards and posts, and camouflaged with brush. There were two chairs inside. He sat me on one with a cushion that he had placed there earlier. I was reminded again how thoughtful and considerate Juan Delgado was with me.

Neither of us had a rifle so I presumed we were not there to hunt, although he had a pistol in a holster at his side. For me, just being there was enough. I was overwhelmed by the beauty and by the fact that I was on this wonderful ranch on the same day I was discharged from the hospital. It was hard to believe.

For about an hour we sat there in silence, looking down the hill toward three big oaks with large branches, on the bank of the

Blanco River. Farther down the hill, a lot of cedar and brush covered the area to the right of the big oaks. Beyond the river there was a small hill, quite rocky and void of vegetation. At the feet of the big oaks we saw two raccoons playing, oblivious of our presence. A few minutes later, a hundred yards to the right of the oaks, three does and a large buck appeared. Immediately I felt excitement. The deer walked in front of our blind about fifty yards away. The antlers on the buck were ten points, and surely a trophy. For twenty minutes they grazed, and then slipped into the brush on the other side. We still sat silently in the blind.

An hour later, the sun started to set below the small hill behind the oaks, causing the sky to turn many shades of red with yellow and blue streaks. Then Juan reached out slowly and gave my arm a gentle squeeze and nodded toward the left. Thirty yards away, two big wild turkeys had appeared.

My heart started beating faster. I could feel my pulse pounding at my temples. My hands began to shake. One of the gobblers was a large tom with a long black beard hanging from his chest — one of the distinctive marks of the wild turkey. The other was a younger bird. The big tom's head was blue and bright red. His steps and movements reflected pride and dignity. His presence was majestic, with an air of alertness that made us freeze as both turkeys looked directly at our blind. We dared not move, not even blink an eye.

Suddenly, giving no warning, they took flight toward the top branches of the big oak — evidently their nightly roosting place. It was a flight of some two hundred yards. I was stunned to see how beautifully they could fly. Although it must have taken only a few seconds, it seemed like minutes to me, and — magically — half-way through their flight their movements became like slow-motion and music filled the air. "The world has music for those who listen." Gracefully they landed on the top branches of the trees. My heart swelled and tears came to my eyes.

I turned to Juan and his eyes were also red, and in a whisper he said, "Wild turkeys can fly, and you, Señor, you too can fly. Last night your uncle told me to tell you that you must fly."

His words startled me . . . but then I could feel Uncle Jonathan's presence. There was no doubt. He was there.

We sat in silence for awhile until finally, without another

word, he picked me up and stood me outside the blind, and standing next to me grabbed my belt at the back. Then, remembering that I must lock my left leg, I walked.

I walked twenty-five yards.

I walked, by God, I walked!


When we got back to the ranch house, Juan asked if I would like to spend the night. I simply answered, "Absolutely."

When I left the hospital they had given me specific instructions about my diet. I was to eat very lightly, mostly soups, if possible, and only boiled vegetables; they should be mashed, similar to baby food. No spices of any type, and in general, I should make an effort not to enjoy my meals. But that night at the ranch I ate pinto beans that were full of spices, garlic, and onions, a huge bowl of chili, very hot with pepper, and corn tortillas that Juan had made for the occasion. It was one of the most satisfying meals of my life.

After supper we sat by the big pot-bellied stove and recalled some of the events that had happened on this ranch. We talked of Uncle Jonathan. We remembered sad times and happy times. It was a wonderful evening. Juan took a chair outside, beyond the porch. He picked me up and sat me on the chair, and we looked at the night sky. The stars were incredible. He had turned off all the lights in the house, and there in the darkness together we became part of the night. For over an hour we sat in silence, transfixed in the enchantment of that unforgettable evening.

That night I slept like a log. I woke at sunrise and found Juan sleeping on a pad on the floor next to my bed. The moment I sat up, Juan jumped up. He helped me dress, but I managed in the bathroom alone.

For breakfast we had huevos rancheros, some more corn tortillas, and strong coffee. Two hours later, with Juan's help, I walked into my own home. My two children were playing in the living room. When they saw me, my little girl turned to her brother and said, "You see! I told you he could walk."


Sunday afternoon I lay on my bed in the living room and watched the children play on the floor and purposely tried not to think of anything of importance. I fell asleep early that evening and there followed the most fragmented night of my life. I would fall into a deep sleep and have vivid dreams for about an hour; then I would awake with a start, and for the next thirty minutes I would recall the dream vividly and submit it to my conscious mind where it was etched into my memory forever. This occurred four times during the night.

The first dream found me in Mexico, walking along the bank of the enchanted El Rio de los Santos. I was nude, except for my white scarf around my neck, and sublimely conscious of my body, erect, vibrant, and strong. There was not one single blemish on my body and not one scar. I felt invincible. I was walking toward Concha who was standing twenty feet in front of me, also nude, looking at the crystal waters of El Rio Santos. She turned toward me, smiled, and said, "Come no closer. If you touch me I will disappear."

I stopped and stood, almost hypnotized by her graceful natural beauty. The sky was a brilliant blue, the trees were vibrant green, and the singing of the birds most beautiful. But it was the fragrance of the flowers that seemed to overwhelm me.

Concha looked at me and said, "I must go," and pointing, added, "She is behind you," and ran away.

I turned. A hundred yards away, a tall young woman with a very graceful figure, with soft brown hair hanging to her shoulders, was bathing in the river in water waist deep. It was a delightful charming sight to behold. I could not see her clearly because she was facing toward the center of the river. The sun was beyond her, and its rays glistened on the water all about her, creating an illusion of unreality. She started to turn toward me, but it was difficult to make out her facial features because of the back light created by the sun's rays. I called to her . . . and I woke with a start.

I lay awake in the darkness of my room, trying to find the significance of the dream. Then I questioned: Are dreams conscious thoughts which have been submitted earlier to the subconscious and which return after a dormant time?

I fell asleep again, and another dream came. My mother came to my bedside, and once more she reigned over my heart and over my mind. "Life to you," she said, "will always be a bold and dash-

251

ing adventure. Let your heart lead you to your destiny. Fulfill what life asks of you."

As she rose to leave, she turned and said, "The girl with the brown hair loves you. Be patient. Your day will come."

My eyes opened slowly and I was awake. I was happy to be so. Life is wonderful indeed, I thought. I was smiling in the darkness as I felt sleep converging upon my conscious thought. I dreamed again.

This time I was in the middle of a bullfight arena awaiting the charge of a huge, vicious, black bull. In one hand I had a sword, and in the other a muleta — a small red cape. The bull charged and I gracefully led the beast around me. Over and over he charged, only to be frustrated by my skills. I looked up to the judges, and the judges were Uncle Jonathan and Uncle Jesse. They waved at me. The bull charged again and I daringly led the beast closer to my body. I looked up at the crowd and found, sitting together, Frank Montez, Juan Delgado, my brother Paul, and Mike Pruske. I waved at them, turned back to the bull, only to find the beast upon me. He gored me on the left leg and slung me to the ground. He hooked my left arm and his horn grazed my body.

When the bull was finally drawn away by the other bullfighters in the arena, my left leg and left arm were bleeding profusely, and my body was covered with bleeding gashes.

I was carried to the infirmary where Colonel Shields was waiting. "He will live," I heard him say, "but without spirit or independence. This you will have to believe."

I shouted, "No!" and I woke to discover that I had broken out in a sweat. I sat up on the edge of the bed and waited for my heart to slow down. Soon, there in the darkness, I felt calm again. I lay back and went to sleep.

Once more I dreamed. I was driving a car up a long formal driveway toward a large white house with big lawns and flower gardens everywhere. I stepped from my car, went toward the window, and looked in. Joyce, Annette, and Mary Alice were dressing a girl with a lovely graceful figure, tall, with brown hair to the shoulder. She was facing away from the window; her feet were bare and she wore only a half slip. Her back was straight and graceful. "I must see her face," I called out. Joyce turned, came to the window, and pulled the shade down.

From that moment, my sleep must have been very deep. I woke and looked at the clock. Eight thirty. The sun was shining, but the trees were swaying from a norther that had blown in during the night. I saw a neighbor across the street wearing a hat and an overcoat as he walked toward his car in the driveway.

It is Monday, February the fourth, the first day of my second life, I thought. I asked myself again, what are you going to do about it? The riddle. Mama's riddle. I must answer the riddle today. I picked up the phone and called my brother at his home. He was just about to leave.

"Paul, can you come to my home in an hour?" I asked. He promised to come.

Next I called Homer Smith. He was delighted to hear from me. I asked how things were going. He said, "Better. I think I am breaking even now. Next year I hope to grow and expand."

I said, "Homer, from this moment on, we are partners. We are going to grow and expand *this* year."

He gave a rebel yell. "If you're sure of that, I'm going to make us both some money."

"I'm sure," I said. "Come see me tomorrow and let's work it out."

I called Diane at the office and told her to phone Juan Delgado. I gave her the number where she could reach him and said to ask him to come to the office at noon. Also to try to find Reverend Neeley. And to tell Manuel that I wanted to have a meeting with all the supervisors at two.

Diane, surprised, asked, "How are you going to get here? Who's going to bring you?"

"Just do it," I answered. "I'll explain later."

Miss Parsons, who had a door key, let herself into the house and walked into my room. I thanked her for her services, but told her that she would no longer be needed. She said it was most irregular, and quickly left.

I lay back on the bed and activated the electric switch that lifted the back of the bed to a sitting position. Then I asked myself the first part of the riddle. Who are you? I thought for a moment, and then I knew the answer. I am Don Quixote. I am Jonathan Reese. I am Ernesto, El Matador. I am Juan Delgado. I am Harvey Reese. I am Delia's son. I am a man on a quest.

Where do you go? Wherever life calls with *honor*.
Whom do you challenge? I challenge myself, always.
Whom do you fear? I fear no one.
And what do you seek? I seek God and Truth, and I seek her with the soft brown hair.

I add one more. *When* will you do this? Now! I have the scars — my body testifies to that fact — the scars that awaken consciousness to the keenest sense. The wind, the trees, the earth have music for those who listen.

I was sitting on my bed smiling when my brother came in. "Paul," I said, "quickly, help me dress."

"Dress?" he questioned.

"Yes, Paul. I'm in a hurry. Look in the closet there in the hallway and get whatever you think I need from there."

He came back with some clothes and helped me dress myself, then slipped my shoes on. I swung my legs around and slid onto the floor. I put a hat on my head and started cautiously out the back door with Paul at my side.

At the car, I said, "Help me into the driver's side."

"Harvey, you can't," he objected.

I opened the door and fell onto the seat, pulled my legs around, and started the motor. The weather was quite cold and the wind was still brisk.

"Paul," I said. "Go back to my closet. There's a blue box on the floor. Inside that box there's a white scarf. Please bring it to me."

He dashed into the house and came back at a trot, carrying the scarf. I wrapped it around my neck.

"Harvey, you can't," he said again. Then as he saw I wouldn't be stopped, he added, "Do you think you'll be okay?"

"You're damn right," I said.

"But, Harvey," he protested. "Why today? Why so soon? Why now?"

I looked up at his face, which was full of concern. I smiled and said, "Because, my dear brother, wild turkeys can fly."

As I drove off, slowly and carefully, I said to myself, "Life must be a bold and dashing adventure. Let's get to it! Let's go live life!"

★  ★  ★